BOOKS BY WILLIAM DIETER

Beyond the Mountain
Hunter's Orange
The White Land

BEYOND THE MOUNTAIN

BEYOND THE MOUNTAIN

William Dieter

ATHENEUM New York 1985

Library of Congress Cataloging in Publication Data

Dieter, William, ———
    Beyond the mountain.

    I. Title.
PS3554.I36B4   1985   813'.54   84-45052
ISBN 0-689-11477-X

Published simultaneously in Canada by McClelland and Stewart Ltd.
Composition by Maryland Linotype Composition Company, Inc.,
Baltimore, Maryland
Manufactured by Fairfield Graphics, Fairfield, Pennsylvania
Designed by Mary Cregan
First Edition

Once again for BETS

One too, like thee, tameless
and swift and proud. . . .

SHELLEY

The hero is not fed on sweets,
Daily his own heart he eats . . .

EMERSON

BEYOND THE MOUNTAIN

CHAPTER 1

Brook was down in Denver when it happened, running an errand for his uncle Caleb. It was possibly more a favor than an errand, for Caleb was interested in the Mack Truck Company's new Bulldog model and wanted Brook to get him some information on it. "Peach of a truck," Caleb told Brook. "I think the dealership is on Broadway. Just slip over there and get prices and delivery times. Pick up some literature too if they have it, okay?" He watched Brook's face. "Of course I could mail an inquiry in. Or I could phone down and get the information."

"Hell, don't do that. I can get the information for you. Besides, I'd like to go." This conversation had taken place the night before Brook left, out on the front lawn between the twin fir trees, and afterwards he'd gone into the house to see his mother, not to ask if he could go, that would be stupid, but to see if he could take one of the cars.

"Absolutely not," she replied. There was no possible way he was going to drive to Denver, she went on to explain, not that far, not that eighty-five miles or whatever it was. "You'll have to take the train." She was at the dining room table and there was a scatter of papers in front of her. She had stopped looking at them and was studying him across the table. The windows were open and the evening wind was sweeping down from the mountains and into the room. She had switched on the chandelier but had also lit a table lamp because of the close

3

work she was doing. There was a generator in the basement that supplied the electricity but it often got weak and the lights dimmed badly. The coal oil lamp flared now in the breeze, sank, flared again, making it look as if her eyes had fluttered. They hadn't. Nothing in his mother's face ever fluttered, Brook knew. It would have been a weakness. Through the door that led into the parlor, Brook could see his father asleep in his favorite chair with his legs stretched out on the ottoman, his boots off. It was Sunday night and the cooks had prepared the usual big meal and his father never lasted long on Sunday nights.

"Tell you what I'll do," Brook said, "I'll drive the Oakland as far as Jefferson and just leave it at the depot." Jefferson was where he would catch the train, a mere six miles down the east meadow road.

"No," his mother said. "Take the Model T."

Brook shifted his feet, getting ready. "Meaning the T is the lesser car and more to my lesser purpose, is that it?"

The lamp flickered again but this time it didn't touch his mother's face. He thought that nothing would ever touch that particular arrogance. "I'm saying that you're not going to leave the good family car at Jefferson while you go stomping off to Denver."

"I'm not stomping off. Caleb asked me to get something for him down there. And I'm using my own money for the trip. He certainly doesn't have any to give—"

"I understand that motor cars are being stolen left and right all over the county."

"I don't know about left. Right maybe." He waited, watching her face across the room. She didn't react to it. "Not only that," she went on, "but who would drive the Oakland back after the train left?"

"The boy at the depot. That's his job. He was hired to drive cars home for people who left on the train."

"The boy at the depot," his mother said coldly, "is the closest thing to a village idiot we have in South Park. He cracked the running board on the Oakland the last time he drove it back, the time your father took the train to Colorado Springs for

4

that horse sale. I know it was that depot boy who did it. He can't wait to get behind the wheel of someone's car so he can go racing away. You can see it in his face. All he thinks about is going fast."

"Well, he's screwed sure if he drives the T. I could put up the canvas top as a sail and fart into it and still go faster than that boy could drive it."

"Don't use that common language with me, Brook," his mother said, but she didn't raise her voice. He couldn't remember when she had raised her voice to him. She used intensity instead of volume; she arched her eyebrows or squinted her eyes or set her jaw, but her voice remained uninvolved. "When you leave tomorrow ask Caleb to take you to Jefferson and drive the car back." She tightened her mouth somehow. "The Ford, Brook," she added, and then turned back to the papers in front of her. He was dismissed; she had wearied of the interview. The evening wind penetrated the house again and reached the table, jingling the glass prisms of the chandelier, flaring the lamp and throwing an outsized shadow of his mother against the wall. It looked like one of the tricks the clowns performed during the intermission of a magic show when they were trying to frighten the children.

When Brook left in the morning he threw his suitcase into the back seat of the T, set the choke, and put the spark on magneto then cranked the car himself. It was difficult for Caleb to crank a car, having only one arm, and the left one at that. Caleb slid into the seat beside him and Brook backed out of the shed in a short arc and then shifted into low and the car jumped forward. That was one of the drawbacks to the T, it would leap on you, whereas you didn't have to put up with any flaws at all in the Oakland. The Oakland had an electric starter and eight cylinders and a sedan body and there were times, like when his father drove to Fairplay on the good state road, when you couldn't even hear the motor running. It sounded the way velvet felt. Another thing the Oakland never did was rattle and shake, which was inborn in the Model T.

In fact, Brook had named the T the Rattler when his father first bought it. That was in '17, just before the Great War.

Now it rattled down the lane and through the gate and into the meadow road that led to Jefferson. Going down a grade, even a grade this slight, you could get the T up to what Brook guessed was about thirty-five miles an hour. *Guessed*, because the car had no speedometer. It seemed to rattle less at that higher speed but Caleb was hanging on to the door just the same. He wasn't afraid of speed—hell, Caleb wasn't afraid of anything—but May's mud had dried into some fierce June ruts and they could throw you if you went too fast. The Ford's top was down. It was a Touring, marvelous in summer but brutal in the winter months, and they were creating some wind with this speed, although Brook noticed they weren't sending up much dust. A morning in mid-June at ten thousand feet altitude after a typical heavy dew wasn't going to produce much dust anyway. Brook saw that the grass alongside the road was clotted with the dew, elegant and blue-white and sparkling in the sun like a Park drifter's dream of riches.

Brook took a chance and advanced the throttle and the car began to bounce even more. With just one arm it was difficult for Caleb to hang onto the door and his hat at the same time. He wore his usual dress hat with the severe snap to the brim that made it susceptible to blowing off at high speed, but he didn't ask Brook to slow down. Brook did anyway, and Caleb spoke to him immediately. "What did your dad say when you told him you were going to Denver?"

"I didn't tell him," Brook answered. "I told the Queen."

Caleb cleared his throat. "You shouldn't call your mother that."

Brook turned to him. "The Queen of Colorado? Why not?"

"You just shouldn't, that's all."

Brook cocked his head and stared at his uncle, making a sort of game of it, using it to reverse the way the conversation was going. It worked. Caleb grinned and stared back at him, and Brook returned to watching the road. His uncle had a decent smile. A decent face, actually. The Kraut artillery shell that had blown Caleb Hartman's right arm from his body

6

hadn't touched his face. Brook often thought it might have been better if the metal had sculpted a little nick in the cheek or the chin for distinction's sake, for there was certainly nothing memorable about the face the way it was. The features fit the shape of the head well enough but they were innocuous. They didn't command the face, even though the man himself was commanding. Why didn't faces fit people? The mean face on the mean man, the sappy one on the fool? The science of phrenology made easy. Or was it physiognomy? To complicate matters further, Caleb's coloring was off. Where Brook's father leaned somewhat toward a dark complexion, Caleb's was pink. Well, maybe not pink, maybe . . . what? He smiled to himself. There it was. His inability to describe his uncle's face proved his point. The face needed peculiarity, otherwise the man was doomed to carry his blandness into perpetual anonymity, the one face in the crowd you could never remember, the man you spoke to and then forgot once you looked away.

"While you're in Denver," Caleb was saying to him now, "you ought to run out to Golden and talk to the School of Mines. I'm sure you'd have no trouble getting enrolled for the fall term. Like I told you, once you actually sign up for classes and get a schedule of some kind to show your dad his objections will evaporate." He watched Brook across the sun-flooded car seat. "Now that you're old enough to vote you're old enough to go to college, that's what I'm saying. You're old enough to do what you please."

"Hell, I've been doing that for a long time."

It was possible Caleb didn't hear. "After all," he went on, "there's nothing like an education. That's what wins today. Technical knowledge. What you've got to do is go out to Mines and sign up for those mineral courses. Just a couple for now and then you can pick up the others later, in your second year." He looked out across the meadow to the mountains. "If anyone thinks these mountains have given up the last of their wealth, they're crazy. There's bound to be veins of gold and silver and lead still around. The real rich stuff. What you've got to do, Brookers, is learn how to tell those metals apart. Lead from zinc, gold from pyrites, you know what I mean? If

7

you can do that you can write your own ticket in this life. Travel first cabin." He shook his head wistfully, staring out over the radiator of the car. "I wish I'd been in your shoes and had your opportunity. I could have really taken hold of some things."

"You mean gold versus pyrites?"

Caleb gave up the wistful look with a quick smile. "Exactly," he said.

When they reached the depot in Jefferson, Brook parked the Ford and cut the motor. He was wearing the fancy leather vest Etchevarl had made for him and he took his watch from one of the pockets and checked the time. He had no sooner informed Caleb that they had maybe ten minutes to wait for the train than they heard it whistle and looked up and saw it approaching across the floor of the Park. The train was still a long way off but there was never any difficulty hearing a whistle in that country. Huge empty scooped-out places like South Park always treated sound as if they had invented it, pressing it into giant blades that could slice through air easily, making distance a negligible thing. In the Hartman sawmill, at the base of the mountains behind them, the headrig man, whose name was Polite, must have heard the whistle too. Perhaps he merely glanced down the meadow and saw the train approaching and anticipated the whistle, but in any event he walked over to the steam boiler and yanked the lever and let loose a tremendous blast of his own. The whistle struggled for power and then broke free, piercing the morning silence in competition with the train. But its sound changed before it ended, changed drastically. It started out as a scream of combat and ended up as a sob. It became a wail that hung on the air, dying slowly of its own sadness.

"Don't forget," Caleb said after the whistle had dissipated, "when you get to the Mack dealership I want you to pin them down. Make them give you the actual prices and delivery times on the Bulldog. Don't let them blow any smoke." He made a clucking sound in his mouth that was part disbelief and part admiration. "In France our division had Mack trucks. Not the Bulldog of course, it wasn't out yet, but a truck they called the Baby Mack. They were a bit light on weight and guts but they were still the best truck over there. The Frogs and the Limeys both were constantly trying to borrow them from our motor pool." He laughed. "We even heard a rumor once that the Krauts would be willing to trade a hundred prisoners for just one Mack." He broke the laugh off abruptly. "Now Mack's come out with the Bulldog and from what I hear it'll outpull anything going. Seventy-four horsepower, can you believe that?" A blaze of intensity surged through his face. "If we had one of those babies we'd build a road into those big spruce stands on the upper slopes. We could get out of this nickle-and-dime roughcut business and into some real lumber." He slapped the windshield post. "I tell you, Brookers, if Warren Harding gets into office this fall the good times are really going to roll. This whole country will explode. It'll be Buckle Down time for sure. Denver will double its size, you mark my words. Just think of the construction that'll start up down there. Think of the lumber they'll need, and not just softwood boards either." His face flushed with eagerness. "Polite was telling me about a new laminating process that's come out. They use a thin peeler or veneer for the outside and then glue lesser wood together for the inside. Plywood, they call it. Hellish strong, I guess. Thing is, spruce is the best tree in the world for that kind of peeler and we got hundreds of acres of spruce. We could be sitting on a fortune up here."

"We?"

"Your dad could, I mean. If he'd just listen to reason. If I could just convince him to make some changes." His one fist opened and closed in his lap. "It's going to take changes, you know. Lots of them. It's going to take a whole new way of thinking to keep up with the times. New investment. New equipment. If Aaron would just take the first step now and order this Bulldog." He stopped then and sagged a tiny bit against the seat. "But he won't. Your dad hangs back. He likes the old ways."

The approaching train blew for the depot and Brook pushed out from behind the steering wheel and vaulted over the left side of the car and pulled his suitcase from the back seat.

9

Caleb said, "Take your time down there in Denver now, okay? Don't push it. Don't think you've got to get right back to me. Have some fun for yourself. *Relaxez-vous,* like the French say. You've earned it, buddy." The train blew again. "Listen," Caleb blurted, "I've got an idea. This is Monday, right? What do you say I catch the late train Friday and join you for the weekend. How'd you like that? We could have us a real old-fashioned blow-in."

"Hey, that'd be keen!"

"A real whoop, like Polite says."

"Maybe I can line us up something. Something you don't need two hands for. I'll bet I can do it."

Caleb laughed heartily, throwing his head back. "I know better than to bet against you, Brookers. You're the original Peck's Bad Boy!" and he followed that with something else but the locomotive had reached the depot and the roar drowned out his words. Brook motioned for Caleb to set the spark and he bent down and gave the T a good crank. The train noise was so overriding that he couldn't be sure the Ford's motor had caught until he saw the fenders shaking. He grabbed his suitcase and ran along the depot platform to where the conductor stood guarding the steps to the last car. Brook was the only passenger getting on the train and he tossed his luggage onto an empty seat and walked straight back to the platform at the rear of the car. Caleb was still sitting in the Ford watching for him and when he spotted Brook he stood up and raised his arms over his head. He looked so strangely partial and off-balance, one arm full length and the other truncated, that Brook instantly regretted his earlier remark about not needing two hands for certain things. But his uncle was smiling at him now, a big white mouthy smile that was like something shouted over the noise and the steam. Brook shouted back, "See you in Denver!" although he knew when he said it that his uncle was never going to hear the words.

Brook went back inside the car when it started to roll and tossed his suitcase into the overhead rack. When the conductor came by and asked Brook for his ticket he also asked him if he were leaving South Park for good. "So many of our young people are now, since the war."

"I'm not sure yet," Brook answered. "I'm going down to Denver to look things over."

"Your first trip?"

"Oh hell, no," Brook shrugged, pocketing his ticket stub. "I've been to Denver lots of times."

The conductor looked at him sharply. "Not on the train you haven't. Not this one. Not since I've been making the run."

"How long is that?"

"Since the first of the year."

"Shit," Brook snorted, "that's not very long," and he left his seat and walked back outside to the observation platform.

The train had only a few miles to travel before it reached the north wall of the Park and began its climb out, and it did not have to stop and search for the way to go. The white man had long ago replaced an old Indian exit trail with a graveled state highway and laid a narrow-gauge railroad track alongside it. Then, after his fashion, he had given that exit gap a name. Kenosha Pass. Now, from the top of that pass, everything Brook looked upon was down—down, below, beyond, sinking away to the horizon in a magnificent panorama he had known all his life. South Park was a huge bowl set in the earth, a basin fifty miles long and thirty-five miles wide filled with an ocean of grass and rimmed with mountains. It was a storybook plateau, an upland meadow nestled in the lee of the Continental Divide that was equal in size, Caleb had told him once, to the state of Rhode Island. The remarkable thing was that on a clear day the Park lay wholly within the reach of vision, hazy and distorted at its southern end but etched in perfect detail here at the northern where the struggling train paused in the pass to catch its breath. Above him the sky was as blue as flax flowers. Below, Brook could trace the frail white track that was the state road, could pick up the tiny clot of buildings that represented Jefferson, make out the smoking sawmill and the sleepy hay barns of his own family, all scaled by height to mere reproductions of themselves, pressed against the earth like pictures in a book, always in the same position, forever on the same page.

Then the train jerked forward and the vista was gone, the majesty shut out by colorless right-of-way banks and the mundane shelf of roadbeds, and gradually the train nosed down and picked up speed and then barreled with a victorious scream into the narrow valley that would carry it, along with the cascading stream it likewise bore, down the eastern slope of the mountains and into the great shining city at the edge of the plains.

Back inside the coach Brook propped his feet up on the opposite seat and leaned his head back against the fat plush of the upholstery. He had lied to the conductor about traveling on the train. He had actually been to Denver only once in his life and that was the summer before when he had gone down with his parents to meet Caleb, who had finally been released from the English convalescent hospital in Liverpool. Brook remembered the unique sound their train made as it entered Union Station, squealing under its own weight, spitting steam from its head like a monstrous speeding insect outraged because it had been forced to stop. Brook had waited in the lobby with his father and mother and then gone back out when the train from the east arrived. There was a funneled rush of sound and the scrape of wheels and then the steam parted and there in front of them on the platform stood Caleb Hartman, a big, lumpy duffel bag sprawled at his feet like an obedient dog. Not quite stocky, not quite tall, Caleb was wearing a rumpled khaki uniform with one sleeve pinned up over his stump. It looked almost ceremonial. Brook remembered how his father walked up to Caleb and shook his left hand and said—Brook would never forget the awkwardness of the left hands—"Welcome home, brother. Welcome back to life."

Brook's thoughts pulled away from the memory and returned to the burrowing train and to the river that shared the narrow canyon with it. Occasionally the hills crowded the river, shouldering in like burly outriders from the back country who had heard stories about the fast water and had come down this morning to watch it run. The river was the middle fork of the South Platte and it showed now blue and now black and now silver, depending on which side of the canyon held shadow and at what angle the sun struck its surface. But it never quit tumbling, never quit plunging down the fall line. Brook kept watching the water through the window and it lulled him. He leaned his head back and pulled his cap down over his eyes. The wheels went dut-dut-dut in a rhythmic unvarying cadence. If this were a troop train going to the front the wheels would certainly make the same sound but his cap would be a helmet. When the enemy artillery barrage crept too close the train would be forced to stop and he would transfer to a lorry along with the other doughboys. They would form ranks in the middle of a wide white road and then the lorries would carry his company directly to the front lines. They would file into the trenches and crouch on the parapets, checking their rifles and their ammunition belts, their bayonet blades glistening in the sun. Their captain would blow a whistle that he carried around his neck on a steel chain and then with a great shout they would go over the top. The shells would scream and the Boche machine guns would do dut-dut-dut, stitching a fierce hem in the meadow grass before them. He would suffer a wound, and fall, and a nurse in a starched white uniform and a stiff blue cape with a prim little hat would run to him with water and bandages. Soft eyes . . . gentle hands. She would weep and call him a brave young hero while they lifted him into an ambulance. It was in Flanders Field, he knew that. He had always wanted it to be in Flanders Field . . . where the poppies grew. . . .

Brook didn't realize he had fallen asleep until a sharp grinding noise woke him and he looked out the window and realized that the train had stopped and he was in Union Station in Denver. He grabbed his suitcase from the overhead rack and left the coach. There was no one to meet this time. It was noisy on the platform and there were baggage wagons everywhere, some full, some empty. The faces in the windows of a departing train alongside him looked like tiny puffs of escaping smoke.

CHAPTER 2

Brook decided against a hotel and took instead a sleeping room. It was on Stout Street, within easy walking distance of downtown. The house was extremely narrow and had absolutely no tree of any kind in its yard, if in truth it had a yard. The room itself was cramped and the furniture and the bedclothes smelled of cigar smoke, and it had a single window facing north. But the bed was a good sleeper and that was enough.

He spent the first night walking up and down a six-block stretch of Curtis, one of the downtown streets. He had never seen so many lights in one place in his life. He left his room just after dark and walked three blocks south to twentieth and then turned west two blocks to Curtis and there it was, a tunnel of lights carved through the city's heart. A blur of lights. So many lights, so many lighted signs that the street seemed to be moving, flowing magically around the tiny black squares in the middle that turned out to be automobiles. It was the Great White Way and over it all, like an indolent evening breeze, drifted the whine of gears and the bleat of electric horns and the heady bouquet of automobile exhaust. Brook loved Curtis Street, and doubly so because it was also theater row. The New Isis was there, and the Strand and the Victory and the Paris and the Colonial. Vitagraph, Pictograph, Vaudeville, he could see them all on Curtis.

He went early next morning to the Mack dealership and then

hurried back to the Victory and plunked down fifteen cents for a five-reeler entitled *Miss Arizona*. When the curtain came down he bolted out to Sam's Coney Island No. 1 for hot dogs and chili, took in a "Select Attraction" at the New Isis where the drop curtain was a huge florid painting of India or Burma or some such faraway land, raced over to the Manhattan Cafe on Larimer Street for country steak and fried potatoes, and then rushed to a late matinee at the Colonial, where a Wurlitzer played from a stage of its own right in the center of the seats. "The movies are king here," he wrote Caleb from his room later. "I especially like the ones with Hazel Dawn in them. She's a real looker. Charlie Chaplin is a favorite. Fatty Arbuckle too. Very funny. I never thought I would see so many automobiles in one place. The streets look like a parade, one that never ends. The folks at Mack were quite accommodating. The five ton Bulldog is priced at $3500 and the seven ton at $4500, FOB their floor. The salesman said delivery was real tight and the best thing to do was sign an order and make a down payment. If Papa is going to do anything tell him to send some money along with you Friday. I can sign the order for him. To tell you how I feel I am thinking seriously of buying something for myself. The place next to Mack has a Stutz Speedster for only $1775. It's a stunning car. Wire wheels. Super tonneau. If I buy it I will take you for a spin when you get here." He signed the letter and immediately added a postscript: "Going School of Mines Golden probably tomorrow. Fare $1 on Interurban. All electric no smoke no cinders. Details when I see you Fri night. B." He sealed the letter and mailed it at the Roman-looking Post Office building downtown and then shot over to the Paris for a swashbuckler starring Douglas Fairbanks. Later, at the Pantages, he caught the "Midnight Only" performance of the "Special Imported New York City Vaudeville Show and Burlesque."

He slept until noon and his eyes were so swollen when he got up that he decided not to go to Golden. That night when he got dressed to go downtown he wore the overseas cap and the dress tunic Caleb had given him. The people on Curtis Street were as fascinating as the lights. Within the first three blocks he heard a gaunt man give a fiery speech about how rotten governments were and how quickly and ruthlessly the current one in Washington should be overthrown. He met a man who offered him a virgin. He saw a white woman walking with a colored man who reminded Brook of True Jackson, the ex-cavalry sergeant who had once bought horses for the Army from Brook's father and then came to work for him when he mustered out. But of course it wasn't True, otherwise he would have waved.

He hadn't gotten far into the fourth block before a tall thin figure slipped out of an alley and fell in beside him in a kind of march step. Brook guessed the stranger to be his own age, maybe a little older. He was hatless and wore a suitcoat that didn't match his trousers. He eyed Brook's tunic and cap and gave him a snappy salute. "What outfit, Dough?"

Without planning it, Brook answered, "Eighty-fourth Infantry." It had been Caleb's brigade in France.

"What Division?"

"Forty-second. Rainbow."

"Hey, tough outfit." They stopped for the corner and when a gap opened in the cars the stranger crossed the street. But Brook didn't follow and the stranger had to cross back over in the next gap. He came up to Brook less resolutely this time, his hands in his pockets, his eyes hiding in the glare of lights along the street. "I'll tell you," he said, "all this traffic and crowding up makes a guy thirsty."

Brook shrugged.

The stranger moved a step closer. "Maybe you're not a drinking man."

Brook kicked at a cigarette butt lying on the sidewalk. "I didn't say that."

"What do you drink when you get going at it?"

Again Brook shrugged. "Depends on what's available." He let his eyes graze the stranger's face. "I won't drink just anything."

"That's the way I had you figured all along," said the stranger,

16

"a real connoisseur," and with that remark his head lifted up out of his shoulders and Brook could see his face clearly. It was swarthy and sharp-featured with a strangely unrefined look. His hair resembled a piece of black patent leather that had gotten wet and dried too fast, splitting right down the middle. The young man's hands came out of his pockets and he began an elaborate study of the buildings on both sides of the street, of the parked cars, the signs and the dark featureless windows above the signs. "I used to know a place," he began hesitantly, busy with his search. Then a disgusted look crowded into his face and his hands went flying up in irritation. "I can't think here. Too much noise. What do you say we get off this corner. There's a little park over on Lawrence," and he led briskly away, Brook following closely this time.

When they reached the park they sat on a bench that stood back from the sidewalk and was flanked on one end by a row of lilac bushes. "I think maybe I could find us something to wet the old whistle," the stranger began confidentially, "but I'm not sure. . . ." He trailed off.

Brook leaned back against the bench and extended his legs and nonchalantly crossed his boots. "Well, I'm not against having a little drink when I come to the city."

"But I'm not sure," the stranger went on, finishing his remark, "that you could swing the price."

"Sheee-itt!" Brook drawled, uncrossing his boots.

"I mean, this is top shelf goods I'm talking about."

"That's the only kind."

"Can't everybody swing a premium deal like this, given the times and all. You gotta have contacts."

"I know what you mean."

"I'm talking imported stuff." He leaned toward Brook and lowered his voice. "Canadian," he said.

Brook sat straight up on the bench.

"Even if I could ring the right bell," the stranger went on, "these people are not going to sell it a thimbleful at a time."

"Right. Who wants to fool with a thimbleful?"

"If you look at the transportation costs and the bribes to get the shipment into the city, I'm guessing a pint could go for as much as. . . ." He stopped and made a humming noise in his throat, ". . . twelve bucks."

Brook tipped his cap forward. "That's not out of line. Not for imported."

The stranger eyed him warily. "You game, Dough, is that what you're saying?"

"Hell yes, I'm game."

But the stranger didn't get up and leave the bench as Brook had expected. "You understand, don't you," he said to Brook, "that there's no cuff with these people, none of that catch you payday crap."

"Good way to do business. A lot like selling horses."

The stranger squirmed in his seat. "What I'm saying is, you're going to have to give me the buy price now. First. I've got to go into the deal with the do-re-mi in my hand."

"Hell, why didn't you say something?" said Brook, and he dug in his pocket and pulled out twelve one dollar bills, which is all he'd brought with him from the room, and laid the bills in the stranger's hand. The stranger got up from the bench and strode off quickly across the grass and disappeared under the streetlight at the far end of the park.

Actually, he was back in an amazingly short time, considering that he'd forgotten exactly where he had to go and how to make contact with the Canadians. He was carrying what was obviously a bottle in a brown paper sack and when he sat down beside Brook he opened the sack and screwed the cap off the bottle. There was an immediate overwhelming odor of perfume. "If it tastes good it ought to smell good," said the stranger, hearing Brook sniff. He took the first drink, a quick one, and handed the bottle to Brook. "No glasses," he said. "I hope you don't mind sharing. I guess you got used to that when you were in the trenches."

Brook tipped the bottle up and took a healthy swig and then turned to the stranger and said, "Well, there's the first dead soldier." At least that's what he meant to say. Actually, nothing came out of his mouth. It couldn't, his throat was closed off. Besides that, his breathing had stopped. At the same time, something hit him in the stomach and then hit him again;

it was what he guessed they called a jolt, and he didn't know whether to spit or cough or stand up and shake himself. Finally, after a lot of swallowing and head twisting and trying to blink away the water in his eyes, he turned to the stranger and said, "Those Canadians sure know their booze."

"He-man stuff," the stranger said. "And it's popular too. It's what the real drinkers always ask for." He took the sack from Brook and wiped the neck of the bottle on his sleeve and took a drink. It was a bigger one this time but it might as well have been milk for all his reaction. Brook's next drink was much easier on his throat, although it was obvious his stomach hadn't gotten accustomed to it yet. They took turns after that, wiping and drinking, talking about what it meant to find real quality in this age of shabby goods, and after a particularly long drink Brook took a package of tailor-made cigarettes from his tunic and began smoking one cigarette after the other.

The night air turned very warm and the streetlights on Lawrence grew fuzzy and the bottle gradually got empty. At some point, somehow, the stranger disappeared and the last thing Brook remembered was sitting alone at the extreme edge of the park bench talking to the lilac bushes. He must have fallen off sometime during the night because when the pack of dogs came up and nosed him at dawn, he was lying on the ground. He managed to get to his feet but his stomach was so bloated he couldn't stand up straight. His head throbbed and there was a curious metallic taste on his tongue. When he finally got back to his room on Stout Street he realized that his overseas cap was missing.

It took Brook all the next day to get his stomach to stop burning and he spent the night in the restaurants on Larimer, eating thick creamy chowders and drinking cold milk, for he wanted to be in top shape for Caleb's visit the following night.

In the morning he bought a new cap at the Daniels & Fisher store and to test his stomach he rode up on the elevator to the tower at the top of the building. The stomach was fine. A man there who was dressed in some kind of uniform told Brook that from the tower one could see two hundred miles of the front range of the Rockies, but what was harder for Brook to believe was how much prairie he could see. When he went to the opposite railing and faced east the prairie looked like what he thought an ocean might, an ocean lapping at the town and threatening to engulf it with the Daniels & Fisher tower a kind of lighthouse on the shore.

That afternoon he put on his best clothes and bought a ticket on the high-speed electric train that he believed would carry him out to Golden but took him instead to Boulder, a town thirty-five miles to the north. On the return trip his stomach began to roil with actual hunger pains and when he got off the train he went immediately to the Oxford Hotel, which was only a block from Union Station, and ordered the hotel's deluxe turkey-and-oyster dinner. Brook had been at the table only a few minutes when he realized that his father had brought them to this very same dining room the year before, immediately after meeting Caleb at the station. Brook could even remember the table the waiter had given them, the one directly beneath the magnificent stained glass window, and he stared at it now as though he could see the four of them still sitting there, his mother in her big European hat and his father in the pin-striped suit and the rolled-brim Stetson, with Caleb looking rumpled in the khaki uniform and his face thin and sallow from the long hospital stay. How grim and inward his uncle had been at the table that day, Brook remembered, how painfully red-faced when his father insisted on buttering his dinner rolls and cutting up his beefsteak for him.

When he had finished his meal, Brook ordered coffee and ran through his mind a list of places he might take Caleb. Vaudeville at the Pantages was an idea but it could prove embarrassing to Caleb, especially during those doctor-and-nurse skits when the words got smutty and the drums rolled and the girls tripped across the stage with their breasts jiggling and nearly falling out. The Photo Plays were definitely wrong; Caleb Hartman wasn't going to come all the way to Denver just to sit through a "Douglas Fairbanks Double Bill," not a man almost forty years old who had been in half the world. There had to be plenty of nice speakeasies in town where he could take Caleb for a few drinks and a floorshow, but he didn't know where they were. And he should, damn it! Caleb would think he was nothing but a wet-eared kid if he didn't know where the night life was, the fun and excitement. Caleb would expect it. *We'll have a real whoop down there!* Isn't that what he'd said? Brook grew suddenly nervous. He didn't dare repeat a dumb-ass trick like walking Curtis and getting hustled again. Where *would* he take Caleb?

He left the hotel and walked through the Welcome Arch into Union Station. It was crowded and boisterous, Friday night, a summer weekend coming up. The train from Leadville, Breckenridge, and South Park was scheduled in at 7:30 and Brook took a seat on one of the high-backed benches and watched the people and waited for his uncle.

But his uncle wasn't on the train. It was announced at precisely 7:25 and Brook went out onto the platform and watched the train stop and the people get off, but Caleb Hartman wasn't one of them.

Brook walked back through the Arch and down Seventeenth Street, and where it intersected with Lawrence he stopped. It was getting full dark and he stood on the corner and watched the lights come on. It was exciting. It was as if the streets were veins and when the lights came on the blood began to beat faster. People multiplied. Sound intensified. The sidewalks gave up their heat and the air got cool. The stream of cars swelled and an exotic oil-and-leather smell rose from the streets. Brook could see a group of theatergoers gesturing to each other under the arc lights a block away, like puppets in a show that had no sound and no music. A big touring car drove past the corner at that moment, full of girls. They were chattering excitedly to each other, laughing, their hair streaming and their arms lifting as if to catch the lights, their faces glossy as wax and white as moonlight.

Brook walked to the corner of Champa and Sixteenth and a man stepped out of a doorway and approached him. He was dressed in white flannel trousers and a blue blazer. His shirt was smartly starched and his cuffs were lacy. The crisp straw hat shaded his face but his shoes reflected every light on the street.

"You looking for something, Slim?" he asked, and his voice was satiny as flax seed. "Something special? A few turns and issues maybe?"

Brook was ready this time. "That depends," he said.

The man winked at him. "You can't be too careful down here on the streets. Some of these slickers are disreputable. They'll try to sell you stuff that's almost straight wood alcohol. Oh, they'll squeeze a few juniper berries in it and add some coloring and give it a lot of fancy names but it's still pure old Blue Ruin."

Brook fixed his eyes on a point just above the man's straw hat. "They couldn't fool *me* with it, I can tell you that. I'd know what it was from the perfume smell."

"Good thinking," the man said. "And you'd be right."

"Right," Brook said, and looked away.

"Listen," said the man, stepping closer and lowering his voice. "How about a nice club?"

Caleb could possibly come tomorrow on the morning train. "How nice?"

The man's hands came up, rings flashing, his voice strangely unexcited. "Dance band. Lots of bimbos. Real knockouts, too. Go all the way for the right guy." He stopped and took a breath. "What I'm talking about here," he said, and his fingernails glistened intimately, "is a little place just outside the city. All the fun you could ever want. Write your own ticket, you know what I mean?"

"Sure, I know what you mean. You're talking about the Sunshine Rescue Mission."

The man laughed effortlessly. "I like a sense of humor in a young fella. Keeps him out of trouble." He made a sly motion with his head. "Look, Slim, I got a Marmon 34 Touring with twelve cylinders parked around the corner just raring to go. Thirty minutes gets us there. Thirty minutes to the sweet life. What d'ya say?" and he shot his cuffs and touched a single finger to the snappy straw boater.

For a fleeting second Brook suspected that it was clothes that made the man, made whole classes of men and then kept those classes apart. Or was that false? Could the roughest blackest heart be put behind starch and lace and made to be a gentleman? The insight was tenuous, lasting only as long as the bootlegger stood perfectly motionless in his elegant tableau, and when he moved, asking breathily for Brook's answer, the moment was gone.

It was a keen ride, Brook thought, faster than he had ever gone and not far off the promised time, although on a couple occasions he nearly lost his new cap. Their destination was the Moonbeam Ranch on Morrison Road, his host explained. "You're going to like this place, Slim."

"That depends on what they're serving for drinks."

They drove around to the rear of a low hacienda style building and went in. It was crowded in an intimate comfortable way. There was a big dance floor and a six-piece band playing "The Sunshine of Your Smile." Brook and his host took a table near the front and a waiter came gliding up, smiling pleasantly, and explained that a half-pint bottle was the minimum order per person. A highball glass was included in that, of course, plus a water or soda chaser. That's what they ordered, both of them, and Brook sat stiffly in his chair with his hands pressed together, not looking at his companion, waiting for the drinks to arrive so he could smell them.

He needn't have worried. The colorless minty liquid the waiter brought to their table was the smoothest concoction he'd tasted since Etchevarl made the *tesuin* out of yucca blades to celebrate Caleb's return from the California gold fields at Christmas in 1916. Lord, was it smooth! "Best stuff I've had since I came to the city," Brook announced.

"Have fun, Slim," his companion winked, removing his straw hat. "It's the sweet life, just like I promised."

The orchestra swung into a peppy version of "It's a Long, Long Way to Tipperary" and then played "Home Fires" next, with a lot of emphasis on the saxophones, and the room got smoky and the people at the tables got murmury and a tall girl with bobbed hair and sore-looking eyebrows and a dress that looked like crepe paper came over and asked Brook to dance— which he thought he faked real well—while the band played "A Pretty Girl Is Like a Melody." Another girl came over later when Brook had gotten a good start on his second half-pint and they danced too, but the band played an especially mournful rendition of "Long, Long Trail A-Winding" and followed that with an even more poignant "My Buddy" and damned if Brook didn't get to crying so hard the girl had to lead him back to his table and leave him there. It was all so sad, he explained to his companion, holding his head in his hands, so terribly tragic that the finest and best had suffered so much in that war. The Great War. The Doughboys . . . so heroic . . . so brave . . . his own dear wounded uncle among them. . . .

Brook had to pay in advance for the return to Denver when his host announced in a disgusted voice that the last thing in the world the Moonbeam Ranch needed was a damned bawler. When the Marmon 34 disgorged Brook on the corner of Sixteenth and Champa his new cap was gone and he couldn't find in any of his pockets the brass-plated trench lighter Caleb had taken from a Heinie officer in France and brought back for him.

When he awoke in the morning Brook had no hangover but his crotch was full of fever. All he could think of was flesh, female flesh. When he shook himself after urinating he got instantly hard. He went down the hall of the boardinghouse and sat in a tub of cold water, and then shaved and dressed and went out and the fever subsided somewhat.

The sun was already hammering the streets, there was no wind, the air was sticky with heat. He went to Union Station and met the morning train from South Park but Caleb wasn't on it. He had a breakfast of oatmeal and toast at the Olympus Cafe on Arapahoe and bought a new cap at Albert Brothers, and then began a tour of the downtown streets, determined to walk off the remaining fever. The street vendors were starting up for the day, shabby heavy-coated men pushing their carts and calling out a list of their wares.

Brook turned down to Thirteenth and walked east, his head clearing and his nerves settling with every block, and when he came to Welton Street he took a seat on a bench that was out of the sun and studied the tall isolated building that stood on the corner. He recognized it right away. It was the Opportunity School his father had taken them to the summer before, him and his mother and Caleb, after they had finished their dinner at the Oxford Hotel. "There's a staff of occupational therapists employed at this school," Brook remembered his father explaining to Caleb. "Their purpose is to teach vocational skills to disabled veterans. A very high-minded program."

Brook remembered how instantly stiff Caleb had gone at the words, how his calf muscles bunched under the wrinkled puttees, how his single hand kept clenching and unclenching as though he were trying to work out a cramp.

"We should go in and speak to the administrator," his father said to Caleb. "A Mrs. Griffith, I believe. I'm given to understand that one of the courses she offers here at the school covers what they call the 'one hand skills.' Telegraphy, calligraphy, basket weaving, that sort of thing." He had been looking up at the building as he spoke but now he turned to Caleb. "You'd think that weaving with only one hand would be impossible, wouldn't you? But obviously it isn't. Men can actually be trained to make baskets—"

Caleb turned on his heels at that point and marched down the sidewalk and then stopped, his back to the three of them, staring rigidly into the distance. He had walked so hard, been so angry, that his stump sleeve had come unpinned and now hung emptily at his side like a strip of bunting from one of those temporary platforms that traveling dignitaries had used during the war to sell bonds.

Brook left the bench and took a turn on Broadway. He sat for several minutes on the cool stone steps of the capitol building and then walked west on Colfax. He went back to the Olympus in mid-afternoon for lunch and it was when he was coming out of the cafe that he met the girl. She was standing in the shade of a building with a parasol at her shoulder. "Hello, soldier boy," she said, for Brook was wearing the khaki tunic again.

"Mademoiselle from Armentières," he said to her, smiling wanly, making it all seem a little weary and at the same time struggling to remember some of the French phrases Caleb had taught him. "*Comment ça va*." That was one. "*40 Hommes et 8 Chevaux*." His mind raced to recall the others. "*Combien . . . avec . . . relaxez-vous. . . .*"

She stopped him with a laugh. "I like it, even if I don't understand it." She twirled her parasol archly. "Would you like to go to church with me? Confess your sins?"

"I don't have any sins."

"You will if you go with me." She smiled impishly and stepped forward and took his arm, nearly suffocating him with a blast of perfume. She had a hard little chin and her cheeks looked stretched. There was a lot of rouge on her face but she wasn't unpretty and she made Brook think of the Pantages girls. Her room was on upper Arapahoe and once inside they both took off their clothes. The girl's body was much fuller than the dress had suggested and her flesh smote him in its abundance. Her breasts were large and hard and her belly was a soft white pod. A wave of his earlier fever surged through him and when she bent forward to remove her stockings he grabbed her by the hips and ground himself into her buttocks. 'Oooh," she squealed, "you got hard fast!"

"I'm ready."

"I like the way you get ready," she laughed, turning to him, admiring him. She pulled him roughly onto the bed and ran her tongue into his ear. She grabbed his penis at the base and rolled it in a slow circle and then pointed it at different objects in the room like she would a stick. But she must have sensed his urgency for she stopped abruptly and pulled him on top of her.

He didn't last long. The pressure in his loins was quickly dissipated.

The girl got up from the bed and put on a blue kimono with huge red flowers in the print and then laid back down beside him with an overdone sigh. Brook was up on one elbow watching her and he saw that some of the paint had rubbed off her face. It was as if he had interrupted her in the middle of dressing and she would stop and talk to him for a minute and then finish. She spotted his khaki tunic on the chair and he could see in her eyes that she was going to turn it into conversation. "My soldier hero," she said. She put a smile with the words but it only heightened her unfinished look. "You seem so young to have fought in the war."

"I'm twenty-one. Hell, you can be a soldier at eighteen."

"Were you a hero?"

"My uncle was," he said. "He lost an arm in the Meuse-Argonne. It was just three weeks before the Armistice. He'd been fighting in the trenches all year."

"I'm sorry." She was concentrating on one of her fingers, and Brook hardly heard her words. "Where is your uncle now?" she asked, and it was more distinct this time; she had raised her head to inspect her whole hand and not just the one finger.

"He's living with us. At least until he moves on. I suppose he'll move on. He always has. He was coming down to Denver last night to see me. On the train. I guess he couldn't make it. But he's a great guy."

"Uncles usually are." She gave a blunt laugh. "Except one of mine. He was always trying to get me into his bed." She started to laugh but when Brook didn't join in she made a quick switch. "Are you from Denver?"

"No."

"Where then?" And before he could answer she said, "What do you do?"

"I'm a student. I mean, I'm going to be a student. Just as soon as I get out to Golden and sign up for classes."

She laughed fully this time. "Baby doll, you can sign up for my classes anytime you want!" and she rolled over and pinched him on the stomach. But she didn't keep her hand idle for long. She slid it down into his crotch and began to rub him. She hadn't bothered to close the kimono and he could see the swollen eddy of her navel and the black swatch of hair between her legs that was like part of a costume she hadn't taken off. Her breasts were so big they seemed to be holding the kimono open for him. She was suddenly a rack of weak faceless flesh and he mounted and thrust savagely into her, pummeling her body with his own. She moaned theatrically and pretended to bite her lip. She was faking the passon but he was actually abusing her and she didn't know it. She didn't know it in the same way a hen doesn't know that people eat her eggs.

When they had finished dressing he put some money into her hand. She didn't count it. "You don't know gold from pyrites either, do you?" he said.

"What?"

He laughed, but he didn't look at her. "Go," he said. "Go from this church of yours and sin no more."

Back in his room he lay perfectly still on his bed as though the heat would prick him if he brushed against it. He was relaxed, the session with the girl had eased him. He felt lazy and his thoughts wandered, seeking something to fix on. Through the window he could see the parched yellow grass of the vacant lot across the street and it made him think of the prairie. The prairie fascinated him. He had seen it first from the top of the Daniels & Fisher tower and again from the window of the mistaken train to Boulder. He wasn't accustomed to seeing that much horizon all at one time, seeing anything that flat. It was almost frightening to look upon, an ocean you feared to enter and could never survive long enough to cross. The prairie was his mother's country. Kansas prairie. She had never talked to him about it personally but he'd heard her tell a woman at a Social one time that the sky was so big in Kansas it smothered you, that as a child she had believed that if you fell when you were out alone on the prairie, the sky would swoop down and press you into the earth and hold you there forever.

His thoughts drifted back to the scorched yard beyond his window, empty of trees. He missed the trees. Behind his home in South Park there was a grove of aspen that covered half a mountain. The wind sang in it in summer like a thousand jays and in autumn it sang with color as well, a thick rich spill of gold. . . .

He dozed, woke when the sweat ran into his eyes, dozed again, never moving, chained to his bed by the heat. The afternoon died. Evening came and narrowed fretfully into darkness. He dreamed of the huge lofty Park and the way the mountains lifted it up from the rest of the earth, held it like a separate kingdom, kept it cool and green. He dreamed of his people, saw them standing strangely blurred and phantasmal in a golden clearing beside a silver stream . . . the people he loved . . . Caleb, his mother and father, his father's ancient friend, the sad-faced Basque herder, Arranz Etchevarl. . . .

It was an apologetic sunrise that slipped in from the prairie and crept through the Denver streets the next morning. Brook woke, saw it and went back to sleep, rising for good sometime closer to noon. He ate breakfast at the cafe and brought a newspaper back with him and was sitting on the porch reading it when he heard footsteps approaching on the sidewalk. Without looking up from the paper he knew the steps would turn in toward the house, that they were for him, that Caleb had finally made it down, that his welcome of his uncle shouldn't be *too* warm—

It wasn't Caleb. It was Etchevarl.

Brook rose to his feet and in that moment a terrible dread rose with him. The big graceful man he had known all his life stood in front of him now without a shred of grace. He seemed shrunken. The corduroy trousers, the cuffed gloves, the great faded beret all seemed too large for his body. The long mustached face was pinched with dismay, the eyes bleak. Then he spoke and the quaint stilted baritone voice was a voice Brook had never heard before: "You must come home, Brook. It is your father. He is lost in the mountains. He went up into the pass and did not return. You must come home with me now."

CHAPTER 3

What Margaret Pendleton saw from the porch of the house was a flash only, a brief sun-catch of something shiny in the trees on the other side of the meadow, maybe two miles away. She wasn't watching for anything in particular, just standing there looking across the immense sloping meadow at the mountains. She had arrived only the day before from Kansas City in response to Caleb Hartman's concern for Ruth, his sister-in-law, whose husband was missing. He was lost in some topmost part of the very mountains Margaret was studying. In the pass, they said. Up on the Divide.

Actually, it wasn't Margaret who had been asked to come to the Hartman home in South Park but rather her mother, who had been a childhood friend of Ruth's and had graduated from Normal School with her. But Margaret's mother was ill and her husband was away on church business in England at the time, all of which freed Margaret to come to Colorado in her mother's place.

And so she had, traveling all the way from Kansas City on the train. She had traveled on a train before, to camp meetings at Wichita and Great Bend but never out of the state, so that when the train crossed into Colorado Margaret began immediately to search ahead through her coach window for the mountains. She had never seen mountains before and when she finally did see them she didn't realize it. There was a density on the flat line of the earth far to the west, like a bad water-color that kept blurring. She even tried looking away and then looking back, quickly, trying to catch the blur for the mirage it surely was. Possibly it was a large cloud or even a whole line of clouds shouldering up over the horizon, jostling for a place to look out from, like children wanting to see how big the prairie was.

But finally she realized that what she was seeing was the mountains, there was no mistake. They darkened perceptibly as the train crept westward, they grew, they got some outline to them, some permanence. But slowly, ever so slowly. It wasn't until she was much closer to Denver that the Rocky Mountains began to look like she'd always thought they would. Purple cones spaced against the sky in a geometry that was perfect because it was so unmoving. Majestic pyramids tiering back-ward from their own front, rank on rank.

Then, strangely, when the train got very close to Denver, the ranks disappeared. The mountains got smaller. Entering the foothills on the far side of the city they failed her altogether. The earlier image broke apart, changing to sunless canyons and cramped slopes choked with a black gloom of trees that simply would not lift.

But South Park, when they reached it, took her breath away. It soared. She thought later that what it did most was surprise her. So many shades of green! So much snow remaining on the peaks. And the air! The air was thinner and lighter and no matter where she looked there seemed to be a blue tint to it, as if it had melted out somehow from the deeper blue of the sky. She wasn't prepared for what the altitude did to her either, for even standing directly in the sun didn't cause her to sweat. There was a coolness that lingered everywhere shade stood. A faint pine incense filled her lungs constantly, luring her into indolence and sleep.

Now, after having gotten Ruth to lie down and rest in the back bedroom upstairs, Margaret had come to the porch to stretch and rub the weariness from her eyes and to look out at things, simply that, and to get away for a few minutes from the other woman's terrible silences. Then she'd seen the flash

31

in the timber at the base of the mountains on the far side of the meadow. And it was just then that a man came up onto the porch and stood beside her, eyeing her with a bold civility, introducing himself as Grant Pickens. "Did you see that?" Margaret asked, genuinely puzzled and also a little embarrassed by the man's sudden appearance. "There's something in those woods over there. Probably livestock."

Grant Pickens didn't answer immediately but when he did there was a tone in his voice that sounded like disgust. "You haven't been around stock much, have you, Missus?"

Margaret delayed answering the question, using the time to inspect her companion more closely. He was actually as sullen faced as she'd first suspected. His clothes were greasy and he wore on his head one of those leather aviator helmets with the chin straps hanging loose instead of snapped shut. His top teeth protruded so badly that when he opened his mouth it looked as if he were about to spit them out. In that stupid leather helmet he reminded Margaret of some Kansas City street tough, and his coming unbidden to the porch was beginning to annoy her. She asked him if her not knowing a great deal about livestock had even the remotest connection with what she'd just seen in the woods.

"Well, it could," Grant answered, drawling it out in the same patronizing manner as before, "considering the fact that the stock we got up here in the Park is all meat and they don't flash when the sun hits them. It's metal that flashes, Missus."

"Really," Margaret said, and turned away, dismissing him, going back to her study of the mountains. They were so green with timber they throbbed; it seemed almost a movement. The slopes were so steep and the colors were stacked against them in such a way—the darker greens higher up, heavier, denser—that it seemed the whole range of mountains must surely topple over into the meadow, even as she watched.

But Grant Pickens hadn't deserted the porch as she had hoped. He was speaking again, almost confidentially this time, hoping to rebut the dismissal. "What you seen there," he explained, "was somebody coming. There's a road in amongst those trees, the old road from the town of Como. Something's on it. Team and wagon maybe but more'n likely it's a motor car." He pursed his lips smugly. "We got a few motor cars up here, you know."

Margaret ignored it. "Perhaps it's Ruth's boy returning from Denver," she said.

Grant let out a breath that fluttered with exasperation. "You flatlanders don't know directions real good either, do you? That timber we're looking at, Missus, that's south. Denver sets to the northeast. That's the way Brook will come home. That is, if he comes at all, if old Etch ever found him." He gave one of the dangling chin straps on his helmet a scornful tug. "I'll tell you, they'd play Billy Hell trying to find *me* in Denver."

"I can't imagine their wanting to," Margaret said, but before she could savor any of the victory in the remark, the sawmill whistle blew. It was terrifying in its shrillness. It knifed down the meadow and slashed at the porch as if pressing on the watchers a personal attack. Then it drew back as though reconsidering, and keened away across the lawn and down the east meadow, fading from anger to a strange remorse as it went. "Why must it *do* that?" Margaret demanded when the stillness had returned.

"Do what?"

"Be so sad at the end like that. It's the saddest sound I've ever heard. It's like . . . something dying."

Grant tossed his head contemptuously. "Not if you're standing next to it, it ain't sad. It's just plain dangerous. It'll blow both your eardrums clean out if you don't cover up."

Margaret started to ask why they blew the whistle at all but the strange light flashed again from the timber. It was splintered and brief and in some ways like another sound, leaving its own peculiar silence when it disappeared. Margaret scouted the dark edge of timber beyond the meadow, waiting for the flash to come again, but it didn't and she went back to what they had been discussing before the whistle. "What was Brook doing in Denver anyway?" she asked, but she kept her eyes on the trees.

"Who knows?" Grant shrugged. "Brook's like a calf charging

a gatepost, time he gets there he forgot why he started." He glanced at Margaret suspiciously. "But you probably know Brook. You're probably family."

Margaret answered curtly that she was not family. "And I've never been here before in my life. I don't even know what Brook is like."

"Well, you ain't missed much," Grant drawled, and he shook his head ruefully as though the terrible responsibility of exposing a friend's true character had fallen on him unavoidably. "They say the best steel has got to go through the fire, but hell," and he paused dramatically, "Brook ain't even felt a *spark!*"

"Is he bright?" Margaret asked, and her lack of reaction to his analysis shook Grant briefly.

"Oh, Brook would like you to think so," he answered, recovering, "but the fact is he'll go dreamy and bookish on you when you ned him most. It was his old man's weakness too."

"I can't believe," Margaret came back, and there was a snap to her words, "that a man who's building a successful business like Mr. Aaron Hartman is, could be seriously flawed."

Grant wasn't sure of *flawed*, but he didn't want to lose ground, especially now that he believed he was ahead. "Well," he began carefully, "Aaron was a man who liked to stick with the tried and true. He wanted to keep doing what he'd always done. Maintaining the cow herds, buying up land, building the horse business and selling mounts to the Army. That's what he wanted Brook to concentrate on."

"Is that what Brook wants?"

Grant sniffed and said nothing.

"Is Brook close to his father?"

Grant grunted.

"His mother?"

A snort now. "Brook ain't close to nobody, especially her. I don't think they're even friends, not that I can see." But he cocked his head just a little then, like a chicken reconsidering a pebble. "Well, maybe Caleb. You could say that Brook's kinda close to Caleb. In fact, I understand he even tried to

34

enlist in the Army when Caleb got hurt over there in France. He was packed up and waiting for the train in Jefferson when Aaron found him and brought him back." He paused. "I guess you could say Brook thinks Caleb's all right."

"*Is* Caleb all right? You seem to be the expert on the family."

Grant was flattered by the request for an additional opinion and ignored the insult. "Well," he began, sucking a front tooth, "Caleb's a mover, number one. He's got his eye on the main chance, as they say. He claims selling horses to the Cavalry is out. The Cavalry is going to be tanks from now on, he says. Caleb came out of that war full of ideas. This new lumber business we're into, that's one of them. He tore down the old mill that had the water wheels and brought in a big steam boiler, just to prove to Aaron it could be done. Now we're cutting five times the boards we used to. He wants to buy a truck and he's even thinking about a little locomotive and a set of rails leading directly from the mill to the depot at Jefferson. That's one of the reasons Caleb hired Polite. Polite was a lumberjack. He's run one of them steam donkeys before. And he's the one built the millpond and the flume."

"The flume?"

"Where we float the logs down the mountain on a scaffold full of water. Like a trough." He waited in a rare politeness for an additional question from Margaret, and then went on. "And there's this new plywood thing Caleb's been kicking around. He says they're starting to use plywood in motor cars now. Running boards and door panels and such. Caleb claims that's where the future is, in wood and motor cars. Not horses. All horses are good for, he says, is to curry and comb and ride around on Sunday afternoons. He claims it takes three acres of land to raise enough food to feed just one horse. Waste of effort, Caleb says. Misuse of land and resources. But of course that wasn't Aaron's opinion. Aaron believed raising horses was a noble thing that a man should do well and care about, like raising a family. Horses was like children to him."

"You keep referring to Brook's father in the past tense. Aren't you assuming a lot?"

35

A series of silver flashes issued suddenly from the distant trees and Grant pointed at them. "Your livestock turned out to be a motor car, Missus, just like I told you."

Margaret had seen the reflections but nothing else. "What makes you so sure?"

"The flashes. They're coming too fast to be a horseman."

Even as Grant spoke, there was emergence on the opposite slope. It looked for a moment as if a knot of trees had broken loose from the bottom edge of the timber and slipped down into the meadow, unable to hold the slope. But it was obviously not trees, it was some object in motion whose identity the distance had cloaked. When it dipped at the creek to make the ford it was a long time out of sight, as if it were some sort of animal drinking. But it broke into view again and began to take on a certain blocky form, however indefinable. Margaret thought it looked one moment like a building and the next like a giant hearse and finally a railroad car that had gotten misrouted. But in truth she couldn't decide. "What is it?" she demanded of her companion, her eyes riveted on the approaching object. "Do you know?"

"Sure I know," Grant beamed. "It's Ess Cohen in his Freighter."

The vehicle grew steadily in size and finally reached the sawmill complex—the flume scaffolding and the millpond and the wigwam burner and the neat squares of curing boards— and as if in recognition someone inside the mill gave two quick toots on the steam whistle. In response, a shrill glottal bleating sounded from the huge truck, which immediately afterward appeared to gain speed as if it had divested itself of some troublesome gas. It lumbered up the meadow road and when it reached the gate it wheeled heavily into the lane, shuddering in certain of its parts and rocking in others, the dust rising up behind like a delayed ovation. The dogs barked and Etchevarl's pet guinea hens went flying and with a last groan of its chain drive the truck stopped in front of the house and went still.

Truly, it was an incredible machine. The vehicle had originally been a standard truck—a Steurer Pioneer Freighter—but

Cohen had had it converted. There were so many motor vehicles in South Park now that Ess had installed a garage next to his Fairplay store and hired a mechanic. He had extended the wheelbase eighteen inches and installed heavy duty wagon springs over each wheel. The original truck bed and side boards had been replaced by an open spruce frame that contained various showcases and compartments and drawers, a veritable department store on wheels. A fringed canvas roof had been built over the top with a canopy extending out over the cab. The cab was likewise open but it had two supporting struts and on each one fluttered a two-foot-square American flag. On the bottom beam of the truck frame was printed in stern block lettering:

S COHEN
SOUTH PARK MERCANTILE.

The first thing to move was the driver, Ess Cohen himself, as he descended from the cab. He stepped down to the small top running board and then to the larger bottom one, sending up puffs of dust with each step. He wore a shapeless garment that had a hole for his head and which flared down over his body like an oversized poncho, concealing everything but his gloves and his black galoshes. He stepped to the ground and brushed himself, causing more dust to fly. He wore goggles and when he flipped them onto his forehead he revealed a pair of dustfree eye sockets so perfectly white and circular that he looked like a raccoon who had learned how to drive a truck and then got lost.

Grant and Margaret walked out from the porch and Cohen stood waiting for an introduction. When none came, Margaret announced herself to Cohen: "I am Mrs. Emerson Pendleton from Kansas City. A temporary guest of the Hartman family."

Ess Cohen nodded graciously, it was almost a bow. "How fortunate that you are here, Mrs. Pendleton. And how tragic the event that brings you." He then turned to Grant and in an abruply changed voice asked where Caleb was.

Grant shrugged. "He's around somewhere. What you got for us?"

"What Caleb ordered yesterday. Can you get him for me, please?"

Margaret ended up doing it. She found Caleb sitting in the kitchen drinking coffee and he came back out with her to the truck. Cohen spoke a few words to Caleb that Margaret couldn't hear and then started unloading a stack of gear from the back of the Freighter—a bundle of yellow slickers, several coils of three-quarter-inch rope and some small hand picks, a few tents, a litter made of folded metal and canvas, plus a shapeless baglike affair that Margaret couldn't identify. When the unloading was complete, Cohen held the clipboard firmly while Caleb scribbled his name across it with his left hand.

"I'm sorry about your brother," Cohen said.

Caleb acknowledged the remark with a brusque military nod.

"Is Brook back yet?" asked Cohen.

"I expect him this afternoon. I sent Etchevarl down to Denver to get him."

When the Freighter had gone and Caleb had returned to the house, Margaret asked Grant about the mysterious sacklike object Ess Cohen had delivered. "That leather thing," she said, pointing to where it lay on the edge of the lawn.

Grant shot her a hopeless look. "It ain't leather, Missus, it's rubberized canvas. And what it is, it's a body bag. A bag for carrying dead bodies."

Margaret studied it solemnly. "You seem pretty sure of what happened to Mr. Hartman."

Grant glanced up at the Divide. "When a man's missing for four whole days," he began, but then trailed off.

Margaret turned and looked into the south meadow, watching the retreat of Ess Cohen's Freighter. Its progress reminded her of the smart-aleck projectionist in Kansas City who had run an entire half-reel of film backward one Sunday evening at the church. "Has Mr. Hartman lived all his life here?" she asked Grant, turning back to him.

"Born here. Never lived anyplace else. Not even in a different house."

"It seems so strange, him getting lost like this. Doesn't it seem strange to you?"

"What's strange about it?"

Margaret shook her head and looked away across the meadow to the dark crowding mountains. "Never mind," she said. "I expect I'm still tired from my trip. And I'm not used to this thin air yet."

CHAPTER 4

It was late afternoon. Brook sat in the parlor with Caleb and Etchevarl and studied his mother. It was very curious. She held herself as though she were waiting for something, eyes open, head up and inclined slightly to one side, her body expectant, her hands closed upon each other and not rubbing together, not pinching at the dress, not wanting the noise or the distraction of that but wanting only to be ready when it came—the voice, the touch, the presence, whatever it was she was waiting for.

It wasn't Brook. She had watched him cross the lawn to the porch when he came home earlier in the afternoon but she hadn't gone down the steps to meet him, hadn't sought him out later in any private way. If she had spoken to him at all he had forgotten. Now, sitting in her husband's favorite chair that had been pulled back to the darkest corner of the room, she did not sob or press her temples or wring her hands and Brook did not expect it. It was not his mother's way, she would never crumple, never break down in any circumstance, the appearance would be wrong. But she was definitely changed, he saw that clearly enough. She was somehow askew in that room, awkward and disrupted like a portrait that has fallen from the wall.

Caleb's voice came then, tight and officious, a reminder of why they were there. "I did everything I could to find your father, Brook," and Brook could actually feel the formality take over the room. It was as much in the silence as in the voices. "Yes, Uncle, I'm sure you did everything you could."

"When I realized your father wasn't coming back to the stone shed when the storm passed, I began a search."

"Yes."

"We looked the rest of that day and all of the next two. We looked everywhere. We did all the things you'd have done if you'd been here, Brook, but there was no trace of your father. No signs. No tracks. Nothing. He was gone."

The words were quick and concise, practically identical to the report Etcheveral had given Brook on the train coming from Denver. It was as if the two men had prepared these brief summaries together, believing that one last recounting of the thing that had happened would absolve them of it, that they would be free of that part of the tragedy that clung to them because they had been there and he had not. Brook could sense in the growing tension of the room their need to shift responsibility to him, and as if to verify it Etchevarl coughed dutifully and said, "Now that you are home . . . if there is anything else you wish us to do . . . after all, he was your father—"

"And your friend of forty years," Brook came back, suddenly quick, suddenly loud. "Caleb's only brother. My mother's husband. But of course his fathering of me is the only important thing right now, that and the fact that I wasn't here." His voice rose even louder. "If you want to know, damn it, I had a good reason for being gone and I'm surprised as hell that no one has mentioned—"

"There's no need for that kind of language," Ruth broke in, and they all turned and looked into the corner at her, more in surprise that she had spoken than in any immediate grasp of what she had said. "We were here, Brook, and you were not," she said tightly, voicing the reprimand outright. "We bore the brunt." And then she stopped. She didn't stand up or reposition her hands or do any of the things that might have acted as a sort of physical summary of her words. She just sat perfectly still in the deep oversized chair in the corner.

Caleb broke the silence. "I've tried to comfort your mother

in every way I could," he said, but he wasn't speaking to Brook. He was looking at him perhaps, but his words were meant for Ruth. It was quite obvious. "She's had a difficult time."

Brook turned to her. "Well, Mother, that's refreshing. I'm glad to see *something* has touched you finally." But that wasn't what he said, it's what he *thought*; he might have said it if they'd been alone, if her eyes had looked different, more like the old eyes, haughty, unpained. He didn't say anything to her.

He turned to Caleb then, more out of avoidance of Ruth than anything. His uncle had a way of standing that was somewhat sideways, that put his good side, the whole one, out in front. He wasn't wearing his customary dress hat and his face looked younger. It occurred to Brook that the man was out of place in the room. His being in the house at all was unusual, for Caleb had been gone from the Park so many times and for such long periods during the years of Brook's growing up that when he did return home it was as a visitor only. In fact, Caleb didn't even have a room in the house anymore, he had an apartment in the employee's building, a small but homey set of rooms furnished by Ruth and cleaned by the maids. On occasion, when Caleb was home, Aaron would invite him to dinner on Sundays and to the music sessions afterwards in the parlor where Ruth would play the piano and Etchevarl the guitar, and all of them would sing. Sometimes Aaron asked for a poetry reading, which he generally preferred to the music. Now Caleb was standing in this same parlor room without his host, full of involvement and a new importance. Brook felt the thrust of transition again and sought to blunt it. "Both you and Etch mentioned a storm that day," he said to Caleb. "Tell me about it."

Caleb did, sounding almost grateful for the chance to fix on specifics. "It was a bad storm. I'd say that more than any other factor it was responsible for the accident." He moved his lips slightly, organizing the words. "We'd been up on the other side of Saddle Pass, six of us, looking at that quarter section of spruce that stands just under Mt. Guyot. Polite's been wanting to put a rough road in there so we can get those sticks to mill, especially if we buy the Bulldog." His eyes brightened. "That's a great stand of timber, the best on the place. There's got to be five million board feet of lumber in there. Virgin stuff, just waiting for the axe." He paused as though he were actually standing in the timber again, dwarfed by it, admiring. "We could see the storm," he went on, "but it wasn't doing much of anything. When we were finished in the spruce we rode back across Saddle and turned down into Right Hand Canyon, heading back to the shed where we'd parked the truck. We'd gotten maybe halfway down the canyon when all at once Aaron stopped and held up his hand and said he'd heard something. A sound like a calf bawling or a mare in trouble. Maybe a rogue cat. Something." He glanced at Etchevarl. "Isn't that the way you remember it?"

"I was riding in the front row," the older man answered, but to Brook, not Caleb. "Your father rode forward and told me he was going back to check out a sound. We were right by the rock face where the canyon turns," and he drew it for Brook with his elegantly gloved hands.

"I know what the rock looks like," Brook said.

"It seemed safe enough at the time," Caleb broke in. "The storm looked like it was caught on the ridge leading to Guyot, not going anywhere, so Aaron turned around and rode back up the canyon, toward the pass. We sort of milled around there at the rock face waiting for him. Some of us smoked." His one arm suddenly came up. "Then that storm hit. Wind, rain, thunder, you name it. We couldn't see up the canyon or down it. We couldn't see each other. That thing pounded us like a tidal wave." His eyes sought out Etchevarl, who was staring out the west window as if seeing the storm all over again. "Would you say that pretty well describes it, Etch?"

The old man nodded.

Brook got up from his chair and walked across to the west window and pushed back the curtains. The last of the day's sunlight had trapped the peaks against the sky. Farther down the mountain, in the steep rock plunges that no one could see, the night was already beginning. Brook turned from the window and went back to his chair. But he didn't sit down. "When did you say this happened?" he asked Caleb.

"Wednesday afternoon."

"And this is Sunday. Has it stormed since then?"

"The usual shower in late afternoon."

"No strong wind? No real cold?"

Caleb shot a glance in Ruth's direction and then looked back at Brook. "I know where you're going with this," he said, his voice hardly audible. "You believe your dad might still be alive. To tell the truth, I halfway expected that from you. But I think it's time you looked at the hard parts of this thing."

"He could be wedged in some rocks," Brook said.

Caleb said, "Where?"

"The horse could be lying across him dead and Papa can't get free."

"Where?"

"He can't answer the shouts because his voice has given out. He can't get to his rifle in the scabbard because he's pinned."

"Where is all this happening?" Caleb said. "Give me the location and I'll go there. I searched the whole east face of that Divide but I'll go back right now if you think—"

"Damn it, he's got to be somewhere!" But Brook's shouting the words, his kicking at the leg of his chair, startled Ruth. Her face lifted out of the black case of her body like an exquisite white fan she had decided to show them, however inopportunely. She rose from her chair and Caleb went to her immediately, striding across the room and taking her arm, speaking solicitously, guiding her from the parlor.

He was back quickly enough but he didn't take up his former position by the piano. He crossed the room to a closed door that fronted on the parlor and nodded at it and then glanced at Brook. "I was born in that room," he said, his voice different now, stronger. "I know this house. I know this corner of the Park. I know these mountains and I just spent three days turning them upside down looking for my own brother. I couldn't find him." He hadn't raised his voice the least bit, letting his calm make the comparison to Brook's earlier outburst, and with that same control he waited now for Brook to respond. When Brook didn't, he continued and his voice had

44

changed anew; it was softer. "Life has to do with odds, Brookers," he said, looking at him. "It's like drawing straws. You don't know which one you're going to get, you just step up and take your chance. Look at me," and he glanced down at his stump. "I picked a straw with a piece missing. Your dad drew and he got the short one. I don't know why. It's the odds, they just ran out for him." Again he waited, selecting his words, picking his way as though through briars. "I know what you're feeling, Brook. I explained to your mother and Etchevarl that because you weren't here when the accident happened you'd probably want to conduct your own search when you got back. You need to satisfy yourself, I understand that. We all do."

Brook stood watching his uncle as he spoke. He was wearing a shirt and a bow tie under the usual argyle sweater but the cuffs of the two empty right sleeves didn't join properly where they were pinned against the stump. It gave him an odd vulnerability. "Thank you, Uncle," Brook said, without intending to say it.

"It's whatever you decide. If you want to go up, we'll go, all of us. Same bunch as on that day. Am I right, Etch?" But he didn't wait for the old Basque's answer. He reminded Brook that there were horses up at the stone shed, as usual. "I'll have one of the men go first thing in the morning and get them ready."

"Right," Brook said. "Right. We'll do it. We'll go up."

Caleb let out an audible breath. "It's the decision I knew you'd make," and he stepped forward, smiling for the first time. "I ordered some gear from Ess Cohen based on it. He brought it out this morning. Maybe now," he began, but he didn't finish. "I'm glad you're home, Brookers," he said, and reached out with his one hand and gripped Brook's arm. Then he left the room.

Etchevarl remained, not moving, standing a few feet from the door. Brook thought he looked older and more confused now than he had on the train from Denver that noon when he rambled on about the search and gulches and about ponds with blue ice in them. The man was staring forlornly at the

45

window across the room, not seeing it really, and Brook said to him, "What about it, Etch? Could Papa have survived an accident? Is he still alive up there?"

The words acted as a prod on the old Basque. His head lifted and the huge mustaches bristled with emotion. "Caleb speaks of knowing the mountains but he did not know them like your father did. Aaron Hartman knew the danger places, all of them. Rock slide troughs and the avalanche runs. Lakes that have no bottom. Dropoffs concealed by brush. Bogs in the tundra that could suck a careless creature into the earth. How could the man let himself be caught in a pass with a storm hanging over his head? How?"

"Is that where it happened? Did the storm blow Papa off Saddle? Him and his horse together?"

Etchevarl's outburst was short-lived. The great head sagged and the gloved hands twisted in confusion. "He was there with us in the canyon and then he was gone. Vanished. Plucked from the bosom of this earth. How is that possible?" His head lifted and his eyes, bleak and tormented, sought out Brook across the room. "How could God have forsaken Aaron Hartman on that day . . . a man like that?" He stood motionless for what seemed like minutes and then picked up his odd-shaped beret from the top of the piano and left the room.

Finally alone, Brook dropped into his chair and faced the window. His eyes stung with fatigue and his stomach churned sourly. Across the room the curtains rustled and through the open window came what the room on Stout Street would never experience, what Brook would have waited for forever there—the evening wind. He could feel in it the coolness that sweeps down from high stone places at dusk, the chill that canyons give up when they lose the sun, when they grow shadowy and bottomless and the mists of night push against the walls.

He leaned his head back and closed his eyes and the day rushed him—Etchevarl at the porch steps in Denver and the labored climb of the train; Caleb in the Oakland at the Jefferson depot; the tall reluctant figure of his mother's house guest on the porch and finally his mother herself, her silence not a part of welcome but of reproach. He thought of the kitchen smell he had known all his life and missed without knowing it when he was away—pine wood and ground coffee—as if that alone was what had brought him home. He thought of the relentless formality that had followed him into the parlor, of Caleb garrulous and full of duty and his mother withdrawn so deeply into herself that what was visible of her was a shell she had left behind, an effigy with which to deceive whoever might be counting the mourners. He thought of his father but the face would not form into an image he could recognize; only the body emerged—tall and angular and slouched a little when he stood just so. . . .

Suddenly Brook was falling, tumbling wild-armed and helpless into space. And just as abruptly he landed, an oddly painless strike upon a rock-speared earth with his body exploding, spraying its own shattered members and the mush of its skull back into the ruptured air it had fallen from. . . .

He woke with a start. He sat forward in his chair and his eyes swept the room, searching the shadows, identifying them. He lit a lamp and left the room and moved along an adjacent hall to where the large oval portrait of his father hung in the darkness. He stopped before it and lifted the lamp and stared for a long time at the face whose likeness flickered in the light with a curious unfamiliarity.

CHAPTER 5

Brook woke early in the morning before anyone was up. It was the stillness that did it. It was outside his window, in the meadow, against the mountain, a stillness so pervasive it was like a voice, a voice crying *Wake up, wake up, a sound might come and you will miss it!*

A sound did come. It was the mountain jays in the aspen grove behind the house, scolding the light. They scolded everything. They scolded Brook until he got out of bed and dressed and went outside to the porch and looked up at the Divide. The mountains were high in that corner of the Park but dawn did not come to them easily, not like a softly soaring bird but rather as one exhausted by its climb through the darkness, a giant raptor sticking its talons into the highest peak and then the one below it, and the next, hanging on, struggling desperately to make a morning perch for itself in that towering place.

Soon Brook began to hear sounds other than the jays. The horse herd was in the near end of the west meadow and there was some friskiness at the fence, a half dozen of the younger mares wanting to race the sun, and there was a creek sound trying to make itself heard. The creek came out of Left Hand Canyon swift with melt, roaring and splashing as it cleared the sawmill but gentling down considerably by the time it passed the house.

Caleb came into view at that moment, striding across the yard from the employee's building. He was wearing a leather jacket whose empty right sleeve he never pinned up for fear of damaging the leather. It flopped now as he walked and for a moment he reminded Brook of an injured creature trying to make it to cover. When he reached the porch and saw Brook he stopped. "Are you ready, old buddy?"

"I've got to eat some breakfast, Uncle. My stomach is chewing my ribs off."

"Good idea. I'll join you. Are the cooks up?"

"They're the only ones who are."

Caleb rubbed his boots across the mud scraper on the bottom step. "While we're eating," he said, "I'll have Willy Walker go up to the shed and get the horses ready." He glanced up the steps at Brook. "You're still going, aren't you?"

"If you think it's necessary."

"It's not what I think, Brookers." He turned away from the porch. "I'll get Willy."

Brook stood up. "Let me do that. Perhaps it's my place," but Caleb had already moved away from the steps and into the lawn. Brook went upstairs and shaved and brushed his teeth and when he reached the breakfast table, Ruth was there. So was Margaret Pendleton. Brook had seen her only vaguely the afternoon before, on the porch or perhaps in the kitchen, and now he said to her, "You're Margaret Pendleton from Kansas City, aren't you? My mother's friend."

"Yes. And you would be Brook."

"Obviously your mother didn't come out with you."

"She couldn't. She wanted to but she's much too ill for a long trip. She asked that I extend her deepest sympathies to Ruth and her family."

"And your husband? Will he be coming?"

Margaret's eyes pulsed briefly. "Emerson is in England on church business. He'll be a resident pastor there for the summer. A sort of trade arrangement with his own congregation in Kansas City. It was that assignment that freed me to come here in my mother's place."

Brook acknowledged the explanation by remarking that it was strange what happened to plans, even the best laid ones.

"Yes," replied Margaret quietly, glancing at Ruth, "and

what a sad time for broken ones."

They spoke no more to each other; Ruth's presence made conversation a callous thing. She sat perfectly still at the end of the table, holding her head as though it were a fragile antique she had found misplaced in one room and was returning to another, stopping here at the table merely to rest a moment. Brook sat at the opposite end and studied Margaret when he could. Her hair was long and she wore it flat on her head, the long flow drawn in at the back of the neck with a comb. But sensible and modest as her hair was, it didn't detract from her eyes. Nothing could, he saw that immediately. Her eyes were absolutely alive in her face. Feeling came out of them like words out of a mouth. They were much lighter in color than her hair, and startling to look directly into. They made Brook think of smoke.

On the porch after breakfast Brook lit a cigarette for Caleb and one for himself. "We'll finish these and go up," Caleb said, drawing the smoke in deeply, his lungs releasing only a portion of it, which he blew idly through his nose.

"Did Willy get the buckskin for me?" asked Brook.

"I don't know. I'm not sure the buckskin's up at the shed. He'll probably put you on the roan gelding, the one he bought last summer in Saguache."

"I'm not going up high without a good horse under me."

"The roan's a good horse."

"The buckskin's a better. He walks rock like a spider. He's the one I want."

"Suit yourself," Caleb said. He flipped the cigarette butt into the dew-soaked grass beyond the porch railing. "I'll have Grant look him up."

"Never mind," said Brook. "The horse will probably be down here in night pasture. I'll get him myself." He left the porch and when he got to the car shed Grant Pickens was there. That wasn't unusual. Grant loved cars and hung around them as much as he dared. He fancied himself both a good driver and a good mechanic but neither came close to the truth. He owned no car of his own, which of course didn't prevent him from sneaking into Cohen's branch store in Como every chance he got and buying gummed stickers that he would secretly slap on the Model T:

GIRLS WANTED, APPLY AT SIDE DOOR.
COME ON, BABY, HERE'S YOUR RATTLE.

"Crank it and jump in," Brook ordered as he entered the shed. "You're coming with me."

Grant obeyed and Brook backed the T out. They drove past the corrals and through the gate and onto the west meadow road that led to the sawmill. The mill stood a mile upslope near the mouth of Left Hand Canyon and as they neared it Brook noticed that the wigwam burner was still smoking from yesterday's feed of wood chips and bark. An immense cone that towered over the adjacent mill buildings, the burner looked like a giant tepee that a tribe of giant Indians had erected in the upper end of the meadow, just short of the trees, and Polite hadn't gotten around to running them off yet.

"I seen you coming home yesterday wearing a new cap," Grant called out over the noise of the climbing Ford. "You get your old one stomped on down in Denver?"

"No one stomps my cap, Grant. I'll buy two or three caps at a time and wear them all until I find the one I like. That's my way."

The Ford was beginning to labor now; you could always tell from the pitch of the motor noise how steep the grade was. Grant leaned across the seat and tried to speak above it. "You lay any of them Flappers down there? You know, the ones who cut their hair?"

"Is that what a Flapper is, Grant? A girl who cuts her hair?"

The sarcasm didn't discourage Grant. "The day you left," he went on, "I figured you'd take me with you but you lit out too fast. Maybe next time you'll remember your friends."

"Maybe next time I will," Brook said, but it was a lie and they both knew it. They weren't friends. Grant was more Brook's age than the other employees but he was smart-mouthed and could be mean, especially when he was drunk. Caleb had hired him in Leadville one day and brought him home, a drifter from the Mississippi delta country who slicked his hair down with pomade, peach pomade that got sour and smelly under the leather helmet. Brook told him once that when he had the helmet on and his mouth open he looked like a beaver dressed up for an aviator's party. That was the first time they fought. It wasn't the last, but a lot of the times they were in Fairplay or Como drunk and Brook couldn't remember who won. It didn't matter, the fights hadn't changed anything. Grant still used the pomade, as well as toilet water and some kind of breath sweetener that smelled like the licorice Ess Cohen sold in his stores. Grant was a power with the women, confessing to it without threat or intimidation. Sometimes you didn't even have to ask him. This time, however, Brook did. "You still a power with the women, Grant?"

Grant grunted and turned to Brook in the seat. "How about it, big shot? You get any pussy down there in Denver?"

Brook threw his head back and laughed. "Did Noah get any rain when he finished the ark? Of course I got pussy. I got so much pussy I couldn't handle it all."

Grant's eyes fixed on him, hungry and wet.

Brook fed him. "Let me tell you about this one doll," he began, dropping his voice so low that Grant was practically in his face trying to hear. "Pretty as a rose petal. Smelled like one too. Soft all over. Had the disposition of a cherub and the blood of a Spanish heifer in heat."

"Goddawg!" Grant whispered thickly.

"After me night and day. Got so she didn't even bother to put her clothes back on, just ran around my apartment with her boobs bouncing and those butt moons shining on me like it was harvest time. I'll tell you, Grant," and he shook his head exhaustedly, "that little gal about wore me out."

Grant snorted scornfully. "Some guys just can't cut prime meat. Looks like you're one of them."

They reached the night pasture and Brook grabbed the rope halter out of the back seat and opened the gate and walked in among the stallions. The buckskin stood at the edge of the herd like an obedient lamb and Brook bridled him and led him back to the rear of the Ford, where he tied him. Grant gave the engine a crank and the watching horses went galloping off. But instead of turning downslope, Brook headed for Left Hand Canyon and when they reached it they sat and watched the creek free itself from the mountain with a fierce tumbling thunder. In the steep rock tiers at the upper end of the canyon the climbing sun turned the lingering night haze to a gauzy whiteness.

Brook turned the car around and headed back down the mill road, driving slower now because of the trailing buckskin. The Ford's engine loved the return; it hardly made a sound. "Did you see the fog?" he said to Grant.

"Saw something up there."

"Fog's like being inside a cloud. You've got slippery footing and no vision." He studied Grant. "I imagine that's what you people ran into the day of the accident. Fog."

"Fog my ass!" Grant snapped, immediately wanting to argue. "That was a goddamned cyclone!"

"I understand it hit just before my old man went back up the canyon."

"After. Right after." Grant paused, obviously giving himself a chance to remember events in case the argument went anywhere. "We'd been up on Guyot looking at a bunch of trees and were coming back down Right Hand. I was riding in front with the old Spic and the next thing I know your pap pushes forward and tells us he's going back up to see what that sound was." Grant gathered his thin shoulders and let them drop. "Hell," he said, "I didn't hear no sound."

"You should have gone back with him, Grant. You. Somebody."

"My ass!" Again it was indignant. "Who's gonna tell the boss when he can go somewhere and who he's got to take with him?" He worked his lips over his teeth. "It was about that time the storm hit us. She'd just been hanging up there on the ridge blacker'n nigger piss, not doing nothing, and all of a sudden she decides to come. Never seen anything like it in my life. Horses screaming and biting each other. Water in your eyes. Water running off your hat. Water in your mouth when you

tried to sing out where you were. Jesus Christ in the nail bin!"
He shook his head in disbelief and the helmet straps flew. "We
managed to make it down to the stone shed somehow. But it
wasn't ten minutes later and that storm was plumb gone. They
can move out plenty fast when they want to."

Brook didn't agree or disagree. He waited.

"So I said to the others, Hey, we better wait here in the shed
for Aaron. But somebody started arguing for going back, I
think it was Caleb." Grant scratched his neck. "So we went
back. We scoured that canyon til the light give out. We went
back up the next day and did the same damned thing. And the
next as well. Didn't turn up so much as a boot nail."

"It's like Caleb to stay with a thing."

Grant sucked his teeth. "That's the damned truth. He had
us up on those ridges before the sun got there. Back and forth.
Up and down. In and out. All day long for the fat part of three
days. I never seen nobody hang on to a search like that." He
scanned Brook's face, seeking sympathy. "Automobiles is my
natural thing, as you know. I ain't real good on a horse. I try
but it don't come automatic for me. Result is, my ass is still in
separate pieces from all that riding."

"Caleb said he'd done all he could."

"Done too much. I told him that. I said, Caleb, you are flat
doing too much here. You're gonna lose the whole lot of us if
you don't stop. But he wouldn't listen. There was no reasoning
with the man. This one day he took me and Etch all the way
up to timberline on Big Red. Colder'n the dead Jesus up there.
Spooky place. Finally we come back down and joined the
others." He stared at Brook with a new intensity. "And fire
that rifle? Are you gonna tell me Caleb Hartman can't fire a
rifle with just one arm? Shit, man, he'd jam that stock down
onto his leg and fire away easy as nothing. Then he'd listen.
Fire and listen. Fire and listen. Jesus Christ in the lumber yard,
how he kept it up! And none of us daring to breathe nor make
a sound while he was at it. I thought he was gonna kill Polite
this one day for dropping his canteen in some rocks. It slipped
out of Polite's hands while he was drinking and went clattering
down through there like a stone dancing with a pebble. I

practically had to pull Caleb off Polite's back. He was gonna bust that big bull up, one arm or not."

"Caleb's a brave man. He's proved that plenty of times."

Grant shook his head. "We was so blind tired by the end of that third day we couldn't have found bare tittie. Finally old Caleb he come down off the mountain. That last night, riding through Right Hand in the dark, Caleb said he couldn't go on. God forgive me, Aaron, he said, but I can't do no more. You're in the one place on this earth I can't get you out of." Grant exhaled dramatically. "You gotta hand it to Caleb. He hung in there."

"That's the kind of man he is."

Grant kept his silence after that, licking his lips as though the flood of words had dried them. When they reached the last stretch of mill road the same bunch of young mares followed them along the fence, flicking their ears and nickering saucily at the buckskin stud, but they finally gave up and wheeled away, looking for something new to tease. Below the corrals and the lot and into the lawn of the house, at the farthest edge of what could be discerned clearly out of distance, stood the figure of a woman. In the Ford, both men saw her at the same time. "There's that Kansas City woman yonder," Grant said. "I was on the porch with her yesterday when Ess delivered that gear. She's got a nice enough hip on her but let me tell you something, that is one dumb broad!"

"She can't be too dumb, Grant. She married a minister."

Grant sniffed disdainfully. "That's worse yet. Ministers ain't known for putting out much pecker, which means she wasn't looking for much. Real Miss Priss, she is."

"Well, you should know, Grant, you're the expert on women."

Grant took it as a compliment. "I know her kind like a book," he went on expansively. "She wouldn't pull her bloomers down unless the angels told her to and the choir was singing under the bed."

Just for a moment the soft smoke eyes of Margaret Pendleton flashed for Brook and he wanted to lash out at Grant for the remark. But they had reached the corrals by that time and Brook spotted the Jeffry parked in the lot with three men seated on the truck bed, swinging their legs impatiently. Brook braked the T and shut the motor off and one of the men jumped down from the truck and walked over and cocked one foot up on the front bumper. It was Polite. He was a short thick man, dressed all in red and wearing a bowler hat. His face was like bad wood, knotty and stained and full of blemishes. "I thought we were going up," he said to Brook. He had a keen booming voice that cut like an axe blade.

"There's fog up there," Brook said.

"I don't see no fog."

"It doesn't matter what you see, Polite. There's fog on the mountain."

Polite spat a stream of tobacco juice into the dirt but it wasn't belligerence. It was more delay, the same as if he'd shifted his feet. He smiled next, showing his brown teeth. "Never knew a little fog to hold you back, Itty Bitty Boy. What happened down there in Denver, you get too much of that cup of life?"

"Can you get too much, Polite?"

"Best to get it while you're young, in any event." He wiped his chin. "I imagine there's some real sweet ladies down there to help a guy with it too. Got them pretty little pungs on 'em. Make a rabbit think he can whip a bear."

Brook didn't answer and Polite spat again, differently this time, and his eyes changed. "You ride on any of them aeroplanes while you was there?" he asked, but before Brook could answer, Caleb approached the car. "I see you found your buckskin," he said to Brook. "I also heard what you said about the fog. Is it true?"

"I figured it might be dangerous up there. But if you think—"

"Good decision, Brookers. Why take a chance? June weather can be treacherous when you go high." He turned and glanced up at the Divide. "The last thing we need now is another accident."

The noon meal was a confusing affair. Ruth seemed alternately brightened and dulled by the company. She would attach herself to the conversation sporadically and a look of amusement actually escaped her face when Margaret told of one or two comical things that had happened on the train ride from Kansas City. But that was the peak of her involvement; she turned morose following that. Caleb stepped in then, talky and cheerful, trying to make amends, and at the end of the meal he even attempted a toast over coffee: "To Margaret's visit and Brook's return home." But it failed. Ruth didn't participate. She sat looking at them as if they'd made some kind of breach, or perhaps said something unacceptable, and she had resolved never to forgive them for it.

After the meal, Margaret went outside to the porch and Brook followed her. She spoke to him immediately, the words tumbling out. "It's so hard to know how to talk to your mother. I never know what to say. I don't know if I should try to keep the conversation light and get her mind off what's happened, or if I should respect her situation by staying quiet. She's just full of grief. If she would only let it out, maybe that would help. If she would just cry."

"I don't believe she knows how."

That elicited some surprise from Margaret. "Well, she'll have to eventually, won't she? I mean, we all have to cry. Maybe not right at first but it has to come. It's the only way grief has of ending itself."

"I don't know," Brook said. It was true, he did not. "Time, I suppose." He was struggling, thinking more of how to answer Margaret than of his mother. "Time will help," he said, and winced at the shallowness of his remark.

But Margaret was grateful. "Yes," she said. She was obviously relieved that he had answered at all and when she spoke again her manner was much less desperate. "Yes, time is essential now. And having the body would help too. That way she would know it was over and that her husband was really dead." She stopped abruptly and her eyes pulsed. "Oh, I'm sorry. I shouldn't have said that. He was your father, not just her husband." Her shoulders dropped in a sort of physical apology and she looked away into the lawn, avoiding Brook's face for the first time. "It's so difficult all of a sudden. I feel so inadequate. I'm new to things like this. New to . . . tragedy." She looked back at him and there was pain in her face. "That's awful, isn't it? I know there's tragedy in life. I've heard about it and I've talked about it and I've been with Emerson at funerals and wakes. I've just never experienced it."

"You sort of stumbled into this one, didn't you? It's probably not fair. I suppose things should be fair." He hesitated and this time it was his turn to study the lawn. "If you want to leave," he said, "if you want to go home, we'll understand."

"Oh, no," Margaret replied, and it was strong now, emphatic. "I didn't mean that. I would never run way from this. Your mother needs me. And it's not finished here. I can't leave until it's finished."

That afternoon, Brooked cranked up the T and took his friend Willy Walker with him to check on a birthing mare in one of the corrals down by the highway, near Jefferson, where the line fence ran. They were about to head back when a Baby Grand Chevrolet drove by on the state road and honked insolently. Brook let out a shout and slammed the Ford into high gear and crashed right through a wooden gate onto the highway and raced after the Baby Grand. But he couldn't catch it and at the Como junction he finally gave up the chase and turned off and drove up into the town proper. He bought a dozen bottles of home brew from a trainman he knew, and he and Willy drank them on a sunny little hill overlooking the railyards.

Going home on the old road that ran through the trees at the base of the mountains, the sawmill whistle blew. Brook announced that he was going to race the whistle and Willy replied that if he wasn't so damned full of bootleg beer he'd know you couldn't race a sound.

"Well, I'll beat it to a certain point then," Brook shot back. "I can reach the edge of the trees before the whistle dies out. What do you say, buster, what's your bet?" He was already gunning the Ford pretty good because the south meadow was even then visible through the trees. But he levered it too hard and going into the last curve the car started to slide and coming out of the curve it was whirling in circles right down the middle of the road, spitting gravel, shaking the fenders, throwing dust up everywhere.

When the Ford finally stopped, the edge of the woods stood no more than twenty feet away and there was no sound about them anywhere. Certainly not a sawmill whistle. Willy took off his hat and slapped at the dust. "What did I tell you, you dumb ass? There's some things you just can't beat!" Then a grin split his face and he started to laugh and didn't stop until they'd reached the lane.

Neither did Brook.

CHAPTER 6

Brook's grandfather, Julius Hartman, built the house, as well as the outbuildings, in the 1870s. He had actually arrived in South Park in 1864 with a party of Kansas prospectors who had heard from an old pioneer come home to Kansas to die that a man, if he kept sharp, could pick gold nuggets off the ground in the Rocky Mountains anytime he damned well chose.

So the party got some money together and started out for Colorado, putting Julius, who was the youngest, in charge of the wagons and the oxen and a few head of livestock. They left Shawnee County early one morning and started west across the Great Plains and six weeks later they reached the foot of Pike's Peak. They rested one week and then entered the Rockies proper, climbing over Ute Pass and rumbling out a few days later onto the lofty flatness of South Park. The entire party headed immediately for the mountains that rimmed the basin and started kicking at dirt and picking up rocks, but Julius stayed down below at the camp, walking in disbelief through the richness his companions had completely overlooked—*the grass.*

Before he said good-by to his fellow Kansans two weeks later, Julius had bought for ten dollars a head the same bony footsore livestock he had herded across the plains for them. He fattened the stock on the lush wild hay that grew in the Park and sold every last one the following summer to a Fairplay butcher for ninety dollars each. The next year he filed homestead on a quarter section in the northern end of the Park and proceeded quietly to buy up water rights in that area, which was full of creeks, Michigan and Jefferson and Tarryall. Water was the gold Julius Hartman sought, clean sweet water to nourish the grass, and he had found it. He soon held claim on South Park's first two permanent ditch rights, one to turn a water wheel for churning butter and the other to drain his hay field, which eventually became the east meadow.

That was in 1866. In 1867 Julius borrowed several thousand dollars from a banker in Colorado Springs and brought home three dozen top quality Shorthorn cows with which to build a proper herd. As the stock prospered on the rich mountain grasses, Julius began to sell meat to the mining camps high in the adjoining Mosquito Range, as well as in the towns that were springing up in the narrow valley of the Arkansas just beyond. With the profits, and after first paying off the banker, he bought more Shorthorns. He took up another quarter-section of land below Jefferson Lake and two years later he bought another one-hundred-sixty acres whose northern edge sloped up to Kenosha Pass. A Sheriff's Sale netted him an entire half-section the following year on the rich flats of the lower Tarryall, more to the south. Two years after that, in 1872, Julius hired a Cousin Jenny to cook for him—Cousin Jenny being the name given to immigrant Cornish women, Cousin Jack to their fathers and brothers who worked the mines—and that same year he started building his house. He built it on the original homestead in the extreme northwest corner of the Park in the first meadow below the timber and directly under the half-dozen massive peaks that formed that part of the Continental Divide. He built a mill race on Michigan Creek where it broke free of a canyon he named Left Hand. He hitched up the sons of the Kansas oxen he had bought that first year and snaked logs off the lower slopes and got ready to build his house.

There were no dormer windows in Julius Hartman's house, no cornices, no Georgian columns. There was no fancy scroll-work anywhere, he owned no jig saw. Solid simplicity was what he was after. He handsawed a few of the boards, for the parlor and the stairway in particular, but the bulk of the lumber came from the big circular saws of his own water-powered mill. He made the roof of the house steep so it could shed snow quickly, and covered it with shingles he split with an axe. He built a big root cellar on one side of the house and a wide high-stepped porch on the other, and erected a summer kitchen. The kitchen was to please the Cousin Jenny who became his wife in 1875, the year the house and the outbuildings were finally finished. She wanted a summer kitchen—it was to assuage her homesickness for Cornwall—and he did it for her gladly, building it thirty feet out from the north wall of the main kitchen, separate from the house but connecting to it with a walkway made of red flagstone.

Julius had a good year in 1875. He put up his first hay barn at the lower end of the east meadow where the state road was beginning to take shape. He sold off forty of his acres to the Park County Land Commission so the town of Jefferson could have a place to build itself, the sole proviso being that a parcel of land one acre in size within the town limits be held free of taxes to Julius and his heirs and assigns for a period not to exceed twenty-five years (this particular number was at the County's insistence; Julius had wanted ninety-nine). The land was for the building and grounds of his newly conceived business venture, the Hartman Hay & Cattle Company. He hired local workmen to construct the building and contracted with a Buena Vista firm to landscape the grounds. The rugs and the furniture for his office he ordered from Colorado Springs, and he placed on the paneled wall behind his desk a plaque bearing a philosophy he especially liked, one borrowed from the young Illinois rail splitter who became a president: *I will work hard, and watch, and my chance will come.*

Julius signed an additional contract that same year with the Denver, South Park & Pacific Railroad, which made him the sole supplier of roadbed ties for the new trackage the company planned to push up the Platte River canyon and into South Park within the next five years. The following year his Cornish bride presented him with his first child, a girl they named Elizabeth.

62

The Shorthorn cows thrived on the bounty of grass in that end of the Park and the winters hardied their blood line, and with every two hundred increase Julius bought up another section of land until he had swelled his original homestead to six thousand acres. His tie contract paid off handsomely—the railroad traversed the Park in 1878, the year his first son Aaron was born—and he used some of those earnings to build new hay barns. He also purchased five hundred head of sheep over in the San Luis Valley and brought them in, along with the young Basque herder who insisted on coming with the animals and whose name was Arranz Etchevarl. In 1880, Julius needed shearing pens and he hired two local Ute Indians to build them, paying them off when they were done with a Henry rifle and a quarter of beef apiece. But a few months before the birth of his second son Caleb later that year, he squabbled with those same two Indians over the theft of some lambs, and one afternoon while Julius was up panning gold in his mountain streams the two Utes raided the house, knocking his wife unconscious with one of the Henry rifles and killing the baby Elizabeth with the other.

Julius and his wife and Etchevarl buried the child in a tiny plot in the upper corner of the west meadow under a stone Etchevarl had carved: *Elizabeth. 1876–1880. Our Darling Sleeps.* Julius never again touched a pan nor built a sluice nor turned a spadeful of dirt to tunnel a mine shaft into a mountainside, and he turned savagely away from his gates any rider seeking work who carried that type of gear.

But the little kingdom in the mountains thrived, despite the loss, although Julius came to realize that he didn't like sheep and he sold the whole bunch off. He started a horse herd with the proceeds from the sale and turned the shearing pens into corrals, and he tore down the original hay barn at the base of the east meadow and built a new one twice its size. In 1898, the year his son Aaron married the Kansas schoolteacher who was teaching at the Fairplay School, the Hartman Hay & Cattle Company shipped one-hundred-two railcars of prime hay from the depot in Jefferson.

Julius got into some hard business with the government at

the turn of the century when they informed him without a great deal of preliminary discussion that in order to protect the watersheds of the public domain in that part of Colorado they would be forced to convert most of the higher timberlands into what they decided to call Forest Reserves. Julius had enjoyed free access to those lands for a quarter of a century and now a government agency was saying it was going to start charging him fees. "By God, you won't!" he thundered at them, pacing from window to window in their elaborate offices on Fifteenth Street in Denver.

But in the end the new agency won, although it assured Julius that he would be granted grazing permits and stumpage contracts to the land just as before, provided his requests were within reason and his fees were paid on time and that he promised never to enclose any of the Reserve acreage on all four sides. Fences and gates were acceptable to the United States government on three sides, but not on four.

That episode marked Julius' first defeat in business, but it wasn't his last. Nothing dramatic, but he began to experience a gradual decline in motivation after the century turned. He had met his goals in life—he had built and amassed and left his mark—and he looked forward to growing old in a sunny tranquility, lord of the manor he had built with his own hands. But burying a child was a pain that grew rather than diminished as the years went by, and then there was the matter of his son Caleb.

The boy grew up with absolutely no feel for husbandry, no love for the land and what it represented or what it could produce, nor did he have the constancy of his older brother. Caleb sold the small herd of starter cows Julius gave him on his twenty-first birthday, using the money to buy into a hydraulic placer outfit that proceeded to hose away the banks of the Blue River on the other side of the Divide, looking for gold. They found it and Caleb made a little money from the operation, but when he came back from the Gulf Coast the next summer he was broke again. He immediately took a job with a company that was working a huge gold dredge on the river above Fairplay. They scooped enough of it out of the bed gravels to

64

make it pay, but Caleb was forced to quit the job when the company accused him of stealing a ten-pound bar of gold-and-silver amalgam. Julius had to make some kind of settlement in order to get the dredge company to drop charges, but it was when he caught Caleb building a secret sluice in a creek running back from Right Hand Canyon that he'd finally had enough and ordered Caleb off the place.

Brook's grandmother, the small quiet Cousin Jenny from across the sea, died shortly after that and Julius buried her next to Elizabeth in the meadow plot and then retreated to the house to live out the balance of his days. The summer kitchen was closed down and the building given to Etchevarl for living quarters, with some renovation of course, but the kitchen in the main house remained exactly as Julius had built it, a large echoing room with a labyrinth of cupboards along two walls and a giant woodbox near the door.

The room was hearty and bright always; it became the center of life in that huge house. Aaron's wife, Ruth, made it so. It was her room more than any other, although she did none of the cooking, and as Brook was growing up he could find his mother there at almost any time of the day, and often late at night, surrounded by the seductive smell of pine wood and freshly ground coffee that forever filled the room. Brook found her there now, in midmorning of his second day home. He had slept late and missed breakfast. His mother's eyes followed him when he came into the kitchen and he saw that her face appeared haggard and severe. He took a chair at the table and her voice came at him immediately, flat, barbed, a kind of attack. "What happened to your search yesterday?"

"I was ready to go up," he said. He tried to make it sound indifferent because he suddenly wanted to thwart her, to force her either to do something with the petulance or abandon it. "But I decided not to go. The weather wasn't right. There was fog up there."

"What about this morning? Is there fog up there this morning or did you sleep through it?"

He didn't respond. He felt he had stalled her for the moment and didn't want to risk a reversal.

65

"I know what *is* up there on the mountain, Brook," she said, but she didn't go on with it. It was as though she meant to punish him with the omission in some way.

Brook took in a breath and let it out and almost began with something sharp but at the last moment he changed it. "Fog is dangerous on steep grades," he offered instead. "And Uncle Caleb agreed with me, in case you're going to ask about that too." He paused. "I'll go up tomorrow. I'll take Polite."

"Polite? Why would you take Polite away from the mill? He's the headrig man. Very valuable. Caleb promised him good money to get him."

"I didn't know Caleb had any money."

She waited with a visible patience before she spoke. Brook searched for some sort of wavering in her but didn't see any. He always looked for it, he always failed to find it. "Taking Polite doesn't make sense, Brook. He can't be much of a horseman. Why not ask Arranz to go up with you? At least he knows the mountains."

"Because I've decided on Polite."

"Fine," she said, looking directly at him, setting her shoulders in a way that he could see. "At least it's a decision. Any decision from you is encouraging." She moved resolutely to a small table under a window and placed some pieces of cloth in a basket and left the room. Brook remained seated and after an interval he heard a door close in an upstairs room.

But a voice sounded suddenly from the rear of the kitchen, startling him. "I could stay back here until you left the room but I don't think I will," came the voice. "It would look like I'd been hiding." It was Margaret Pendleton. She came forward and stopped at the far end of the table. "Or it might appear as if I'd been eavesdropping. Neither is true." She eyed him warily. "What's true is that I'm a little embarrassed."

"Did you hear us talking?"

"I couldn't help but hear." She started to move around the table and then didn't.

Brook looked down at his hands, avoiding Margaret's face. "My mother and I rub each other."

"Yes," Margaret said. "You do." Her words were cautious

and subdued. "It's a little hard to understand. I mean, at a time like this a mother and son usually draw together out of need."

He looked up. "Wrong. My mother doesn't need anyone, least of all me. Never has. Why should this be any different?"

Margaret was slow to respond. "Your mother's troubled, Brook. Deeply. But I'm sure she's glad you're home. I'm sure your uncle is too."

"Yes," he said quickly, "it gives them both a chance to forgive me for not being here when the accident happened." He grinned at her. "But it won't be for a while yet. They need to impose a little more guilt first. Make me do some penance."

She didn't laugh and he had hoped she would. "I don't know if I agree with that."

"I suppose it doesn't matter."

She studied him. "You don't like to be headed, do you? You're like a proud horse."

"Do you know horses?" he asked, needing something quick to say.

Margaret answered that she did.

"Would you like a job? You could help Willy Walker green break a bunch of the newest ones."

She didn't answer but she didn't look away from him either. The moment grew long.

"You're different from what I thought you'd be," he said then, not planning it, not thinking ahead to how it would set. "You look younger, for one thing."

"Do I?" Her face lightened with the words and she attempted a smile. "Younger than what? What age should I be?"

Brook regretted his remark then and shrugged guiltily. "I'm sorry, I shouldn't have spoken so personally. It's just that I've never met a young minister's wife before. I mean, a minister's young wife. Most ministers I've met . . . I mean, the wives of most the ministers. . . ." He stopped completely. "Help," he said simply.

She laughed outright and the laugh surprised him. It was throaty, he hadn't expected that, and her mouth was wider than he thought it would be. And her eyes went quickly dark. "Well," she said, "my age is not a secret. I'm twenty-five. That's somewhat younger than my husband. Perhaps, knowing Emerson's age, you would expect me to be older. That is, if Ruth told you his age . . . if she knew it . . . if she discussed my husband at all. . . ." She trailed off and a brief confusion showed in her face. "I may be the one who needs help," she said. But she smiled when she said it, holding it a moment, using it as an opportunity to start over. "I heard you say you were initiating a new search tomorrow. I hope it's successful. I hope you find. . . ." Again she didn't finish. "I hear your mother and your uncle talking in the kitchen a lot. He's glad you're home but he doesn't hold out any hope that your father's still alive. It must be hard for him to say that to her, but he does. He's not afraid."

"Caleb's not afraid of anything. He was a hero in the war, you know. He won two medals. One from the French and one from the British. I've seen them. I made him show them to me once." He laughed. "I had to. He never offers to show them."

"Your mother's frightened and bewildered still," said Margaret. "She's very raw."

Brook didn't answer.

"If the body could be found it would help her. If it's God's will, you'll be successful, you'll find the body."

"If it's God's will?"

"Yes."

Brook worked his face into an exaggerated frown. "That confuses me a little. Do you mean that God will show *me* where the body is but wouldn't show Caleb? Am I more worthy, is that what you're saying?" He waited but she didn't respond. "Another thing I don't understand, will God be *with* the body when I get there or will He just point to it from a distance? Maybe He'll call to me from a bush or a rock and tell me where it is, what do you think? I have a lot of trouble with that part of God's will. I don't know whether I should go up there and *look*, or just *listen*."

When she spoke, Margaret's voice had changed. "Death is difficult for us," she said. "In our grief we sometimes overlook

68

the reasons for it. We fail to understand its true place in God's overall plan—"

"Is that *you* saying that? I though you were new to death and tragedy."

It surprised Margaret and she showed it. "What?"

"Do you believe what you just said or is it something you've heard your husband say at countless funerals and wakes?"

She had a way of holding you with her eyes as though she were using them to look inside you, to comprehend your meaning. They flickered a bit now, some of the intensity drained away and they lost some of their dark color. But none of their eloquence. "When you're in the mountains tomorrow," she said quietly, turning to leave the room, "please be careful."

CHAPTER 7

The day came in undecided. There was a wind that gusted up at times and then died down. There was some blue sky overhead, there was some cloud. It was going to be hot but not yet. It could still turn.

Brook overslept again and it was perhaps two hours short of noon before he and Polite left the lot. They took the Quad, which is what they called the Jeffry truck, because it had four-wheel drive and because, as Polite was fond of saying, "it would just flat get out and climb!" It needed to climb, for the road up Right Hand Canyon was over a mile long and steep all the way, except for a short stretch at the very top. There were two other trucks on the place, the Double T Ford stake bed and a second Jeffry. The Ford was useless on any serious slope and was used mainly to pull hay wagons around the meadows. The second Jeffry was out of regular service; Polite had jacked up the rear end and replaced one wheel with a special drum and pully and was using it to drive a barking saw up on the ridge at the head of the flume. Polite was a good mechanic, a genuine one, not like Grant. He wanted the Mack Bulldog badly and he never lost a chance to talk about how the truck would make it easier to get the big sticks off the higher slopes and "down to splash" as he called it. But he hadn't stood around idle while he was waiting. He'd built a tractor, built it from scratch. He traded Ess Cohen some new shelving for an old White truck frame and engine, and then adapted it. He doubled the spring strength and welded cleats on the rear wheels and added a water tank for additional cooling by sticking a thirty gallon drum on top of the radiator. He also installed front wheel brakes, which even the standard tractors didn't have yet. Ugly looking contraption, but it could skid logs.

The two of them crossed the north meadow in the fickleness of wind and cloud and when they entered Right Hand Canyon the road tilted immediately upward. The sensation was unsettling because the Quad had no body, it had no cab or top or sides, just a bench for the front seat and a flatbed behind. Polite was driving and perhaps a quarter of a mile up the canyon he turned to Brook and said, "I see you got a new cap while you were down in the city."

Brook took the cap off and turned it lazily in his hands and then restored it to his head without looking at Polite, or answering him.

"A couple bucks more," Polite said, "and you could have got the cap in your size." There was no malice in the remark; Polite gave insult and took it with equal indifference. It suited him; the man was hard. His body was a stump and his face resembled wood that had gone pulpy. Willy Walker said he looked like a barrel of lye soap that hadn't set up properly. Polite had come from the South originally, Georgia or Florida or another of those flat steamy states where the pine forests stretched in every direction but up. Polite had hated that. "Those trees were nothing but toothpicks trying to keep the land from washing into the swamps," he told Brook once. "I wanted trees!" So he left home to find some. He worked in Wisconsin and Minnesota and eventually ended up at the mouth of the Columbia where the states of Oregon and Washington glare at each other across the river. He worked around Aberdeen and Gray's Harbor in timber so dense the sun never reached the forest floor. He spoke of trees it took two days to fell, of stumps that two dozen men could stand on at one time. "Now that's *trees*, Itty Bitty!"

Like a lot of Southerners, Polite made a fetish of the language and the expressions he used. A "sawdust savage" was a lumberjack and a "peavey" was a cant hook, and a "cant dog" was a logger with a big mad on. A rookie logger was a "whistle punk" and if you'd held every job there was in the timber business you had "gone through the chairs." When a man got cabin fever he got "staky" and when he died his buddies said he'd "gone up." Most of the Hartman employees called Polite the Bull of the Woods. He liked that title and he dressed the part—cutoff high-water pants with galluses, wool shirt, wool socks, flannel long johns, a plaid mackinaw—all in varying shades of the original red. He topped this outfit off with an incongruous bowler hat that never left his head. He knew his job and he was absolutely without fear concerning it. When he had finished supervising construction of the flume that ran down part of the mountain to "splash" (which was the mill-pond adjacent to the sawmill) he rode the first log down himself, negotiating the curves of the elevated water trough with just his hobnail boots and a cant hook for balance.

Polite was about Caleb's age, perhaps a little older, and he never went to town. He occasionally played cards with the men after supper and sometimes hunted with them, and he practiced throwing the axe out behind the sheds almost every Sunday afternoon.

The Quad finally reached the stone shed and they parked it and switched to horses, customary procedure for anyone planning to go higher. A string of horses was kept permanently in a small corral behind the shed for that purpose. Brook mounted the buckskin that had been taken up the day before, while Polite picked out a stubby paint for himself. With his outlandish clothes and the ridiculous hat and multicolored horse he looked like a clown at a kiddy's rodeo. He shifted a massive wad of tobacco from one cheek to the other and spat wetly and grunted to Brook, "How long this gonna take, Itty Bitty?"

"Why?"

"Too long and my ass'll splinter. Saddles and me just don't plumb."

"Bullshit," said Brook, and they rode out.

The creek in the upper canyon was not the same as in the

bottom end. It hid itself behind boulders and brush for most of its lower length, as if ashamed, but at the top it reappeared, thudding brazenly against the canyon wall as though it wanted to be remembered as a boisterous thing that didn't give a damn. "Water's up," Brook called out. "Lots of melt. Did you people check these creeks on your search?"

"We checked all the running water we could find. Your pa ain't floating."

"What makes you so sure?"

Polite spat compulsively. "I ain't. If I knew where your pa was I'd take you to him. But it ain't no creek, that I know. If he was crossing water that day and fell in and drowned, then where's his horse?" He watched Brook's face, seeking praise for his judgment more than agreement with it. "Your pa was riding the Alma gray that day. No horse that big is gonna drown in a mountain stream."

Brook pushed the buckskin ahead and when they reached the rock face where the canyon turned, Polite reined in his paint. "Just here is where your old man stopped and went back," he said, nodding at the huge outcrop. "We were coming down from the Guyot ridge on the other side of Saddle. Caleb had been pushing me for some time to show his brother that stand of Englemann up there. It's prime wood, number one sawlogs and a lot of high grade peelers. But you can't flume those sticks off the mountain, they're too big. With the Bulldog maybe. . . ." He let it drift away, surveying the rich green geometry of the spruce high above them, and then he came back. "We were riding down in threes. I was up front with the Spaniard and I think Willy was the other one. Maybe Grant, no matter. We'd reached the rock face here and all at once your pa went back."

"Did he say why?"

"Not to me. He spoke to Etchevarl. I only got a little of it. I guess there was a sound and he was going back to see what it was."

"You should have talked him out of it. You had to see that storm up on Big Red."

"It wasn't on Big Red," replied Polite testily. "It was near Guyot."

"No difference. You should have gone with him."

Polite shifted his chaw. "Hell, if I had second sight I would have. But I couldn't see the future that day any better than I can see it on this one." He gathered tobacco juice in the front of his mouth and let it go with a lot of bluster. "Maybe Caleb was right," he said, wiping his mouth hard.

"What do you mean?"

"He said you'd blame us. He said you'd hold us responsible for what happened."

Brook looked away from the mottled face beside him. "I'm not blaming anybody," he said. Then he looked back. "And I don't want to be blamed. That strike you as fair?"

Polite shifted in the saddle, which was too small for him, just like the horse, and eyed the ridge above. "All of a sudden that storm came roaring down through here like a load of runaway logs. Pushing everything in front of it, including us. When we got to the stone shed we piled in, horses and all, trying to get out of the way." His voice slowed. "But quick as she hit, she quit. We piled back out and headed up the canyon. Hell, I'd have bet my mama's Bible we'd meet your old man coming down, soaking wet and laughing about it. You know how easy he was that way."

Brook eyed the silent heights above him.

"But he didn't show," Polite finished flatly. "We never saw him again."

They rode away from the rock abutment and continued climbing. Gradually the canyon lost its depth and shallowed out. The wind pushed at them. The trees that had been watching their ascent began to pull back from the rim as if not wanting to be seen. The trail flattened at the last moment and turned to the north and suddenly Saddle Pass lay directly in front of them.

The pass was aptly named, a perfect saddle of land that bridged one mountain slope to another. It was no more than two hundred yards in length and at its far end stood a knobby

74

shaft of rock that resembled the high pommel of a Mexican saddle. Even the color of the pass was saddlelike, lent to it by a leathery sedge that covered its surface everywhere. The pass could look innocent enough from a distance but to move out onto it was to sense its treachery, to know the deception of its slopes and to feel the wind rushing across the Continental Divide. On its eastern edge the pass beveled down gently into the canyon headlands from which the two men had just emerged, but on the west the ground sheared off abruptly, a cliff plunging into depths which were inaccessible from either top or bottom. "What do you think, Polite? Did my father go off here?"

"That's my guess. I figure he couldn't locate the sound he was looking for and just kept coming up the canyon. He got to where we're standing and heard it again, or else saw something, and he started across. The storm picked that time to hit and he lost his footing and slid down the apron and off the edge."

Brook sat the buckskin in silence and then shook his head. "Bullshit," he said quietly. "Papa knew these mountains too well. Lived his whole life in them. It's what Etch was trying to say. Why would a man cross a pass like this with a storm waiting on the other side?"

Polite let go with a splat of brown juice. "Knowing a place real good won't necessarily save you from it. Your pa figured he could beat the storm. He misjudged and it killed him." Brook didn't respond and Polite kept on. "We did the best we could for your old man, Itty Bitty. Caleb had us turn these mountains inside out. Three days worth. But it wasn't any good." He shook his head. "Your pa's in those rocks at cliff bottom. There ain't no place else he can be. There ain't no place left we didn't scour out."

Brook studied the bridge of earth that lay in front of him. Wind probed its grassy surface as if it were seeking something hidden there. "We'll have to go to the edge of that cliff and take a look," he said to Polite.

Polite gave a snort. "Oh hell, yes. We'll just saunter down

to the rim and visit awhile and glance over from time to time. If we had Etchevarl's telescope we could take turns trying to find the bottom."

"I'm serious, Polite."

"No, you ain't," Polite spat. "You're just crazy. You got too much of that poontang down there in the city and it shrunk up your good sense along with your balls. There's no way you're gonna get a man to walk down that apron and look over the edge. With that grade and that wind his boots won't stick for shit. It's pure suicide. I'd rather ride a tree top to ground than try it."

"It could be done. A few stakes. Some rope. A man could shimmy down to the edge."

"You'd have to tie several pieces of rope together to make one long enough. Tied rope is weaker than bad string."

"There's that new rope Caleb ordered, it might be long enough. There were some hand picks in with that stuff too. And we've got plenty of bull stakes."

"Oh, you got the gear for it, Itty Bitty. What you ain't got is a reason for killing the man you send to do it."

Brook listened to the wind, studied the long rooflike slope that stretched from the crown of the pass to the edge of the cliff. "Tomorrow," he said distinctly, over the wind. "Tomorrow we'll come back up here with the gear. All of us. Then we'll see."

A solitary black cloud had moved in unobtrusively from the west and snagged itself on Guyot. Even as the two men watched, the wind surged and the cloud broke free of the peak and drifted ominously toward them. They turned away from the pass and about halfway down Right Hand the cloud caught up to them and beat at their backs with a savage tattoo of rain. It eased off when they reached the stone shed and transferred to the Quad, and at the bottom when they drove out of Right Hand it was there again, boiling angrily in the mouth of the canyon. But it would not follow.

* * *

76

On certain days Willy Walker worked horses in the high corral. Given the least amount of raw material to work with there wasn't a horse going that Willy couldn't shape out. He usually went forth in the spring of the year with Hartman money in his pocket and scouted the ranches in the San Luis Valley or the upper Arkansas or one of the numerous forks of the South Platte. He bought the raw and the ornery and the spirit broken for a lot of argument and very little money, and sold them in the fall on Hartman Bills of Sale for five times the purchase price. Unfortunately, the market for horses wasn't as good as it had been. Now that the war was over the cavalry officers weren't driving into the lane with a fistful of requisitions. There was a promising new market in the riding academies that were springing up in the Park for the benefit of vacationers, especially the big one at Hartsel that featured the hot springs baths, but it wasn't enough.

Another market was the Easterners who migrated to the Park every year and insisted on farming it—buying machinery, turning sod, planting seed. Every last one of them failed. They failed because the Park was not the lush wet garden halfway up the sky they thought it was, and Willy got most of those horses back at the foreclosure sales that inevitably followed. The Hartman horse herd consequently swelled a little every year, growing fat and lazy on the wild hay, but Aaron wouldn't adjust. He continued to deal in horses because his father had and because he himself loved them, and so he kept Willy Walker on the payroll.

Margaret Pendleton had discovered what Willy did with the horses in the corral and it fascinated her. She was standing at the corral fence watching Willy work when Brook and Polite returned in the Quad. She waved at Brook and he lifted a hand to her, although she believed it was as much in surprise as in greeting, and when they parked he didn't move away from the truck like the other men, but stood knee deep in the grass with the sun in his eyes and the wind batting at the bill of his cap, looking back at her. He wore his hair extremely short and the cap rode low on his head, making it appear too large. He left the truck after a minute and walked toward one of the sheds and Margaret continued to watch him. He was tall and slender and his legs were exceptionally long, giving him a certain rhythm when he walked. She thought he was one of the most graceful tall men she had ever seen.

That afternoon Brook drove the Ford stake bed into the east meadow to check the birthing mare he and Willy had penned there on Brook's second day home. The mare had foaled and was with her colt now but it was obvious she was in serious trouble. She stood splay-legged in one corner of the pen with her colt neglected and her head sweeping the ground and her eyes not seeking Brook where he stood at the fence. She probably hadn't cleaned out properly after the birth and a clot of navel gut was still trapped inside her, poisoning her irrevocably. Brook went to the truck and removed the Winchester from beneath the seat and sighted the barrel across the top board of the pen. *We owe our animals the mercy of a quick death,* his father had insisted; *we share the earth with them, they are our brothers, our love for them has its roots in heaven.*

The bullet in this instance *was* a mercy and yet for the instant of the shot it had a certain cruelty, for it did not simply drop the mare into death but wrenched her there. She lurched hard and fell hard, and when the rupture of the air had healed and the stillness enveloped the pen again there was a moment when Brook caught himself waiting for the mare to rise. It was as if she had gone sprawling at the sudden explosion and would shortly get to her feet and shake her head and look up at Brook in a kind of stunned wonder at all that power and noise. He wondered if the Great War had been like that, if the living soldiers waited for their dead comrades to restore themselves and rise, to brush their uniforms and look around and ask what had happened. Had Caleb himself experienced such a bewilderment when the German shell blew him off the road in that wet murky dawn he spoke of so reluctantly?

Brook tied the dead mare's feet to the truck and dragged her body through the grass to a place by a dry creek and covered her with dirt and then returned to the pen and picked up the colt. It was a beautifully patterned chestnut male with a strong line to its back and good conformation; it needed to be saved. Brook drove directly to the back yard of the house and called for Margaret and she came out onto the porch at once. "Have you ever seen a colt?" he called to her.

"Yes."

"Have you ever held one?"

"No."

"Have you ever weaned one?" but by then Margaret had seen the animal in Brook's arms and was hurrying down the steps toward the truck.

It was difficult for anyone not to fuss over a new colt when they first saw it. They would bend down and peer into that comically helpless face with a predictable reaction. A man would generally say "hey fella" and stick out a hand and rough up the colt's mane, but a woman would invariably gush. Margaret was no exception. She leaned in over the door and crooned at the baby animal and stroked its neck and then nuzzled it. "Be careful," Brook warned her, "he's still frightened. You don't know what he might do."

Margaret lifted her head and looked at Brook.

"Of all God's creatures," he said, "you're looking at one of the dumbest."

"Are you really?" she said, continuing to stare at Brook.

"The colt," Brook countered, recognizing the tease, "I'm talking about the colt." He got out of the truck and set the colt on its feet in the grass, a tiny stick figure with big wet eyes. "Watch him," Brook cautioned. "Don't let those wobbly knees fool you. He can lunge quicker than a mad cat." As if the words had been a command the colt squealed and butted the air. "They'll butt any living creature they see," he told her. "It's a natural instinct in them. What they're doing is looking for the . . . ." He suddenly couldn't say *teat*.

"Teat?" Margaret offered.

He left Margaret in the yard with the colt and went to get a weaner pail. He stopped at the springhouse and poured a few pints of milk into the pail and brought it back to the yard and handed it to Margaret. "Here, you try it," he said. "Keep the pail well out in front of you and just above the colt's head. They like to butt up."

The colt lunged, smelling the milk, and Margaret stepped aside. "If he's ever going to nurse you'll have to stay in front of him," Brook told her. "Try to guide that rubber teat at the base of the pail into his mouth. He'll never find it on his own." The colt made another lunge and banged the side of the pail. "They're stubborn little devils," Brook said. The colt nosed the pail again but couldn't find the teat. "Tip your pail more and hold it a little lower," Brook instructed.

Margaret worked the pail for several minutes, coaxing and offering, but without success. "They're stubborn little devils," Brook kept saying, and finally he got nervous enough to take the pail from her. "Let me show you," he said. "I've weaned a hundred colts." On his first attempt he bent down and positioned the bucket just above and in front of the colt's nose and then sloshed the milk a few times. The colt stepped forward and slid its mouth perfectly onto the teat and began to suckle lustily. "It's all in knowing how," Brook said quietly. He allowed the colt to nurse a few minutes and then withdrew the pail and stood erect. "It comes from long experience with animals," and at that moment the colt butted him in the knee and his leg buckled and he went down instantly. The pail hit the ground and a sheet of milk shot out and struck Brook full in the face.

Margaret knelt over him immediately, her eyes dancing. "It's the knowing how, isn't it?" she said in a choked voice. "It's your long experience with these stubborn little devils that has put you flat on your back with your face full of milk." She wiped Brook's face with the bottom of her skirt and when she had finished she let the *entire* laugh escape. But Brook wouldn't look at her, or speak, and finally Margaret returned to the house.

Brook picked up the colt and carried it to a stall in the stock barn. He brought more milk from the springhouse in another bucket and knelt on the colt's head and poured the milk into its mouth, nearly choking it. When he finished he threw the empty pail into a corner of the stall and kicked at a clot of wet straw bedding on the floor, sending it flying. He returned to the yard and retrieved the weaner pail and then walked to the lot and stood at the fence. There was a flutter in his belly and a weakness in his knees but it wasn't being knocked down by an animal that had caused it. He could have laughed at that too. The reason was that in bending over the colt, coaxing it and cooing at it, Margaret's blouse had sagged open and revealed her breasts and the deep cleaving that divided them, and when he was on the ground she had lifted her skirts to clean his face and in so doing had exposed her legs. They were long and slim and very naked, and it was these images that pulsed through him now. He looked across the rise of the west meadow, hoping the sight of something familiar would relieve him. He saw the mill and the stacks of fresh lumber that looked at that distance like beehives. He saw smoke curling up from the wigwam burner, drifting away to the east, trying to escape the brooding loom of the mountains.

But the flutter in his belly would not diminish and he knew it wasn't going to. It might quiet itself, become tolerable, but it would never go away. He stepped back from the fence and lifted one boot and drove it hard into the bottom board. The board snapped in two, perfectly, with a crack that slammed through the hot afternoon like another rifle shot.

CHAPTER 8

They drove up to the mountain shed in midmorning, parked the Quad and made the switch to horseback, the five of them. Earlier, in the kitchen of the house with Ruth there, Caleb had tried to dissuade Brook from the attempt but as they plodded up Right Hand his attitude changed. "I understand your need to do this, Brook," he was saying. "I don't like it necessarily but I understand it." They were riding in advance of the party with the others strung out behind. "To tell the truth, knowing for sure where the body is will help us all. Maybe then we can get back to normal. There's certainly been no peace for your mother since the accident. It's a hard thing to say but her recovery won't really start until she accepts the body being at the bottom of that cliff."

As Caleb spoke, Brook's mind flashed a picture of his father lying smashed amid the rocks, an object too alien in shape and color for the earth to accept as its own. He shook off the vision and they clattered up the last stretch of broken slope to the ridge.

The pass lay before them in a nakedness of sun and wind, holding the bridge in space like a hard finger. As they rode out onto it the ground sloped gently away from the spine of the pass like the back of a good horse, but it steepened quickly when the back became the belly and halfway down the western side it tilted swiftly into a gulf of emptiness.

They dismounted and unpacked the gear and Polite drove a bull stake into the ground a few feet east of the crest. To this stake Brook secured one end of a massive coil of three-quarter-inch rope and the remainder he threw straight down the west apron. The rope slithered to a stop like an unfinished spring. Polite spat disgustedly. "Just like I figured. She ain't gonna reach."

Grant Pickens studied the frail spiraling of rope in the brown sedge below him. "Stretched out she might."

"We're not dealing with wire here," Polite came back. "It's rope. Rope won't stretch for shit. We're gonna have to tie."

"That's going to be one long rope," Willy Walker offered. "Too long. It puts too much strain on the knot. On the stake too."

"Then we'll divvy up the strain," Brook put in. "Pound a second stake farther down the slope and connect the two with rope. Then to the bottom stake we tie a second rope that will reach down to the edge."

Polite figured a moment and then spit into the grass. "Double stakes, double trouble. We'll have to station two men at the lower stake and two at the top. That splits our strength in case something goes wrong."

"Nothing's going to go wrong," declared Caleb starchily. "We're going to rig this thing properly, the way we know is right. Our main objective is to protect the man on the rope."

It hadn't been announced who would be the man on the rope, although Brook had known from the beginning that he would be the one, as had Caleb. The others did not and on the trip up the canyon they had studiously avoided looking at one another, fearing to see in the other's face their own anxiety. But now their dread was named and they stood on the naked beam of the pass and studied everything in sight—their boots, the sky, the horses flicking their ears against the wind—everything but the rope trailing away forlornly down the west apron. When Brook announced that he would be the one to go, the sound of their combined relief was like a single expended breath.

They decided finally on Brook's plan. He and Polite pounded a second stake at a spot on the slope where a man could still stand upright, approximately one-fourth of the way down, and when both ropes were in place and the two stakes secured to each other, Caleb joined them at the lower stake. He immediately ordered Brook to tie a double knot near the free end of the second rope. "That'll be your safety flag," he explained. "When you're rappeling down the slope and your lead hand touches the knot you'll know your rope has run out." He glanced sharply at Brook. "You've rappeled before, haven't you?"

"I can do it."

"Have you rappeled before?"

"No."

"Then pay attention. You loop a rope around one thigh and up across your chest and over the opposite shoulder. Like this," and awkwardly, with his one arm, he demonstrated the maneuver to Brook. "Then you just back yourself along the rope. See that? Nothing to it, once you know what you're doing. Aaron and I used to rappel the shed roofs when we were kids. The supreme test was the big hay barn down by the highway. You earned your badge the hard way on that baby. The apron here on Saddle isn't much different, just longer. And steeper near the edge." He studied the rope and the stakes and looked down the slope and then back at Brook with some sort of decision showing in his eyes. "I'm going to tie you," he announced, "just to be safe," and he had Polite rig a safety harness out of a short length of rope and attach one end to Brook's waist and the other to the rappeling rope. "Concentrate on your feet and that rope in your hands," Caleb instructed him when Polite had finished. "Just those two things, nothing else. Don't look up here, don't look to the side, don't look up at the sky." He grabbed a hand pick from the pile of gear on the ground. "Keep this in your belt. If you lose your footing, grab the pick and stick it in the ground. Whatever you do, don't let the rope take your whole weight all at once. It would put too big a strain on the stakes. Do you understand?"

"I understand."

"I'll be here at the lower stake with Polite. Grant and Willy

84

will be at the top." He eyed Brook closely. "Do you still want to do this?"

"Like you said, it'll be better when it's done."

"Remember now, the closer you get to the edge," Caleb warned, "the tougher it gets. Your body will begin to feel heavier and the wind will hit you harder. If it gets too strong, drop to your belly."

"Right."

"You'll be going backward down the slope. When you reach the edge you're going to have to turn your head around and lean back in order to see over. Okay? It's either that or go down the apron head first. I don't think you want to do that."

"No."

"Try to pick out the horse first, the Alma gray Aaron was riding. It'll be bigger. Easier to see. When you're ready to come back up, make a signal and we'll haul you in."

"Those stakes have got to hold, Uncle."

"They'll hold, Brookers. I'll see to it, that's a promise. Now go."

Brook moved away quickly, backing down the sedge, feeding out rope, concentrating on the tangle of slack that lay coiled along his path. Gradually the apron steepened and the slack disappeared and the rope grew taut in his hands. The angle between his body and the ground narrowed. In his left hand he could feel his body weight increase as Caleb had foretold. He fed out more rope. He wondered where the double knot was. Would he reach the edge of the apron before he reached the knot? Why hadn't Caleb told him about that? How near was the edge right now? He glanced back over his left shoulder and saw nothing but an enormous expanse of sky. He stopped and looked back up the slope.

It was a foolish thing to do. His stomach lurched wildly. At an incredible angle above him the shrunken bodies of Caleb and Polite bobbed in a brown sea of sedge that writhed in the wind. Brook closed his eyes and the wind roared in his ears. He opened his eyes and played out a little of the rope. Then a little more. The slope was unbelievably steep now. The wind surged at him, wanting to pluck him from the earth and hurl him away across the sedge. He eased his body into still another backward step and his right hand abruptly struck the knot. He stopped and took a deep breath. He fixed his eyes on a spot in the sedge and slowly bent his knees until they touched the ground. He turned first one boot outward and then the other and jammed the inner edge of them into the earth. Slowly, trying to establish his center of balance, he turned his head and looked behind him.

He was at the very lip of the cliff. There was less than a foot of earth between his boots and empty space. He shut his eyes and opened them and then leaned slowly backward and pushed his head out over the edge.

In that instant some inner part of him fell, fell into emptiness, an abyss that held no recognition and offered no dimension he could comprehend. Yet his eyes caught a gloss of something in the depths that was both a dimness and a density, a miscolored formlessness that for a fragment of a second held the plunge of his vision. But the sheer terror of that plunge blinded him to anything further, to detail, to sight itself. His stomach twisted and the breath left his chest and he turned and threw himself against the safety of the earth.

It was a mistake.

The sudden movement caused his boots to slip. Before he could open his eyes and grab for the pick in his belt he fell over the edge of the cliff.

Upslope, at the lower stake, the rope jerked taut with the abruptness of Brook's fall and the knot tightened against the stake. Caught between opposing pressures that were unendurable, the stake pinched itself free of the earth with amazing ease, quivering in its release like a thing alive.

Polite dived for the rope and Caleb whirled to face the crest. "Hold there!" he screamed into the wind. "*Stake's loose!*"

The two men standing at the crest heard Caleb's shout and lunged for their stake but in those few lost seconds the stake surrendered to the sudden force from below. With a speed far greater than the men's it tipped downslope, quivered, and then pulled free of the earth altogether.

The entire lifeline of ropes and stakes lay loose upon the pass.

Polite was tied at the waist with a short subrope looped onto the lower one, just like Brook. He had taken the precaution almost as an afterthought, and it saved Brook's life. His own too, perhaps, but it destroyed his hands. When he grabbed the rope it was already flowing swiftly after Brook's plummeting body and thirty feet of it tore through his hands before he could get his feet planted and the rope slowed. Twenty feet more burned through before Caleb could grab the rope with his single hand and help get it stopped. The two men stood frozen to the earth in a tug of war with the invisible weight of Brook's body before Willy Walker and Grant Pickens could grab the upper rope and get their feet planted.

Wordlessly, battered by wind, the four men hauled steadily away on the rope.

When it reappeared at the rim of the cliff, Brook's body was limp. The loop of safety rope had jammed in his armpits and his cap was gone and his arms hung at his sides like braided rags. But fifty feet later he began grabbing at the rope like a man in a nightmare, and during the last one hundred feet he had struggled to his knees and then his feet, gripping the rope desperately in both hands. His face was bloodless and his eyes were locked. Caleb grabbed him when he reached the lower stake and guided him to the top of the pass, where Willy helped him into the buckskin's saddle.

Only when Polite reached the crest himself did he release his grip on the rope. Then he screamed and sank to his knees, holding his torn hands above his head like a crazy man in prayer. His mouth dripped tobacco spit and his face was a mask of pain. Willy took off his shirt and tore it into strips and wrapped the strips around Polite's hands and with Grant's help got the stricken man to his horse and into the saddle. "Jump on behind," Caleb ordered Willy. "Hold him good. He'll fall off if you don't."

They rode down to the stone shed in a single file and made the switch to the truck and no one spoke. Grant Pickens sat next to Brook for the entire trip down the canyon and when they emerged at the bottom he finally spoke. "Jesus Christ in the stone quarry," he grunted, "you lose more caps than anybody I ever seen."

Willy Walker didn't know how to drive a motor car so it was Grant who took Polite to the hospital in Fairplay. Caleb sent along a pint of whiskey but there was no conceivable way Polite could have held the bottle. That flesh in the palms of his hands that wasn't gone was mangled. His left thumb was shredded to the bone and loose from its socket. The mottled purple of his face had faded to the stale gray of old dough and he sat in the front seat of the Ford moaning and rolling his head from side to side. Caleb threw a blanket over the man's shoulders and barked a command and Grant jammed the T into gear. The skinny wooden wheels fired gravel bullets as the T went out the lane.

Caleb led Brook into the kitchen of the house, followed by Etchevarl. Ruth seemed to set her jaw when she saw Brook but it was not a grimace, and there was no escaped cry. She went to him and took his arm and led him to a chair at the end of the table. She filled a basin with warm water from a jacket in the stove and set it in front of him. Working carefully, she began to remove Brook's shirt.

Strangely unsettled, Caleb told Ruth what had happened on the mountain. He seemed unable to look at her while he spoke. "It shouldn't have happened. The ropes were tight and we got good depth on the stakes and the instructions were clear for when he got to the edge. But he . . . the sod must have been soft because the stakes. . . ." He glanced at the kitchen window and at his shoes and then continued. "Polite caught the rope. He was standing right there and he had Brook all the way." Now Caleb looked at Ruth for the first time. "There's no guarantees up there for anybody. Not on these mountains. But the odds were right for him and he came through like a champ. He's going to be okay." He let out a breath and the expression that had been masked in his face all along seemed to surface in words. "And I'll bet he got a good look at what was down there at the bottom."

"What hurts the most?" Ruth asked, not physically acknowledging anything Caleb had said but still administering to Brook. She had unbuttoned his shirt and removed his arms from the sleeves and now he sat naked from the waist up.

A thick discolored bruise had formed under Brook's rib cage and red burn marks arced across his upper chest where the rope had jammed him. "The rope burns bother me the most," he said, answering his mother finally, but watching Caleb. "And my ribs hurt when I take a deep breath."

Ruth probed gently at his chest just above the circular bruise. "Feel any pain there?"

"No."

She repeated the movement, higher up this time and a little harder.

"No."

"Well, there's nothing broken," she announced clearly, stepping back. "Caleb was right, you're going to be okay. But sore, you're going to be real sore for a few days." Wetting a cloth in the warm water she bathed the long angry welt at the top of Brook's chest and then covered it with a strong smelling salve. With Margaret's help she cut a large piece of muslin into strips and wound them tightly around Brook's ribs. "There," she said simply, "that should do it," and she stepped back from Brook's chair and watched him with a faintly quizzical expression as though she were waiting for his answer to a question that someone in the room had asked earlier and all had forgotten but she. But Etchevarl must have remembered too, for he moved forward silently from his place just inside the kitchen door and stood next to Ruth. Just as intently, Caleb stepped up to the table and looked down at Brook where he sat waiting in the chair. "Well?" Caleb asked softly, and they all knew then what the unspoken question had been.

As he studied the circle of faces above him, some part of Brook left the room and returned to the mountain, passed the sleepy stone shed, climbed the raw tumbled slope below the pass. He saw the wind-battered saddle of earth and its stark precipice, saw the terrifying plunge beyond that and then the bottom far below. "I saw something," he said, looking away from the faces. "Lighter in color. Different shaped. It must have been the horse Papa was riding that day. The Alma gray. It was in the rocks at the bottom."

Ruth dropped into a chair that stood near the table. Her eyes closed for a moment but no expression crossed her face and she made no attempt to speak.

Somehow, Brook knew the first voice would be Caleb's. "You did your duty, Brookers," it came, terribly loud in that hushed room. "You accomplished what the rest of us could not. What perhaps we were afraid to try. It took a great personal courage and I'm proud of you. Your mother is proud too, I know she is. We all are." But when Caleb moved around the table it was to Ruth he went, not Brook. "Aaron is dead," he said to her, bending down and touching her shoulder with his one hand. "We have had witness to it. Let it be finished now. Let life go on." Then he turned and left the kitchen. Etchevarl bent his great leonine head to Ruth's and whispered something only she could hear. She reached up and squeezed the old Basque's hand and his chin dropped to his chest. He remained thus for several minutes and then he too left the room.

Ruth remained in her chair and Brook, still naked above the waist and bound in bandages, remained in his. He thought several times that his mother's face was on the verge of brightening, that it would at any moment release the emotion it had held captive for so long, but just when he most expected to see the lifted brows or the clearing eyes that would signal such a surrender, nothing happened. The old singular privateness still bound her, the tight blur of restraint remained. At one point she lifted one arm from her lap and rested her elbow on the table and very deliberately placed the tips of her fingers against her forehead. Her hand shielded her eyes and she sat in this position for several minutes.

From the interior of the house, with a dull muffled formality, came the striking of a clock.

As Brook continued to watch his mother it dawned on him that once again he was in attendance upon her, waiting like an obedient subject for a dismissal that would send the world into movement again. His mother the Queen. Dismissals, not emotions. She had no emotions of her own, he realized, none except what others were willing to lend her. He saw clearly the stoic avoidance that was Ruth Hartman's true face upon the world, inviting reaction and feeling but never offering any.

From across the room, Margaret coughed or stirred or did something interruptive and then came forward and took Ruth's hand from her face and led her from the room.

When Margaret came back downstairs ten minutes later, Brook was still in his chair, sitting so motionless he seemed almost a waxen figure. "Your mother's in her room lying down," she reported to him. "She's strong and can handle this. She needed to know about her husband and now she does. Thanks to you."

Brook remained unmoving and expressionless in the chair.

"Caleb said you were very courageous up on the pass," she went on. "That's got to mean a great deal to you."

"Yes," Brook said finally. "Coming from a man like that, it means a lot."

"Yes." The atmosphere seemed to be tipping back toward the earlier formality and she searched for something to say that would right it. "Well," she began, "you certainly have a gift for turning dull days into exciting ones. If you're not being knocked flat by an orphan colt, you're falling off a mountain."

He smiled then, shattering the somber image completely. "Anything to please the guests."

She watched his smile, which was perhaps his own attempt to circumvent the growing stiffness in the room. Perhaps his being bandaged and only partially dressed caused her to look at him somewhat more critically. He had long arms but his wrists were thick and his hands large. His skin looked smooth, lighter in color than his face and neck. His features were quite ordinary except for one. His mouth. A single front tooth in his lower jaw had grown in crooked. It was minimally visible when he talked but much more so when he smiled, as now, and it committed his appearance to a certain uniqueness. It wasn't a boy's smile, although there was in it that same wistful quality, that careless charm which sometimes borders on the oafish. She broke off her appraisal then, aware that she was being too long at it. "Well," she said, "no more search parties for you for a while."

"I guess not."

"And no riding either."

"I suppose you mean the Ford. It's rougher than any saddle."

"Either one. They'll both be too painful."

"That sounds ominous," he said, smiling again. "I'm sure you're saying it just to cheer me up," and with that he started to rise from his chair. But when he tried to stand erect he stiffened suddenly and all the color drained from his face.

She crossed the room to him instantly, acknowledging his pain even though it was obvious he was trying to conceal it. She reached out and gripped his arm, not because she feared he might fall but because he seemed so vulnerable and defenseless standing there in the middle of the room, bound in bandages. A wave of concern swept through her like a surge of fever, so intense that for a moment she was sure he could feel it.

Perhaps he did. The color came back into his face; there was a certain high heat in it, like a blush. He stepped back and an odor of turpentine and menthol rose up from his bandages, something of the salve Ruth had administered. "Not altogether a bad smell," she was going to say to him, perhaps to relieve his embarrassment or simply because something needed to be spoken at that moment. But she didn't say it. For some reason she didn't understand, she reached out and touched his chest instead, just above the bandages. Then she immediately withdrew her hand. "You'd better let me help you into your shirt," she said quickly, and began to maneuver first one arm and then the other into the sleeves of his shirt. "Does it hurt when you move your arms?" she asked.

He groaned a denial and smiled at her and the earlier impishness was back again. She finished buttoning his shirt and then stepped back and surveyed him. "There," she said cheerfully, "now no one will ever suspect that you took on a mountain single-handed."

But she didn't feel quite so cheerful when she went upstairs later and started a letter to Emerson. She kept remembering the feeling she'd had when she helped bandage Brook's injured chest. She felt that for the first time since her arrival she had actually been able to help someone in the family, to share in some part of their tragedy, however slightly. But that emotion had been swept completely aside when later Brook had tried to rise from his chair. It wasn't his pain she felt, for that was to be expected. It was something else. Perhaps it was that he looked so helpless standing there, so excluded from his family, so oddly alone. She pushed the unfinished letter aside. No, it wasn't Brook's pain she had felt. Strangely, it was some part of her own.

Polite came back from Fairplay the next day, spitting great dollops of tobacco juice and pawing at things with his bandaged hands like a clumsy bear trying to mimic the humans who, having somehow managed to capture him, had decided to dress him in the ridiculous plug-hatted red-shirted costume of a clown.

CHAPTER 9

Nature had given Arranz Etchevarl's face but one expression with which to face the world. *Sorrow.* If he felt the other emotions known to humankind—joy, wrath, avarice—they remained alien in him, incapable of representation. The old Basque's eyes were mainly responsible, for he was of Latin blood and the Latin eye was created for sorrow. The sockets are deep and the lids are heavy and a refined satiny darkness, the very paint of sorrow, pervades the entire well of the eye. In Etchevarl, there were additional enhancements. His face was long and its tendency downward, the jaws being in some mysterious way wider than the upper part of his face as though the perpetual sadness had swelled them outward. And then there were the mustaches. On an Anglo-Saxon face they would have been ludicrous, an overblown theatrical disguise, but not on Etchevarl. The great drooping horns of misfortune were a natural part of him. He did not twitch them for effect, did not lick at the thick curved bars of hair in any self-conscious awareness. The mustaches were not an appendage to his face, they were *of* it, like the sorrow.

It was this melancholy countenance that Brook looked into when he sensed a new presence in the car shed and glanced up from his work. He was repairing Plain Tread casings for the T. His chest had continued sore and he had puttered for the better part of two days, allowing the ribs to heal. What it was that Etchevarl was bringing Brook now, the reason for the interrup-

94

tion, was a complaint. This was unusual for Etchevarl because he was not a complainer. He had never been a servile man, shuffling his feet and averting his eyes and stitching his hat brim through his fingers as he talked. When he felt he had just cause to voice a resentment, and inasmuch as his dignity allowed him, the old man would voice it. In his own style too, which was unremittingly formal. Formal English was the only English Etchevarl had ever spoken. It was an adopted tongue, for when he came to herd sheep for Julius in 1879 at the age of twenty he spoke only Spanish and of course Basque, a flawed undisciplined language that no one could understand. The one who had taught him English was Ruth. She was concerned in those early schoolteacher days with the rules of syntax and elocution and not at all with the commonness of idiom, and Etchevarl spoke the language now as she had taught it to him then, grand and reverent and pure.

In such a way did Etchevarl speak now to Brook, face up, chin out, a huge lumpy beret draped over one side of his graying head. "Caleb has removed me from the summer kitchen," he announced solemnly. "As of last evening I am no longer quartered there."

The announcement caught Brook by surprise. He stood staring at the old man, feeling his own awkwardness, struggling to separate the manner of the words from their meaning. "So," he managed limply when Etchevarl stopped. He took a deep breath, needing more time. "So, what will you do now? Where will your new quarters be?"

"In the employee's building," answered Etchevarl promptly, scanning Brook's face. "In with the regular workers."

Unable still to think of a suitable reply, Brook repeated the word that had won him delay earlier. "So?"

"The summer kitchen was given to me by your grandfather many years ago, about the time you were born," Etchevarl went on, as if he were explaining it to a stranger. "He promised it would be my personal quarters for as long as I wished. Your father continued that policy while he lived. Now it is abandoned."

"Well," Brook replied, speaking carefully, organizing what

he realized now must be his defense, "who did Caleb give the summer kitchen to?"

"To no one. He took it for himself."

"I see."

"I was not even consulted in the decision. He simply took it upon himself to break the agreement."

"But it wasn't a treaty, was it, Etchevarl? I mean, we're not talking about a contract here. Hell, things change. People change."

"But I do not." It was controlled, resolute, delivered nearly at attention. "I am the same as when the summer kitchen was first given me. It is others who have changed, who have come and gone with fortune and the seasons. The improvident Caleb—"

"Caleb had good reason for being gone, old man. We mustn't forget that. He was away in a foreign land making a sacrifice for his country. I think that earned him some special rights."

"The right to reward forty years of loyalty with an eviction? The right to ignore even the common courtesy of a discussion?"

"Look," Brook broke in, stopping the older man with an uncertain shrug, hoping the gesture would make the words more a plea for understanding than a statement. "Sleeping quarters are a place where you can fart all you want and not have to deny you're doing it, okay? They're a bunch of blankets you climb into at night and crawl out of in the morning and wash once a month in a tub out back. No big matter." He waited for a reaction and when he didn't get one he reached out and laid a hand on Etchevarl's shoulder in a comradely way. "I'll tell you what I'll do, Etch. I'll mention it to Caleb at dinner tonight. Maybe I can talk him into changing his mind. Hell, he was gone for a lot of years and he may not remember that Papa made that promise to you."

It was Brook who didn't remember. He didn't remember to mention the summer kitchen to Caleb that night because Caleb began telling stories about the war and Brook forgot everything else. He had never heard his uncle do dialect and was pleased to discover he was so good at it. The British speech was Brook's favorite and seemed to be Margaret's as well.

"I got to France with the first group of Americans," Caleb began, "but the Frenchies didn't know what to do with us. They finally assigned half the division to the French Second Corps up in the Vosges, which was at the western end of the front, and the other half went to the Amiens salient to relieve some of the British troops. That was me." He set his jaw, just a little. "It was trench warfare of course. Trenches everywhere. Sometimes I think the whole north of France was one big trench. The British had been in that sector for two years and had some real elaborate fortifications built up. I remember one afternoon we were sitting around in this three room dugout waiting for a German gas attack to clear—you could always tell the German gas because it smelled like apple blossoms—when we looked down into what they called No Man's Land and spotted a bunch of rabbits hopping around the shell holes. Must have been a family of them that the gas had rousted out. They were bouncing all over the place, looking real white against that black mud. Without saying a word, a bunch of us Yanks grabbed our Enfields and started banging away."

"At rabbits?" Margaret asked, incredulous.

"What happened to them?" inquired Ruth.

Brook discovered right then that his uncle was possessed of excellent timing. There was a dead moment following Ruth's question and Caleb made expert use of it, making it longer by leaning forward and eyeing each of them, pinning them in their chairs with the suspense of his impending answer. There was a sense of waiting for a timed explosion. It came swiftly. "Killed in action!" Caleb announced at precisely the right moment, and their laughter was the explosion. It filled the room.

"Were the British upset?" Brook asked when they had quieted down.

"Just the opposite," replied Caleb, sitting straight up in his chair and making a sort of haughty face. "The Tommies took off their gas masks and looked at one another and said, 'I say, jolly good shoot, what?' And their officer stood up and

97

tipped his helmet to us and said, 'Top-o, Yanks! Absolutely top-o!' "

Oh, it was marvelous, all that noise and mirth flooding the table. It lasted much longer this time, not an explosion now but a wave.

Caleb's French dialect didn't need any apologies made for it either. Margaret began to clear the table after the rabbit story, with Ruth actually helping her so it would go faster, and when they came back Caleb poured brandy for everyone and began a new story. His face was flushed with involvement. "The French people were mostly peasants. Very poor. Wooden shoes, stone houses with dirt floors, that sort of thing. Nothing like it in this country. Thank heavens." His uncle had a good speaking voice, Brook realized, lucid, strong but not so deep that it blurred, like some men. "The people over there were mainly older couples or young girls because most of the young men had beeen killed in the war. They'd been fighting the Germans for three years before we got in." He took a single cigarette from a row he had lined up on the table earlier and leaned toward Brook to get a light, and then continued with his story. "All the mademoiselles in France loved the Yanks. We had the most money, I think was the reason, certainly more than the Tommies or the *Poilu*." He took a drag from his cigarette and explained that *Poilu* was French for soldier. Brook thought his uncle pronounced the word beautifully, although he had never heard it before, not like *40 Hommes et 8 Chevaux* and some others that Caleb had taught him when he'd first come back from France. Brook took a drink of his brandy and Caleb waited for him to set his glass back down and then went on. "The Frogs, that's what we called them sometimes, the Frogs didn't have a whole lot to eat. Onions and potatoes and a few scrawny chickens was about all. But they had lots of wine. Their cellars were full of wine and whenever an American outfit was billeted nearby for any length of time the mademoiselles would set the bottles out on a little table in the doorway of their house and start selling the stuff. Selling it dear too, I might add. Those little gals didn't have the

98

greatest smarts in the world but they knew how to sell wine. When a Yank would walk by their table they'd curtsey and flash a smile and say *Je pense que je t'aime, soldat Americain.* I like you, Yonkee soldyear. You buy wine from me, I theeenk I *lawv* you!"

Again the table erupted. "Oh my!" Margaret cried, her eyes wet with laughing, and Brook almost spilled his brandy.

Caleb took the occasion to offer fresh drinks and everyone accepted. "Another thing," he said, "if mama and papa weren't standing right there next to them at the sales table, some of those mademoiselles would make a date for later that night." He winked suggestively. "A date for out back in the barn."

"Oh dear," Margaret said, and hiccupped just as she said it. Her hand flew to her mouth to cover her embarrassment and everyone roared again, even Caleb this time.

"But the French didn't really like us," he went on, starting to make it serious now, slowing everything. "We were new to them for a while but that changed soon enough. In the end they just tolerated us, although they never quit wanting our money. It got really bad toward the end. For example, if a Yank outfit was marching through a village the people would bring out water but they'd charge us for it. So many francs for a dipperful, so many for a Mason jar. Oh, there were some decent people over there, I suppose, just like in every country. I remember when I got wounded there was a French nurse who was very kind." He stopped talking long enough for Brook to light another cigarette for him and then took a deep drag and exhaled the smoke slowly. "The Americans finally got enough divisions over there to be assigned their own sector. Pershing insisted on it. Said he wanted a separate American command or he wouldn't fight his troops. It was a bluff but it worked. They gave him the toughest front they had, the Saint-Mihiel salient." He let go a soft bark of a laugh. "We reduced it in two weeks." He took in smoke again, watching the fire on the end of the cigarette. "Those Krauts just couldn't beat us, no matter how hard they tried. Slow us down once in a while maybe, but not beat us. As usual, our division got the spearhead in the advance.

We were good at what we did. The best. Some Heinie prisoners said one time they'd rather face anybody than the Forty-second. Der Rainbows, they called us."

"Where did you get wounded?" Margaret asked.

"*Côte du Chatillon* was the name of the place. It was a ridge. My brigade was up there this one morning waiting for the Kraut barrage to lift. When it did we moved out but for some reason the German artillery decided to swing back for one last shot. Maybe they found some extra shells, I don't know. They were firing 155's." He exhaled smoke and it was a streamer now, not a wreath. "It was the twentieth of October, three weeks before the guns stopped for good. I'd been in four major offensives and never even got so much as a scratch. Oh, I burned myself one time boiling clothes in a syrup can. Nothing serious. But I'd lost most of my buddies, those that had come over on the ship with me, plus some new ones." He shrugged tiredly. "It's all a matter of odds. Eventually, they run out on you. The Krauts fired their last round and when that shell hit it knocked me clear to the other side of the road. I laid there a long time. I remember getting terribly thirsty. There was some water in a puddle by my head and I tried to splash some of it into my mouth but I couldn't do it. Next thing I knew they were unloading me out of a lorry onto a depot platform and this French nurse was trying to get water down my throat. '*Bouvez, si'l vous plaît*', she kept saying. '*Il faut que vous bouvez*. Please! You must drink!' A French medical officer came up and tagged me and shooed the nurse away. I understood what he said to her but he didn't know it. He told her not to waste the water, that I'd never make it onto the hospital train. I didn't find this out until later but he pinned a KIA tag on my coat. Killed in action."

No one laughed. It was difficult to picture Caleb helpless; he was not a man to be a victim and that realization was in everyone's face. He tapped his cigarette out in the saucer and when he picked up his story he was grinning at each of them, making it safe again, taking them away from the thirst and the mud in the road and the frightened nurse.

"I don't remember much about base hospital but rehab was

real good duty. It was Mossley Hill Hospital in Liverpool. I didn't get kitchen police and I didn't have to drill and clean harness like those poor buggers in the channel ports who were waiting for a troopship to come and take them home. I had pretty blond nurses to make my bed and draw the shades and push my wheelchair around. They were clean and healthy looking and spoke my language. But best of all, they weren't selling any wine!" and he made them laugh again, it was that easy for him.

"I believe I could sell wine if I had to," Ruth broke in unexpectedly, and Caleb's eyes opened wide and he grinned and said, *"Oui, oui, mademoiselle.* You make good salesman, I theeenk!"

It took them a long time to stop laughing, all of them, Ruth more than the others. It was a strange thing just to see her do it. She'd always had an odd way of laughing anyway, Brook remembered, not an involved thing ever, not an enjoyment so much as a social observance, like the amenity of not talking before another person had finished, or of coughing only into a handkerchief. Now Caleb was urging her to drink her brandy, which finally got her stopped. "You too, young squire," he grinned, turning to Brook. "You'd better drink up."

That pleased Margaret. She laughed that low throaty laugh and raised her glass to Brook and said, "Here's to you, young squire."

Brook had a third brandy after the ladies left for the kitchen to prepare dessert, and Caleb broke out two cigars and they smoked. The brandy was smooth and the room was cool and the chandelier light flowed over the room like liquid. "Keen brandy," Brook said. "Real keen. Not a drop of Blue Ruin in it."

Caleb must not have heard for he leaned back in his chair and blew a lazy ring of cigar smoke. There was a look of contentment on his face and his eyes closed for a moment. "It's good to be home," he said quietly, almost to himself. Then his eyes opened and he turned to Brook. "Brookers, you rascal, how are things going for you?"

"Fine, Uncle."

"Everybody treating you right?"

"Super keen. How about you?"

Caleb held the cigar in his one hand and studied it, pursing his lips as if he were judging its quality. Brook could see the tiny smudge of whiskers under his nose that he obviously couldn't shave properly with just his left hand. "Listen, Brookers," he said, lowering his voice to a confidential tone, "we've got to get over to the hot baths at Hartsel one of these Sundays. It's something I've been wanting you and me to do since I came home. But with one thing and another—"

"I understand."

"We'll take the Oakland, how's that? You can drive. We'll go and splash around a bit. Maybe find the secret bath house and knock back a few bourbons. What do you say?"

"Sounds keen."

"You might want to bring a buddy along. Willy Walker or someone. Maybe Grant."

Brook snorted derisively. "Forget that sonofabitch!"

Caleb gave an answering snort, just animated enough to make it more than a breath and less than an argument. "Speaking of Grant, I've been meaning to tell you this but it slipped my mind. I sent Grant and Etch up to snake out some of that downed aspen in the grove back of the house. We can use it for gateposts and forge wood instead of just letting it rot on the ground."

"Right."

"But I thought that as long as they were in the grove they could cut down a couple of the better looking trees and have Polite slice them up to show to the Denver lumber people. I've asked one of the companies to come up next week and take a look. I think that aspen would make good boards for new houses." His brows went up, bland arcs of hair in a bland face. "What do you think?"

"Sounds good. Too damned many trees in that grove anyway. Hell, you can't even see sunlight after you get in there a ways."

The ladies brought two desserts from the kitchen and then left the room, promising to return. When Caleb had finished eating his he pushed the dish back and said, "When Grant came in this afternoon he told me he noticed something strange at the upper edge of the grove."

"Strange? What?"

"Cat piss, he thought it was. Big cat. He didn't see the animal, just smelled him."

"Smelled her," Brook corrected. "If it's piss Grant smelled, it'll be a female."

Caleb stared at him. "You're right," he said. "You are absolutely right. I'd forgotten it's the females that do that." He knocked a tight gray coil of ash from his cigar. "Anyway, there could be a cougar nosing around up there. There used to be a bunch of them on the place when I was a kid. Maybe they've decided to come back and thought they'd send a scout out first." He started a laugh and then broke it off. "You being the good Winchester man you are, Brookers, I thought maybe you could swing up there and have a look. I wouldn't bother you with it but I can't handle a rifle anymore. Not well enough to kill something."

"I know."

"So if your ribs aren't too sore—"

"Ribs are fine. Glad to go up." He had another brandy and finished the cigar, not touching his dessert. But the cigar had turned strong, he thought. The overhead light began to hurt his eyes and the room got warm and the ladies wouldn't come and wouldn't come and wouldn't come and it wasn't until he woke up sometime after midnight with everyone gone that he realized he'd fallen asleep in the chair.

He stood up and flipped off the wall switch and went upstairs to his room in the dark.

Brook felt fairly decent when he woke in the morning, although it was late. He grabbed a handful of apples from the root cellar on his way to the lot and when he neared the corral he spotted Margaret standing at the fence looking in at the horses. She was dressed in riding clothes, a tailored trouserlike outfit that flared just above the knee and then snugged back in against her thighs. She wore riding boots and had one leg cocked up on a middle board of the fence, drawing the cloth of the breeches tight so that from knee to waist she was one long swelling curve. Something broke open in Brook's stomach when he saw it, as if he'd been hit with a fist, making him feel shaky. He touched the bill of his cap to her and mumbled a good morning and walked straight up to the fence with his eyes down so he wouldn't have to look upon her womanness from the rear again.

Margaret glanced at him and then explained that she had come out to the corral to watch Willy Walker. "I just love to see him train the cutting horses."

"Willy's good."

"Right now he's doing a dally down. At least that's what Grant Pickens called it yesterday. It's when you ask the horse to hold steady against a tightening rope."

"I know what a dally down is."

"Grant said he helps Willy train the horses every chance he gets."

Brook sniffed. "Grant's good-hearted that way but he's got a recurring problem. He can't remember from one day to the next what a horse looks like. He gets them mixed up with chickens. That makes it hard for him to help Willy as much as he'd like. Some days Willy will be here in the corral and Grant'll be in the chicken house."

The remark went unanswered, although Brook could feel Margaret studying him. He turned away from the fence then, keeping his eyes averted, announcing that he had goldbricked long enough and had better get to work. "I just came to the corral to say good morning."

Margaret asked where he was going and he pointed to the aspen that climbed the slope behind the house. "Uncle thinks a cat might be working in the grove. Or maybe just traveling through. I need to know."

"A cat?"

"Cougar," he answered, moving away. "Mountain lion. Colorado panther."

Margaret turned from the fence and followed Brook, her face eager. "May I go?" she called to him.

Brook stopped and turned. "I'd planned on taking only part of a day for this trip, not a whole week." But he put a grin with it, to show her.

"I know horses."

"Yes, you said that once."

"I've ridden quite a bit."

"I figured that from your riding outfit," he replied, but he wouldn't look at it. Then he said, "It's pretty steep where I'm going. Cold. Windy. I don't think you'd like it."

"Please?"

He didn't give her an answer but went instead to the horse stalls where he bridled and saddled a claybank mare and led it back to her. She mounted the mare perfectly, without assistance.

They picked up the grassy ruts of an old wagon road that angled onto the slope and in a matter of minutes the aspen grove had engulfed them. It was an eerie change. The sunlight faded and the air grew chill and the silence rushed up from every side and surrounded them. Moving among the trees was like picking a path through a fairyland of wands. The ground was a sponge of ancient leaves and their passage made no sound. Somewhere above them, perhaps beyond, the wind was a mysterious unfound singing. "Did you know," Brook said to her at one point, his words leaden and echoless in the dense stand, "that if you're in here when it rains you can't hear it falling?"

After thirty minutes of weaving their way through the chalky stillness of the grove they broke out of it, riding into a strip of climbing meadow where the openness was an abrupt green tumbling and the sunlight a glare that hurt their eyes. Shortly after, they exchanged the meadow for the blue-green shades of a pine forest where a pungent aroma rose up to them as if the ground had been soaked for centuries in a vat of pitch. The mountain jays were there too but they were hidden in the trees, scolding the two riders as they passed quietly along.

Gradually the forest thinned and the deadfalls began to appear, swelling out of the earth like strange sores. They encountered small tarns whose waters mirrored the sky from one angle and from another stood so motionless and clear that they appeared empty. Beside them, there were blue-purple plots of wild iris alternating with the gray flinty tongues of talus.

Still they climbed, never attacking the mountain straight on but always crisscrossing it, stopping once to rest the horses and to eat the apples that Brook had brought. The sun was warm and the wind gentle and a sense of drowsy isolation overtook them. Far behind, far below now, the floor of the Park lay upon the earth like a bright green scarf. "Oh, we're so high," Margaret cried, her voice full of wonder and disbelief. "It's as if we're the first people ever to stand here. Breathing air that's never been breathed before."

They rode eventually into a rocky shelflike area shielded on its upper edge by a thick band of fir trees. "If there's a cat around," Brook announced, "I'd expect it to be in these rocks. It wouldn't live in the grove. Never, not a single day. I'm surprised Grant would smell it there."

"Grant smelled it?"

"Caleb said he did."

Margaret looked puzzled. "What does smell tell you?"

"A female cat will set out boundaries with her urine," he told her. "It means that this is her territory and everybody else had better stay out."

Margaret said, "What will you do if the cat jumps you?"

"Jumps *us*," he corrected her. "We're riding together, remember?" He laughed when he looked at her. "But she'll go for you first if she has any sense at all. You smell better."

"Smell different," Margaret came back. "Better is relative. It depends on who's doing the smelling."

A cloud passed over them the next moment, low and speeding, shutting out the sun, chilling the air. A deep rumbling sound seemed to accompany the chill and Margaret reined her claybank and searched for it.

"Wind," Brook explained. "It's up above that belt of fir you see there. In the crooked wood."

106

"The what?"

"Crooked wood. Timberline. Where the trees give out."

"Can we go up and see it?"

"I don't think so. You wouldn't like it. It's not very pretty."

"We've come this far, can't we go just a little farther? I've never been this high on a mountain in my life, let alone timberline."

Brook steered the buckskin alongside Margaret's mare and undid the coil of rope he had placed on the saddle horn before they left the lot. "Wish granted," he said, "but we're going to need this rope."

"I wondered what it was for when you put it there."

"Some horses will lead in rough places but most of them are followers. Your claybank is a follower. This rope will help her. It will take a lot of her fear away."

Margaret made an exaggerated face. "Fear? Just exactly where are you taking me?"

Brook took a firm grip on the end of the rope. "Here we go," he said. He led them through the strip of fir, past pits of crusted pinkish snow and into a steepening growth of scrub that hid the slope beyond. The roar of the wind increased. The air turned cold. At the top edge of the scrub Brook stopped and turned to Margaret. "Hang on!" he shouted, and then jabbed the buckskin onto a slope that appeared to rise almost vertically in front of them. The big stallion seemed to squat against the earth, his back legs quivering with the strain of gravity and his hooves spraying gravel onto the trailing mare. Twenty yards he climbed. Thirty. Forty.

Suddenly they broke over the crest of the slope onto a surface that was naked and scoured and blood red in color. The wind struck like a scream that had been held since the beginning of time and then released at the moment of their appearance. Brook slid from the saddle and made his way back to Margaret and held his arms up to her. "We're here!" he shouted, the wind in his voice. "The crooked wood! Timberline on Big Red Mountain!"

Margaret never moved. She was staring at the mountain, her face a mask of awe and despair. The topmost line of trees straggled away across the slope in an utter desolation. Stunted, barkless, they had been twisted by the cold and the wind into unbelievably grotesque shapes. Some of the trees lay flattened and some had been split in two and others were deformed past recognition. "My God!" she groaned. "They're . . . it's like a death!"

The wind neither surged nor fell but swept in a steady force over the red crest. From the tortured picket of trees rose a dreadful sound, as of moaning. Margaret shuddered. "The wind sounds human . . . like . . . crying." She closed her eyes and an icy revulsion claimed her voice. "Take me down from here, Brook. Please!"

Brook did not remount but led the horses out on foot, sliding down the steep incline and stumbling through the scatter of scrub and the belt of fir until he reached the clearing where they had started. Then he turned back to Margaret. She did not dismount. Her face seemed stricken. "That's a horrible place, Brook," she said, shivering.

"I tried to warn you." He softened his voice. "I came up here for the first time when I was real little. My dad brought me up. I can hardly remember it but I know I was scared."

"Those trees," Margaret shuddered. "They're doomed."

"Yes. The mountain's trapped them. They're caught on an invisible line. Life below the line. Death above. They can't escape." He recoiled the lead rope and edged the buckskin out in front of Margaret and they started back, picking their way around the tundra and the deadfalls, winding steadily down the green spill of forest and meadow. At some point on the mountain, Brook veered away from the trail that led to the aspen grove and rode instead into the bleak ragged stretch where the rocky tunnel of Left Hand Canyon had its origins.

They hadn't descended far into the canyon before they encountered the cougar. The horses caught the animal smell and stopped without being reined. Margaret's mare rolled her eyes and nickered, her nostrils flaring nervously. "I'll be damned," Brook said. He searched for the cat and located it at once, coming up from a crouch on a rock overhang against the south wall, maybe forty yards downslope. Without pointing, or even looking at Margaret, he said, "Do you see the mountain lion?"

Her answer was quiet, careful. "Yes, I see it."

They eyed the cat, making no movement, and the cat eyed them in return. Then, as if in warning, she gave a cry. It was like the ripping of strong cloth. The sound tore the air and then died quickly and everything went back to what it had been, the canyon hot and sleepy and the cat looking painted against the rocks.

Margaret sat motionless, never taking her eyes off the animal. "How gentle," she said. "Who'd believe that the face of a wild creature like that could look so gentle?"

Brook explained that the cat was a female with a nursing belly. "She's probably got her den in those rocks behind her. It's a good spot."

"Why is it good?"

"South face, for one thing. That means plenty of sun. And there's a good ledge to lay out on. She can scout the canyon for food from there. Crippled stock, sick calves, some small burrowing game maybe. That's what she was doing when we rode up, making a scout."

"Are you going to shoot her?"

"No, I don't think so."

"But if she kills calves and crippled stock—?"

"She's got cubs she's protecting," Brook broke in, nodding at the rocks behind the cougar. "If I kill her, I kill them and I don't want to do that. I won't kill something just because I've got the opportunity. Or the power." He pulled the Winchester slowly from its scabbard and pointed the barrel skyward. "Get home, cat!" he shouted, and pulled the trigger. The shot slapped at the walls of the canyon and the cougar turned and disappeared into the rocks before the sound had quite died away.

They continued their descent of the canyon. The heat climbed steadily to meet them and Margaret removed the jacket she had been wearing. She had fallen into a curious silence and

Brook gradually eased the buckskin forward until he was directly beside her. "I'll pay for your thoughts," he said, "if you think they're worth anything."

"I doubt they are," she answered pleasantly, glancing across at him. "Actually, I was thinking about last night, about Caleb. He was funny. He made me laugh. I haven't laughed that hard in a long time."

"That goes for me too. And how about my mother?"

"Yes," she said, "it was a wonderful tonic for her." She delayed a moment. "But Caleb wasn't always funny, was he? I mean . . . he changed."

"Right. It's hard to picture him hurt that badly, that close to death. Can you imagine trying to splash water from a mud puddle into your mouth?"

"That isn't what I meant. I wasn't referring to his war experiences. Or even last night especially. I meant more the way he's been *lately*."

"I don't know what you mean."

"It's as if Caleb's suddenly got a second chance at life, at having a home," she answered. "And I'm glad for that. I really am." But she shook her head as if dissatisfied with the direction her answer was taking her. "What I mean is, he's so *comfortable* with it, with his new chance. Even in the face of a personal tragedy like losing his only brother. Don't you notice it?"

"First," Brook answered, "you have to tell me what you mean by comfortable."

"Well," she began, looking obliquely at him, struggling a little, "for example, he sits with your mother in the kitchen all the time now. I hear them talking constantly. He discusses the future mostly, nothing about what happened, about the accident. He never mentions Aaron's name. It's always Polite or the mill or the Bulldog. And her, of course. How strong she's been. How well she's done." Margaret paused for a moment. "And he loved pouring the brandy last night, offering the cigars, directing things, being the host. He was right at home, taking over like that. You could see it in his face."

"Hell, I thought he did a great job. I really enjoyed the evening." He glanced at her. "I assumed you did too."

"I did but— Oh, never mind," and she broke off, lifting her hand in an apologetic way and then letting it drop. "I don't want to speak out of turn about your uncle. About any of your family. It's not my place. It was an observation, that's all. You asked for my thoughts." She looked at him and her voice dropped. "I *did* have fun last night, Brook. It was a welcome change for me, really." She started a smile but didn't finish it. "This hasn't been an ordinary summer vacation, you know. So much has happened in such a short time. And then those trees back there just now, that crooked wood. Beauty and ugliness. Death and life. So cruel—"

"I tried to warn you."

"Yes, I know. But I'm not looking for protection against the hard parts of life. I don't think anyone should. The hard things are what strengthen us. My husband always says that the best steel has to be tempered, that it must go through the fire."

"Has he been through? Or is it just something he's always saying?"

Her answer was somewhat defensive. "Brook, God's ministers aren't required to walk all the different paths of life themselves. They're more . . . ministers. That's what the word means, to minister. To provide aid, to comfort and protect—"

"No, Mag," he broke in, "ministers can't protect. If the Fates want you bad enough they'll reach in and get you. The clergy isn't going to stop them. Hell, it's just another profession, like law or medicine."

"But there's a calling for the ministry. There's a divine selection that's involved."

"Is there, Mag? Do you actually believe that or is it merely something your husband always says?"

"I wish you wouldn't call me *Mag*," she answered sharply. "It's crude. It makes me sound like a girl of the streets."

"You don't know what a girl of the streets is."

"Really, Brook—"

"And neither does your husband. He stands up there in his pulpit every week and expounds at great length and with divine guidance on things he doesn't know a damned thing about."

She flared then; it was in the way her shoulders straightened.

111

It would have shown in her eyes but Brook couldn't see them. She was looking straight ahead and when she spoke her voice was full of polite indignation. "You condemn me for being influenced by my husband, Brook, but how about you and your uncle? I understand you were going to join the Army just because he got hurt. And your plan to become a metallurgist, wasn't that originally his idea?"

"Hell," Brook snapped, "you're just upset because metallurgists aren't *called*. They're not divinely chosen like ministers are. Maybe like minister's wives too."

She fell instantly quiet, so quiet it was like a retreat. When she spoke it was in a voice much subdued, almost pained. "You're attacking me, Brook. You've been attacking me ever since I said that about Caleb changing. Why? Why are you doing it?"

An unexpected rain struck them at that moment, smoking the hard hot ground of the canyon floor. Brook steered toward a rock overhang in the canyon wall and they moved under it and dismounted, standing quietly against the dry stone, feeling its heat, listening to the new presence the rain made and waiting for it to stop. Margaret was forced by the lack of room to stand close and Brook caught the lilac scent of her, just as he had on the day of his bandaging. She didn't speak and her eyes were half closed, not seeing anything in particular. Maybe the rain.

After a few minutes the rain stopped but the cloud remained, hovering soundlessly above the canyon, and Brook walked out to the buckskin and removed two yellow slickers from a side bag on the saddle. He shook them out and put one on and helped Margaret into the other. He held the claybank's reins while she remounted but still she would not look at him. Her face was closed, drawn in upon itself, set with a disquiet borrowed from the rain.

CHAPTER 10

Brook stood in the door of the machine shed and stared into its shadowy interior. There was a sadness about old machinery parked in a shed. It spoke of time gone, rejection, neglect. It even had an odor, a musty smell that made the air itself seem old.

Once it had been a new smell of course, a smell of factory paint and Number Two gear grease and a shiny coat of Cosmolene. Now the machines sat abandoned and unseen. Their paint was gone and rust had worked into the metal, along with the caked grease, to make a kind of mold that gave the air its dead smell. If you studied the individual machines long enough it seemed they were ashamed of being in the shed; they wouldn't *look back* at you. They sat dumb and huddled in the half light and you could feel them hoping that maybe this time the person watching from the door would give a shout of discovery and get the tractor and wheel them out into the sun again.

But it wouldn't be Brook. Brook was in the shed looking for tire rims, not old machinery. He was trying to stay busy, trying not to think of Margaret. The morning had broken thick and sullen and the light was bad everywhere, not just here in the shed. He sat on a battered mower seat for a few minutes, letting his eyes adjust to the shadows, and it was when he crossed over to the single window to wipe it free of its coarse lace of cobwebs and dust that he saw the tombstone.

Even then, he had to look twice. What he saw was a rough slab of rock leaning against the wall beside the window, leering up at him in the sheared light like a partial face. There were unfinished letters carved into the dull surface of the stone.

AARON HAR . . . .

Brook left the shed immediately and walked across the lot to the employee's building. The central dining area was deserted except for Etchevarl, who was the one he had come to see. The old man was standing at one of the windows staring dolefully into the murk beyond, his mustaches drooping from his face like wilted wreaths. Brook went directly up to him, kicking aside a chair that was in his path. "That stone in the machine shed," he began. "Is that your work?"

Etchevarl turned slowly, absorbing the words, studying Brook's face carefully, his eyes as desolate as his mustaches. "If you mean your father's tombstone, yes."

"Who the hell do you think you are, some kind of stone mason?"

Etchevarl's forehead knotted but his expression didn't change. "You are obviously angry, Brook," he said evenly, "and so I must ask what the anger is for. Is it fright? Did seeing the stone frighten you? Or has it made you remember finally what such stones are for?"

"What I feel is my business."

"And furnishing a tombstone for Aaron Hartman is mine. Obviously," he added bleakly, "it is no one else's."

"That's a shitty stone."

"Then make a better one," the old Basque replied. It wasn't sharp; if anything his voice had softened. "Let us make a better one together. But for the love of God let us do *something*." His eyes searched Brook's. "I can no longer talk to your mother with any privacy. Caleb has become her very shadow. When I talk to you, if I can find you, you do not hear my words or else you make promises that have the substance of feathers. You sleep late in the morning or you ride out with the minister's wife and are gone all day."

"That doesn't concern you."

"Perhaps not. What does concern me is that your father still lies in the rocks where you saw him a week ago. He lies in the rain and the sun alike, unaware of their difference. Strange animals come in the night to nose him. Birds sit on his body in the day and peck at his face."

Brook turned and left the building and walked up to the house. His mother was alone in the kitchen and when he came through the door she glanced up. He started to ask her the date of his father's birth but at the last moment he changed his mind. He went into the library and searched in the Bible that lay in the front of the room on its own stand but he couldn't find the Births section. He left the house and returned immediately to Etchevarl, who was still stationed at the window staring out into the morning gloom. "Your father was born the year I came to this place," Etchevarl announced before Brook ever reached him. "1879."

Within the hour, Brook had changed clothes and located Willy Walker and was headed out the lane in the T. Overhead, the clouds were dense and low-hanging and had cut off the tops of the mountains that circled the Park. The earth seemed jammed in upon itself, huddled under a sky that was not big enough, waiting for a rain that would not come.

Brook decided on the old road to Como and halfway across the south meadow the sawmill whistle blew. It was an unnerving sound. It was like a great bird flying overhead, blinded by the clouds and unable to see the earth, screaming its frustration at what lay hidden below.

When the road left the meadow and entered the timber a new world emerged, a world of gloom, a fuzzy suffocated land full of trees marching ominously toward them through the mist. The road was a frail arrow pointing them to a wall of fog that kept receding mysteriously before them. So heavy and muffling was the air that the T seemed to run as quiet as the Oakland, which became a stroke of fortune a short while later when they rounded a curve in the road and heard directly in front of them the rumble of a heavy truck. Only at the last moment was Brook able to swing left and avoid smashing into the rear end of the lumbering vehicle. It proved to be Ess Cohen's Freighter. Ess himself sat goggled and cloaked in the high open seat between the twin American flags, hunched over the wheel like a desperate racer who has fallen behind.

Brook whipped the Ford in front of the Freighter and took the lead but the dust-bleached merchant arrived at his Como branch store just minutes after Brook and Willy got there. "Jesus, he must have opened that baby up!" Willy exclaimed.

"Yeah, all of fifteen. Maybe even twenty."

When Cohen sauntered out from the back room, Brook saw that he had exchanged his driving cap for a dress hat and was tying a clean apron around his waist. Willy saw it too. He offered Ess five dollars for the hat and two for the apron, final offer, take it or leave it.

Cohen responded with a laugh but it was thin and watery, an amenity only. Laughter had never been for Ess Cohen that instinctive reaction to humor that it was for other men. He must have sensed this lack in himself for he countered it by being eternally pleasant, never grumbling or bursting into temper or storming around wailing at events. It was as if he were locked permanently into the comfortable middle range of human emotion. And he was a consummate storekeeper; that was his supreme atonement. He could do extensions in his head, he could remember the location of every item of merchandise in his stores, he knew exactly what stock was back ordered and when the new supply was scheduled to arrive. Now pleasantly, almost modestly, he picked up a pencil and an order book from the counter and looked at Brook.

"I want to order a tombstone," Brook announced bluntly.

Cohen commenced to write and then stopped. "You've found your father?"

"I didn't say that. I said I wanted to order a tombstone." He felt a burst of annoyance. "*Aaron Hartman*. Write that down. No middle initial."

Cohen wrote and then spoke to Brook as though some sort of ceremonial comment was required with this kind of order. "You're to be commended. A man should honor his father. With love and recognition in life, with remembrance in death."

116

"*Born 1879. Died 1920,*" continued Brook. "Write that down."

Cohen wrote and when Brook spoke no more he looked up from his order book and asked if Brook wanted the stone in polished granite or marble.

"Marble. And I want it big, at least four feet high."

"You want nothing else, just the name and dates? No angels on the base? I can get you some nice angels."

"I'll bet you can."

"How about memorium?"

"Rest In Peace is always good," Willy suggested. "You see that a lot."

"Nothing on the stone except what I ordered," Brook insisted, and then he asked about delivery. Cohen told him to expect two weeks. "And there'll be a delivery charge if I bring it out to your place."

Brook shot a look of annoyance at the storekeeper that didn't stop with the man but swept on across his store, at the long counters and the rolls of wrapping paper with the cones of string hovering above them like a nagging mate, the compartments along the side and the barrels in front and the gorged shelves stretching away into a murky jumble in the back. "By God, you'll find a way to make that extra buck, won't you, Ess?" he said hotly. "Sell it, that's one dollar. Deliver it, that's another."

"Something wrong with that?"

But Brook would not be deterred. "If it can be bought and sold you'll handle it, won't you, Mister?" he went on. "You'd stock Life itself if you thought you could get an exclusive contract." His voice rose rhetorically and he lifted one arm and swept the store with a flourish. "All the Fates and Fortunes of Mankind," he proclaimed grandly, "right here in our store!" He stopped and looked at Cohen. "I'll tell you what you'd better do, Mr. Mercantile," he said, "you'd better give me a sack of Health before I leave today. You still have Health in the sack, don't you? And you can wrap up a couple boxes of Happiness while you're at it. The kiddies like it so. The missus too. And oh, yes, I nearly forgot, you'd better throw in twenty

117

pounds of Good Fortune. I'm getting low. What's that? Good Fortune's still on back order? Well, how about twenty pounds of Opportunity, do you have that in stock? Good! I'll be back next week and pay my bill. In full. You like payment in full, don't you, Mr. Mercantile?" And with an elaborately faked laugh that mimicked Cohen's earlier one, Brook turned and left the store.

Willy was a step behind. "What the hell's eating you?" he demanded when they reached the sidewalk. "You sounded like an escaped loony in there." He studied the street, first left and then right. "I know a place where we can get a drink."

"Moonbeam Ranch?"

Willy looked puzzled. "No, I'm talking about the butcher shop, back room. What do you say? You need something to wash down that Tight Jaw you got ahold of."

Brook replied that he wanted to get back and they climbed into the Ford and headed out of town, the mist barricading each successive side street as they drove past.

On the road, the fog appeared to have welled up from the ground and flooded out the trees. Visibility was less than fifty yards. There seemed no space left on earth, no distances to fit it in. The entire Park had been reduced to a murky tunnel that crumbled silently behind them as they raced to escape it. "You're really a friendly cuss when you go to town, aren't you?" Willy scowled. "I imagine Ess loves to see you come into the store. I'm surprised he even took your order."

Brook had no replay. He was thinking of the order book Cohen had written in. It reminded Brook of the book his father had kept, not an order book but a sort of log about his horses. It had boasted gold lettering on its cover at one time, you could still see the indentation, but you couldn't make out what the letters spelled. His father had kept the book in a separate cabinet in the tack room and in it was listed the breeding date of certain mares, together with their names and the name of the stallion who had serviced them. Later, in a following set of columns, appeared the name and sex of the colt that subsequently foaled. *Belle, stud Jack, Sept 17 1918. Colt male Flory . . . Dixie, stud Diamond Two, Dec 3 1919. Colt mare*

118

Dolly. The unusual thing about the book was that the deaths of the horses were never listed. "Really special," Brook said, looking at Willy. "A book with just births in it, no deaths. The beginnings but not the ends. Not like a stone from your local Merc."

But Willy didn't understand about the book, nor what Brook meant by the words, so he spoke of the stone. "It'll be a good stone. Your old man would have liked it. But I wish you'd had a horse put on the face of it. You know how he loved horses. All kinds of animals actually, but horses most. That's the way I remember him, on a horse. Like he was that day coming off the mountain, just before the accident, before he disappeared. Shit," he added, his round swarthy face pinching out the word, "it never should have happened. It wouldn't have happened except Caleb heard that damned sound."

"You mean Papa."

"No," Willy said, "I mean Caleb."

Brook placed his foot on the brake pedal but he didn't press down on it. "What are you talking about?" he said, looking directly at Willy now. "Are you talking about the accident?"

"Hell, yes, I'm talking about the accident. What else?"

"It was Papa who heard the sound. That's why he went back."

"Well, he went back," Willy answered, drawling it out. "You're right about that part. But he wasn't the one who heard the sound."

Brook pressed a little on the brake pedal, not meaning to, not knowing he did. "Wait a minute," he said. "Wait just one minute. That isn't the story I got. Grant. Etch. Polite. They all told me—"

"I don't know what they told you. I don't care. All I know is what I saw."

"What you *saw*?"

"Yes, saw! And what do you know, for Christ's sake? You weren't there!" He practically spit out the words.

Brook was hot now too. "I'll tell you what I know. Somebody around here is full of shit!"

The little horseman turned toward him in the seat. "We were

horseback, coming down Right Hand from a timber scout that Polite took us on. I'd been working horses real heavy for several days and my ass bones were out. It hurt me to ride and I fell back of the others. Caleb and your old man was riding ahead of me and all of a sudden Caleb stops and sticks up his hand."

"Willy, it was Papa—"

"Will you listen to me, goddamn it? I'm trying to tell you what happened. Caleb put up his hand and said something I couldn't hear. He acted surprised, you know, like when a thing is real unexpected. Your old man pulled in the gray and I could see him listening real hard and then he said something back to Caleb but I couldn't hear that either. Next thing I know Aaron pushed up front where Etch was riding and spoke to him. Then he turned the gray around and went back up the canyon."

The road emerged suddenly from the timber and entered the south meadow. It was as if a stream had borne the car down a crowded mountain and then shot it onto an empty sea. There was nothing visible anywhere, they were adrift in whiteness.

The gate eventually hove into view and Brook turned in, and at the end of the lane he let Willy out of the car. He parked the T in the shed and crossed the lawn and went into the house by the front door instead of through the kitchen. It was extremely quiet. He could hear nothing. There was no sound anywhere. The fog was pressing at the windows, trying to see in. Brook lit a lamp and went into the hall where the portrait of his father hung and held the lamp up to it.

The face seemed to leap out at him, the forehead high and the hair full and the face patrician in its long thin molding. The mouth was firm and well made and the lips sensitive, and the eyes looked back at Brook with that vital brightness of life that the camera had trapped there.

There was a sound behind him in the hall and Brook turned. It was Margaret. She was standing in the shadows without a lamp of her own. She smiled weakly and stepped toward him. "You surprised me," she said. "I wasn't expecting you to be here."

120

"Yes," he said, surprised as well.

She waited, looked at the lamp in Brook's hand and then back at him. "What are you doing here?" It was a curious strained whisper.

"Looking at Papa."

She was silent a long time. Brook could feel her studying him, watching his face. When she spoke her voice was thinned with suspicion. "That isn't it," she said flatly. "There's something else."

He gave no reply, continuing to stare at the portrait on the wall.

"What's the matter, Brook?" Margaret said. "What's happened?" and again it was a whisper, as though the shadows in the hall required it.

"Nothing," he answered.

"It's in your face, I can see it."

"I just wanted to see Papa."

She studied him carefully, not speaking.

Brook shrugged and was almost ready to let the matter go but then he changed his mind. "Well," he began, "this thing is getting confusing all of a sudden." He forced himself not to look away from her.

"What is?"

Brook lifted one hand and then dropped it. "Willy and I went . . . On the way back . . . I hadn't talked to Willy Walker like I did the others."

"What are you saying?"

"Willy was there that day. In the canyon. He said it was Caleb who heard the sound, not Papa."

Margaret kept her eyes fixed on Brook's face.

"The others . . . all the others told me it was Papa. Grant, Etchevarl, Polite, all of them."

"What did Caleb tell you?"

"He didn't. I mean . . . I don't think he did." He looked away from Margaret and concentrated on the portrait. But it didn't last long. "No," he said, looking back, "that's not true. Caleb did tell me."

"What, Brook?"

"Papa. He said it was Papa."

The sawmill whistle blew at that moment. It was reluctant, not wanting to gain the house so much as to stay outside, hidden in the fog.

"If that's true then it means Caleb lied," Margaret said. The lamp flared, throwing their shadows onto the wall. "Why? Why would Caleb lie about a sound, Brook?"

CHAPTER 11

"I've got to think," Brook said to her. "I've got to study this thing." She had followed him out onto the porch, to the far end where the swing was located. Through the fog she could see a few feet of grass below the railing, looking like a narrow beach around an island. Beyond, the twin fir trees stood in the center of the lawn like the masts of a mysterious schooner that had slipped into a shrouded bay and dropped anchor, silent, afraid to move, waiting for the fog to lift.

Brook continued to pace nervously up and down the porch and Margaret took a seat in the swing and remained quiet until Brook stopped parading and came and stood before her. His jaws were set tiredly but his eyes burned. "Maybe it was Willy who was lying," he said, "instead of Caleb."

"Why?" she came back quickly. "Would it do him some good? Does he have something to gain with a lie?"

Brook's shoulders sagged. "No," he muttered dejectedly. "Willy has nothing to gain. All he has is his horses and that's all he wants."

Margaret took the moment of resignation to organize her thoughts; she had her own confusions to sift through. "How did this thing come up anyway?"

Brook took a few steps along the porch and then returned. "Willy and I had gone to Como," he began. "We were on our way back and he was talking about the tombstone I ordered, about horses, about seeing Papa on the big gray he always rode, the one Willy bought in Alma." He looked away into the fog as though he were trying to identify the two fir trees. "Willy said he happened to get behind the others coming down the canyon that day. They couldn't see him, I guess, or forgot he was back there." His eyes flickered momentarily as if he remembered something. "That could be true because I remember Polite saying he thought Willy was in the front line . . . or maybe it was Grant . . . he couldn't be sure."

"Then what?"

"Well, Willy started talking about Papa, how everything would have turned out all right if only Caleb hadn't heard the sound, that the accident wouldn't have happened otherwise. He said it offhanded like that as if he were simply repeating what everyone knew."

"Was there a sound that day, Brook? Is that how it started?"

Carefully, stiff with preoccupation, Brook sat down beside her in the swing. A tiny muscle moved in his jaw. "Etchevarl came to Denver on the train to get me that Sunday," he began. "On the way home he told me what had happened, not in detail but in a general way. When I got here my uncle gave me his version and over the next few days I talked to some of the other people who'd been in the party. I talked to them individually, alone, one at a time."

"Why alone? Did you suspect something?"

He glanced sharply at her. "Hell, no. What's to suspect? I just wanted to know how it happened. I had Caleb's account and Etch's and I wanted a couple more, that's all. I wanted to be sure that nothing had been overlooked, that they hadn't forgotten anything in their search."

"And?"

"They hadn't. They spent three whole days up there on the mountain. Caleb put himself in charge and did a thorough job. Just what you'd expect of him."

"So all the stories matched then?"

"Yes. They were identical. The party was returning down

124

the canyon. Papa heard something. He stopped. He told Etch he was going back to check it out."

"Were those his exact words?"

"That's what everyone says they were. The reports were all alike in that respect and I wasn't looking for any differences. Why should I?" He watched her face closely. "Now this comes up, right out of the blue. Willy says it was Caleb who heard the sound. That it was Caleb who stopped and raised his hand."

"Could Willy have mistaken the horses?"

Brook shook his head. "Not likely. If any man in the world would know who was riding what horse, it'd be Willy Walker."

Margaret looked out into the fog. "Then that's it. Caleb lied."

Brook stirred beside her. "But he *wouldn't*, Margaret, don't you see?" It was impatient, at edge. "Not a man like that. He wouldn't lie about what happened to his own brother." He stood up abruptly and faced her. "Why would any of them lie, for Christ's sake?" and his voice was close to being shrill. "That's what I don't understand. What's the reason? Papa left the group and went back up the mountain. The rest stayed behind. Papa got blown off a cliff when a storm hit. What's a lie about a *sound* got to do with any of that?" He threw his hands up in the air in an act of pure exasperation, and then let them drop.

"I don't know," she said, and the words sounded equally helpless in the thick dead air of the porch.

Brook took in a deep breath and let it out slowly. For a moment it looked to her as if he wanted to lean forward and put his head in his hands.

"I don't know what any of this means either, Brook," she went on, "but from what you've said, it sounds like your friend Willy made a mistake. Either that or . . . ."

"Or what?"

"Or your uncle really did lie." She pressed her hands together in her lap and then opened them, peering in as if trying to see something she had missed the time before. "And if Caleb did lie then he wasn't the only one because the others told the same story." She looked up at Brook. "Do you see

125

that? It could mean a conspiracy. It means that they had to get together before you got home and get all the stories lined up with each other. And if that's true then it makes you question whether there really was an accident at all."

Brook sat down in the swing and stared at the deck of the porch. He looked so distraught, so put upon, that she wanted to reach over and comfort him. "The more I think of it, the more I think that Willy's mistaken," he said, before she could do anything, move her hands, reach out for him. "He admitted to me he was tired that day. Sometimes when you're tired you don't see things right. That can happen to anyone."

"Or he simply got it mixed up with something that happened later in the search. That's a possibility. Perhaps you'd better talk to Willy again."

"Yes," said Brook. "Yes, I'll talk to him."

When Brook had left the porch, Margaret went into the parlor and sat in the big worn leather chair that had been Brook's father's. She undid the comb at the back of her neck and shook her hair out. She leaned her head back and rubbed her eyes lightly with the tips of her fingers, and then dropped her hands to her lap and studied the windows. The fog was like a blind person crouching there unable to see in, able only to press against the glass and listen to the house. That's what she did. From deep in the soft leather chair that had been Aaron Hartman's she closed her eyes and listened.

After several minutes she thought she heard a sound and got up and walked into the hall on the opposite side of the room. She could hear nothing but she saw a light at the far end of the hall, the pale aura of it gradually growing to a verifiable slice of white at the edge of a door. It was the kitchen door and she walked quietly toward it and looked in.

Ruth was sitting at the table in the center of the room and Caleb was sitting across from her. There were two cups beside them and two empty dessert plates between. Ruth's back was turned to Margaret and Caleb sat leaning slightly toward her, talking, his face relaxed and pleasantly animated.

Margaret stood in the shadows and watched the two of them for several minutes and then turned and retraced her steps down the hall and went outside and stood on the porch. The railing, the pillars, the air itself dripped with gloom. She started across the lawn to look for Brook but then changed her mind and returned to the house and went directly upstairs to her room. She began a new letter to Emerson but after a few lines she pushed it aside and went over to the bed and laid down and stared at the ceiling.

The gloom got into the house finally, it was in the dining room that evening at dinner, blurring the lights, dulling the people. Margaret was hesitant to the point of rudeness and what little Ruth contributed to the conversation was sputtering and dispirited. For his own part, Brook was mistrustful. He was convinced that his mother had been staring at him all evening. She had regained that piercing covert look of hers which implied that she knew a secret concerning young men and that when the time was right, in front of others and when Brook was present, she would reveal what it was. It had angered Brook before and it angered him now. When his mother asked after the meal if he wanted coffee, he snapped his reply. Margaret's head lifted and for a moment Caleb's eyes flared, but it was a moment only, quickly past. Declining coffee, Margaret left the table followed soon after by Ruth, and when they had gone Caleb gathered up a handful of toothpicks and formed a network of trenches on the tablecloth. He was wearing his spectacles and they had slipped down his nose to a point where he was forced to peer over the tops of them. It gave him a quizzical look, avuncular, strangely domestic. It was not an unpleasant sight but it had always made Brook uneasy.

After supplying Brook with matches, Caleb asked him to arrange his infantry divisions opposite the trenches and to demonstrate his plan of attack had he been Ludendorff, the German commander. It was an exercise they had played through many times before, sometimes assuming alternate roles, but tonight Brook performed badly. Not only did he fail to reduce an obvious salient but he got caught in a surprise counterattack and his lines were irrevocably breached.

When Brook went upstairs later the gloom had reached as far as his room and he lay in bed and thought of Right Hand Canyon and the storm that day of the accident and of the talk` with Willy Walker that he had postponed until tomorrow.

He was a long time falling asleep.

Like many of the Hartman employees before him, Willy Walker had come up out of the Great Plains, probably Oklahoma or panhandle Texas. He certainly talked like it; he had that region's lispy underbite way of speaking as though he was moving a sharp pebble from one cheek to the other and didn't want to risk a lot of unnecessary use of his tongue. The best judgment had Willy working the rodeos as a youngster and looking at him you knew his chin had plowed up its share of dirt. The way he walked on occasion you also knew he'd been kicked too many times in the knees by too many sulky flat-eared broncs. But he'd obviously graduated from the rodeos to the fancier Wild West Shows, for he had a pure flair for teaching a horse how to step through the rules and the manners.

Yet there was an ambiguity about Willy that puzzled those who worked with him. He owned several pair of good boots but on certain days he would wear tennis shoes. His figure was on the lean side and yet he had an abnormally full face that looked like it belonged on a heavier man. He always wore the same flat black hat and his hair was exceptionally long; some days he let it hang over his jacket collar like a girl's but on other days he tied it up with meat string. Polite said Willy had Indian blood in him sure as a sow had tits. That was possibly open to question but what everyone knew for sure was that Willy was moody. Either you couldn't shut him up or he'd go wordless for a week. All in all, Brook figured it didn't matter. Willy Walker may not have been the brightest guy born but he stayed sober and gave you all the sweat he had in him, and he was exceptionally good with horses.

Now in midmorning with the fog pulling back steadily, Brook found Willy in the smith shop, a squat windowless building with a single wide door and a large forge that sat toward the back. Everything in that building had the same dull iron color —the tongs and the barrels and the rods and the chains and the leather aprons that hung from the wall. There was no sheen to anything, no glisten, and there was a smell to the shed that made you think of fires that had gone out, of metal that had burned hot once and then grown cold. Willy stood in the doorway where the best light was, repairing a cinch strap, and Brook spoke to him immediately. "Let that go for now. I want you to come with me," and they cranked up the Quad and backed it out and drove up Right Hand to the stone shed.

The shed was sturdy. Julius had built it. The roof was corrugated tin that captured the sun in the afternoons and clattered like a pewter plate when it rained, and on the dirt floor underneath could be read the shed's entire history. On the horse side lay an accretion of pine needles and bedding chaff so built up over the years that it looked like a permanent mat, while on the other side lay the spreading black eyes of oil that had dripped from the trucks that were parked there later. There were only two windows in the shed and the isinglass in them had grown cracked and milky from forty years of winter cold; they reminded Brook of the eyes of a blind horse.

Brook loved the shed. It was the place he had played in as a boy, now a castle, now a fort, sometimes a dungeon with only silent dozing horses as fellow prisoners. There had been earlier prisoners too, his father and his uncle. Their initials stood in the base of one wall, AH on one stone and CH on another, weak shallow cuts carved by boys at play. Brook had always envied their having each other and had never cut his own initials in the stone because of it. They would have looked too alone.

Brook parked the Quad on the truck side and the first thing he asked Willy when the engine died was whether he had spoken to Caleb or any of the others since they'd come back from Como yesterday morning. Willy answered that he had not. "But what if I had?" he insisted, and there was a whine in his voice.

He was in one of his moody spells, had acted sullen all the way up the mountain. "What's my talking to people got to do with anything? And what in hell did you drag me all the way up here for?"

"I want to talk to you."

"About what?"

"Papa's accident."

"Naaah," Willy drawled acidly, "you don't want to talk about that. You want to huff and puff and get the black ass again like you did in the car yesterday. I say something nice about your old man, I talk to you about what happened, and you tell me I'm full of shit." He snorted brusquely. "Screw you!"

A sudden anger burned the back of Brook's neck but he managed to keep it out of his voice. He explained to Willy that if he'd been wrong, if he owed him an apology why, hell, he had it right now. He understood how those things could happen but Willy had to understand a few things too. A guy can get sensitive about his old man, especially if he hears a different story about the events leading up to his death. Not grossly different but Willy had to expect some kind of reaction, what the hell. "Some guy tells you a thing is black, some other guy comes along and swears to you it's white, what would you think? Would you get a little hot or wouldn't you? Wouldn't you start mulling the new story over in your mind and maybe want to talk about it again?"

"Well, get talking then," Willy grunted.

Brook traced the circle of the steering wheel with one finger and said, "In the canyon that day, you saw something take place but your mind turned it around and made something else out of it. You were probably tired. I understand being tired, Willy. Hell, my ass has dragged my tracks out plenty of times. I've been so tired, for Christ's sake, I've seen four sets of headlights coming at me—"

"I know what I saw, goddamn it. I saw those reins."

"What?"

"The reins. Caleb had the reins in the hand he held up when he stopped and spoke to Aaron."

130

"So?"

"A man don't lift reins like that when he's sitting a horse. Not if he's got two hands. He'll hold in one, lift with the other. I remember thinking when I saw it, he *has* to do it that way. Old Caleb's got to lift reins with the same hand because it's the only one he's got!"

Brook studied the choke lever on the Quad's steering column, the way moving it up and down hundreds of times had worn the plate shiny. He moved away from the truck and walked across the shed to the west window and looked out as if he could see something. He couldn't. The isinglass had weathered into a jumble of arcs and lines and circles that resembled the ones he used to draw with his protractor when he was a kid alone at the kitchen table doing his homework. He turned and walked back to the Quad and propped one foot up on the massive front bumper, speaking more to change his own inner patterns than anything. "You've got to admit one thing," he said, "Caleb knows how to make a search." His voice was so quiet he wondered if Willy had heard it.

He had. "Hell of a search," he said, getting out of the truck, relief in his face and the whine gone from his voice.

"Five men, five horses, that's a good-sized bunch to pack in this shed all at one time."

"It crowded us, sure enough, but we didn't stay long. Soon as the storm passed we moved outside and split up."

"You split up?"

"Yeah. Two groups."

Brook walked to the door of the shed. The sunlight lay piled up on the road, falling through the trees like premature leaves from a season that hadn't come yet. He glanced up the canyon and then went back to the Quad and stood at the bumper again. "Which group were you?" he said to Willy, who was still standing on the other side of the truck. "Caleb's?"

"Damned if I know."

"Come on," Brook chided him.

Willy's face always looked swollen. It made his eyes appear smaller than perhaps they were. His mouth too. He blew a tiny bubble of spit and his lips pinched weakly and he said, "Too long ago. Can't remember." His tied hair hung like a black tongue at the back of his neck, making him look alien.

"You can't remember who you rode with?"

"I rode with a lot of people those three days. Caleb switched us around a lot. I'd be with one bunch one time, another bunch the next."

"How about Caleb? Certainly you rode with him at least one of those days."

Willy studied the windshield posts on the truck. He took a straw out of his pocket and stuck it in his mouth and bit the end off. He looked at Brook and back at the windshield, at the way the frame was folded forward from the middle but without the glass. There was no glass in the Quad and there never had been. "I was so bushed those three days I couldn't tell shit from good pine tar," Willy said, mumbling the words. "The groups all run together." He spit the end of the straw from his mouth and it made the words come clearer. "What difference does it make who I rode with?"

"It doesn't. It's just that I hadn't heard about this part of the search, about the splits. I didn't think to ask and nobody told me. What this does, it makes the story complete now." He waited, eyeing Willy. "But I'd still like to know who you rode with. It's sort of a finishing touch, you might say. Wraps it all up. Enables me to picture what happened. Maybe you rode with Caleb one of those times and that's when he held the reins up."

Willy muttered something and moved out from behind the truck, then went to the partition and glanced over at the horse stalls on the other side. They were mostly empty, the bulk of the horses having been moved to the corral in back. He took another nip out of his straw and stared into the stalls but Brook could tell that he wasn't really seeing anything, he was just using up time. So he said to Willy, "I've got an idea. As long as we're here and we've got the time, why don't we do that part immediately after the storm all over again? Play it out like we were actors on a stage, what do you say? Maybe it'll refresh your memory."

132

Willy was glad of any activity and put up no resistance. They saddled two of the horses and led them onto the road and mounted. "The rain has stopped," Brook said, and it sounded like a stage instruction. "We're going back up the canyon to find Aaron. It's Caleb's idea. He's formed two parties and you're in one of them."

Willy studied the road briefly and said, "We didn't split up here by the shed, I was wrong about that. It must have been later," and he nudged his mount forward. After perhaps two hundred yards he spoke again. "At this point we're still riding together. We still had our slickers on, I remember that."

They came eventually to the rock face where the canyon turned and Willy started to rein in and then changed his mind and continued on. A quarter of a mile later they passed a solitary fir that marked the mouth of a narrow branch canyon and perhaps a hundred yards past that, Willy stopped. He glanced to the left and to the right as though he were measuring distance and then he turned his horse completely around and faced Brook. "We didn't come this far," he said. "At least I didn't." He pushed his hat back and studied the ground they had just crossed. "We must have formed up back there at the fir," and he moved down the road until he had reached the tree.

And still he took his time, studying the road, the tree, the canyon leading mutely away. "Etchevarl's got that fancy full-stamped saddle," he said finally, his dark round face slowly giving up its glower. "I remember he took his slicker off right here and I could see the saddle real good. The slicker had it covered before. I went with him, with Etch. We went up toward Big Red. To the left."

Brook waited, not speaking. Relief was flooding into Willy's face. Hell, this was easy, there was was no trick to remembering things, regardless of how long ago they took place. "Did you ever in your life," he beamed, "see an uglier hat than that plug Polite wears? Wet, it's even uglier. There was rain standing in the brim and he dumped it out right here where we're sitting. Poured it on the ground, I remember that real good. Polite was with us, me and Etch, in that first group. Caleb and Grant

133

Pickens made up the other. They went on up the canyon." His look darkened again. "But that's just the first day. There was a bunch of different groups later, like I told you. No chance in hell my remembering them. Just forget it."

Brook told Margaret most of Willy's story that afternoon as they sat on the stone bench in the front yard. He also told her how Willy was able to remember that it was Caleb who was the first to stop the day of the accident because he was holding the reins in the hand he lifted up, that only a one-armed man would do that.

Margaret made no comment when Brook finished. The fog was gone and the sun was making a struggle of its return, not separating the clouds but staining them, streaking them with light like paint that hasn't been mixed properly. "It's obvious now, isn't it, Brook?" she said finally. "It's obvious that Caleb's the one who lied about the sound."

"But it probably wasn't deliberate. He could have simply forgotten what he was doing."

"He needed a sound so he made one up."

"Margaret—"

"He needed to stop the party for some reason and that's how he did it. He could have faked a lame horse or fallen from the saddle or pretended to see something. But he didn't do it that way. He pretended to *hear* something."

"For God's sake, Margaret—"

"And it worked. Your father stopped. The whole party stopped. Caleb talks a lot about odds and at that moment on that day, they were all with *him*."

Brook stirred in his seat. "But why? That's the part that doesn't make sense. What would his reason be?"

"I don't know." She took her time with her indecision, folding and unfolding her hands and then watching them as though she wasn't the one who was doing it. "All we've got are the hypothetical things, the ifs. *If* Caleb had a plan worked out. *If* the time was growing short to put it into effect. *If* he wanted an accident to happen to your father in such a way—"

Brook shot to his feet. "Damn it—"

Margaret lifted her hands defensively. "Brook, do you remember the story about the king who killed the messenger because he brought bad news? Don't make me the messenger. There are certain things we know at this point and we have to look at them. They may be unpleasant but they won't go away, will they?" She kept her eyes on him, wanting to show her understanding, trying to include him in it. "If Caleb's purpose was to isolate your father from the others, to get him alone in the canyon, then he accomplished that purpose. But he had to lie to make his plan work and Willy Walker caught him at it. Willy's the only one who saw it, the only one who knows. The rest of the men were riding in front with their backs turned."

Brook sat down heavily on the bench. "But those are the same men Papa spoke to. He told them *he* had heard the sound."

"Did he? He spoke to them, yes, that's obvious from all the stories, but is that what he actually said? Wasn't his purpose to tell them he was going back up the canyon and not who had or hadn't heard a sound? I think so. After all, the men wouldn't necessarily remember your father's exact words." She waited. "Would *you*, Brook? After all that subsequently happened, would you remember every word of a hurried conversation?"

Brook sat perfectly still on the bench. "Tell me something, Margaret." His tone was cautious. "Assuming Caleb did have a plan, how could he get the storm to be part of it? You can't conspire with nature to produce a storm just because you want it—"

"It wasn't a storm that did this, Brook." She looked directly at him. "It was people. It was the people who went back up the canyon and found your dad alone up there. The first group to reach him. Did Willy say anything about who that group was?"

"Why, yes, he said it was . . . Caleb and Grant."

Margaret reached over and touched his arm. "Then that's who did it, Brook. That's how it happened. It was the only way and the only time. A thousand-to-one chance for the scheme to work and Caleb pulled it off. First, he had to pick the perfect time to create a diversion. Next he had to isolate your father and push him—"

"No, Margaret." Brook's voice was controlled. "There has to be some other explanation for Caleb's behavior. He wouldn't kill his brother, his own flesh and blood. I know it. Not a man like Caleb."

This time it was Margaret who stood up. "Then why did he lie, Brook? We're back to that. Why did Caleb tell you and your mother and everyone on the place that he heard a sound in the canyon when he didn't?" She stood looking down into Brook's face. "You know it's true, Brook. You know your uncle lied that day, that Willy Walker is telling the truth. I can see in your face that you know."

Dinner was awkward. Brook discovered soon enough that he couldn't talk to Caleb, couldn't even look at him. He kept seeing a face other than his uncle's but he couldn't determine whose it was, it kept fading out just at the point of recognition. In fact, strange unfixed images kept flashing at Brook throughout the meal, brief fractured images . . . bodies milling . . . bodies falling . . . .

For his part, Caleb seemed especially expansive, smiling briskly, wanting to talk, directing things in that assured way he had. He was wearing the usual bow tie, the only tie he could manage with one hand, and his brightest argyle sweater with the right sleeve pinned up. "We had a couple of lumber buyers come in from Denver today," he said to Brook. "I wanted you to meet them but I couldn't find you. I took them up to the mill and showed them the aspen boards and they came up with a real good price. Sixteen dollars a thousand board feet, would you believe it?" He waited. "But that wasn't the best part." He made a clicking sound in his teeth. "Take a guess on what they offered for the spruce?"

Brook could feel his uncle watching him, poised for his response, the good shoulder slightly forward as always, the whole presence waiting for Brook to raise his head and ask, *"What was the quote on the spruce, Uncle Caleb?"* He could feel Margaret and his mother watching him too, waiting for the same thing.

But what Brook said was, "Did I tell you, Mother, what I did yesterday?" and he turned to her fully where she sat at the end of the table to his left, catching her in her surprise.

"Brook—"

"I went into Como and ordered a tombstone. From Ess Cohen. It will be here in two weeks."

"Oh," Ruth said, and drank from her water glass and set it back down. Her voice had some of the surprise still in it. "How was it?" she asked.

"How was what, Mother?"

Caleb coughed politely. "What kind of stone did you order, Brook?" he asked. "Granite? Marble?"

"Marble," Brook answered, and realized at once that he had finally spoken to Caleb. "Marble is best," Caleb said. "It's what your mother wanted."

"Is that right?" He looked from one to the other of them, first Ruth, then Caleb. "I didn't know that. I didn't know mother wanted marble." He turned to her then. "Is that right, Mother? Did you want the marble?"

"Brook—"

"Marble's perfect," Caleb broke in, directing his words at Ruth. "It's a quality stone. Traditional. Worthy of our lost brother."

Brook studied his uncle as he spoke. His voice seemed unctuous and smug and his head was tilted back slightly so that his gaze was downward, a look not in any appraisal of the table and its setting but an attitude more, almost imperious, nearly possessive. . . .

"*Brook!*" It was Ruth's voice. "Brook, you're staring." She picked up her napkin from the table and touched it to her mouth and then laid it down. "Margaret has spoken to you twice and you haven't bothered to answer her. You're too busy forgetting your manners to answer anyone!"

Afterward, after the dinner lapsed mercifully into silence and was finally finished, Brook went immediately outside, avoiding Margaret. He went into the lawn and walked, circling the trees, smoking cigarettes one after the other and grinding them out angrily in the thick black grass. He saw Margaret come out onto the porch and stand a few minutes and then go back into the house.

Perhaps twenty minutes later Caleb left the house and went to his quarters in the summer kitchen. It was then, after another cigarette, that Brook made up his mind to confront Caleb head on. He would go to the summer kitchen and speak to his uncle, demand an explanation of that day in the canyon, one that answered once and for all the question of the sound.

And he did. He crossed the lawn to the summer kitchen after Caleb had been inside for perhaps ten minutes, opening the screen door carefullly, entering the tiny pantry room and opening the door that led to the larger room beyond. Somehow, Brook expected his uncle to be facing the door and perhaps smoking, waiting to welcome him to the room with some kind of comradely remark. Instead, he was seated at a small table in front of the sink. His shirt was off and he was naked from the waist up, leaning toward something on the counter so that the side of his body visible to Brook was the injured side.

Brook had never seen his uncle's wound before that moment. It stunned him. He actually felt his stomach lurch. Caleb's right arm was vividly exposed, the stump tapering to a blunt point several inches above the elbow, the flesh red and puckered where the bone ended. Across the shoulder ran a whole trellis of scars and on his uncle's body below the armpit there were others, gouges actually, pits in the flesh that had never filled, a splatter of angry discolored mutilation.

Brook closed his eyes and turned his head away, and after a moment he left the summer kitchen.

When he returned to the porch, Margaret was there. He didn't look at her, studying instead the cubes of light that the windows of the house projected onto the lawn. They were so whole, so perfectly precise and geometric. In a weaker voice than normal, Margaret asked where he had been.

"Walking."

"I looked for you everywhere."

138

"Yes."

He struggled to free his mind from the ravaged images of the summer kitchen. "Dinner," he said. "I didn't do well at dinner, did I?"

"You were rude," she answered. It was without emphasis or condemnation. "But you often are. I think people have learned to make allowances for it." She stopped and when she spoke again her voice was oddly flat. "There was something much more apparent at dinner than your behavior."

"What?"

"Your mother and Caleb. Did you notice how protective they were of one another?"

He tried to see Margaret's face but it was invisible in the shadows. "Would you like to walk with me?" he said.

They moved into the lane and once the house was well behind them, the darkness became full. The moon was up but it was distant, it was a light but it cast none, none to walk by easily. They stopped eventually at a fence where the lane met the road, resting their arms on the top board. Far off, down the wide slot of the east meadow and deep within the black pit that was the floor of the Park, a single light flickered weakly. "Did you notice?" Margaret said.

"The light? Yes."

"No, I mean at the table. What I said before, Caleb and Ruth at the table, the way they—"

"No," he said quickly, "and I think we may have jumped to a few conclusions on this thing, Margaret. We're way out ahead of the facts. I think we need to look more closely at the people involved here." Where he had been hesitant before, the words poured from him now. "I think your Cain and Abel judgment is way off the mark. I don't believe men kill their brothers, at least not without some overpowering reason. And you've got to look at the man. Caleb isn't just any man." He turned to Margaret in the darkness. "He's a decorated hero of the war. He literally sacrificed himself, gave up part of his body. For *us*, Margaret." His words picked up a tempo he couldn't stop. "If Caleb had a beef with Papa he'd go to him straight, I know he would. And what's the beef anyway? Uncle wants to drop the horses and get into lumber, maybe buy a new truck. What's wrong with that? It's just a business decision and it might turn out to be a good one. Papa was always slow to make up his mind but that doesn't mean he was unreasonable. If a thing had merit he'd see it eventually. Hell, Caleb knew that. They were brothers, for Christ's sake. They grew up together. They were close, I witnessed that again today. They'd cut their initials in the wall of the stone shed, both of them, when they were boys. Caleb's not going to create an accident and do in his own brother just because they have a difference of opinion. And he's not going to go to a frog-eyed idiot like Grant Pickens for help with it either. That just flat doesn't make sense." He took a deep breath. "Christ, a sound's no evidence at all. I've got to have more than that before I condemn my own uncle."

Beside him, Margaret did not speak. There was no sound from her. Below the fence, an unseen bird called from the meadow grass. Far off, in the unbound darkness of the Park floor, the single weak light that Brook had spotted earlier flickered one last time and went out.

In his sleep that night, in his dreams, Brook saw them for the first time, six mounted riders on a canyon trail, indistinguishable in their sameness, six shrouded travelers in a steep rock hall with a black wind hovering and one suddenly lifted his hand. One. One rider only . . . .

CHAPTER 12

Brook rose early and left the house. The morning seemed free and unrestricted after the nightmares of the night before; it was the space he needed, the house was a prison, suffocating him.

He went to the farthest edges of the lot where the grass stood tall and tangled and he walked there a long time, glancing back occasionally at the house as if seeing it for the first time. As he walked he watched the day begin, saw the people of his life come into it from their individual seclusions. Grant Pickens strolled aimlessly from shed to shed and Brook ignored him. Willy Walker disappeared into the corrals that were his private kingdom. Polite relieved his bladder against the backside of a tree and then took his crew to the sawmill in the Jeffry, blowing the whistle once he arrived. The blast of freed steam probed the morning like a curious finger, poking at the lot, prodding the night stillness that lingered in the passive circle of buildings. But the whistle seemed reluctant to travel too far afield and broke off quickly, satisfied to have rousted at least the near day.

Sometime during the morning, Caleb left the summer kitchen in his dress hat and wearing a shirt and tie under his belted sportcoat. The sportcoat meant he was expecting visitors or that he was going to make a trip. Brook watched him cross the lawn, remembering his nakedness in the summer kitchen the night before, seeing him shielded now by the healing bandage of clothes. It was obviously not visitors, for Caleb backed the Oakland from the garage and drove out the lane.

Sometime later, Etchevarl marched down the shaded steps of the employee's building and stopped in the middle of the lot. Behind him the sun made a silver orb of the giant circular saw that Polite had hung in front of the building to serve as a dinner gong. The old herder stood unmoving for several minutes, studying the sky, and Brook was struck instantly by the feeling of security given off by the familiar figure—the solid stance, the straight back, the whole confident aura of the man who had come so long ago from the old world to find an isolated mountain home in the new.

Brook rose from his place against the fence and headed toward the lot to join the old man. Arranz Etchevarl had always been a force in Brook's life, a kindly comrade hiding behind a *piñata* at a birthday party, a fierce horseman sweeping across the meadows, a Latin face brooding in the parlor when they gathered for the music sessions, Etch playing his guitar and singing the sobby nostalgic *cantes jondos* of his homeland. Having Etchevarl around while he was growing up was like having another grandfather for Brook, one he didn't have to kiss goodnight. He looked up as Brook approached, his face calm and without menace, and Brook almost threw his arms around the old man, so warmed was he again by the overriding sense of security emanating from him.

But at the last moment he decided against embracing Etchevarl and asked him instead if he would like to take a drive. No place in particular, Brook informed him, maybe the west meadow to check hay, perhaps up Left Hand to mark the rise of the creek. "And you can drive," Brook added.

Etchevarl swelled perceptibly, for he was greatly enamored of motor vehicles, even in the face of a vast inexperience with them. He disappeared into the employee's building and reappeared a few minutes later dressed in a flowing ankle-length, cream-colored ulster. He had exchanged his floppy beret for an elegant driving cap, complete with goggles, which he immediately lowered into place. Brook started to laugh, estimating the distance of their trip to be two or three miles at best, but at the last moment he did not. *"El gran señor,"* he exclaimed instead, eyeing the old man approvingly. *"Muy ilustre charro!"*

When they reached the car shed Brook cranked the T and climbed into the front seat beside Etchevarl. The old man hooked his right hand around the gas lever on the steering wheel and pulled down hard, at the same time advancing the spark lever on the opposite side with his left hand. Brook glanced over his shoulder. "You're clear in back." Etchevarl shoved his left foot against one of the pedals protruding from the floorboard and the Ford lurched into gear and shot straight forward through the rear wall of the shed.

"Surprise! Surprise!" Brook exclaimed after he'd finally managed to grab the brake lever beside Etchevarl's left knee and prevent the car from making a second lurching orbit of the lot. "You've been taking private driving lessons!"

There were splintered boards draped over the hood of the Ford and broken ones strewn in a perfect circle in the dirt. Brook got one of the employees to gather and stack the boards and arranged with another to have the rear wall of the shed restored. He then returned to the T and pointed out to Etchevarl which was the low gear pedal and which the reverse, whereupon the old man turned the car around and drove back through the garage, which now resembled a Currier and Ives print of a New England covered bridge. Etch stopped the Ford smartly on the other side and turned to Brook, his face expressionless as always, reflecting neither success nor failure. "Where to?" he asked.

"Well," Brook answered politely, "I hate to plan too far ahead, considering, but why don't you try for the west meadow road? That is, if you think you can get safely past the corrals."

Brook saw to it that Etchevarl drove without haste and when they had gone perhaps halfway up the meadow they began to hear the sawmill and the peculiar high-pitched keen of the circular saws. It was an angry sound, like a host of hornets fighting over a nest, and when they drew nearer, the whole bang and scream of the lumber operation swept over them, the whine of the headrig that Polite ran, the twang of the resaw, the slam and clatter of new boards along the green chain. But when they had driven past the mill and glanced back, it lay perfectly nested and peaceful in the meadow grass, the millpond resembling a tranquil lagoon and the wigwam burner sending up idle wreaths of blue-white smoke.

When they reached the tiny cemetery plot, Brook motioned for Etchevarl to turn in. The cemetery lay at the extreme upper edge of the meadow, almost in the trees, and driving up to it like this from downslope they couldn't see the three headstones and the weathered picket fence at first, only the tall cross-shaped cairn of rocks and wood that Etchevarl himself had erected above the first grave a long time ago. It was this first grave that they stood at the fence and looked in on now, the oldest grave, the smallest. The inscription had faded into the stone; only the grime of years delineated the lettering. *Our Darling Sleeps.*

"The day I carved those three words on that stone," the old man said, "I didn't know what they meant. They were English words and I didn't know English. But I knew the sorrow Julius and his wife were feeling. They stood right here where we are standing and gave it voice. I can hear their sobs even now."

The wind soughed in the adjacent trees and made a whispering in the grass that cemented the graves to the earth. The plot was a solemn place, even in the sun. A formality clung to it, a drapery of old grief and sad lost times. "I try to keep the place up," said Etchevarl reverently, looking in his flowing coat like a misplaced cleric. "I've never allowed the ground to sink. I keep the fence standing and sometime this summer I will whitewash it again. And I will take a scythe to the grass as soon as . . ." he left the remark hanging and looked at Brook . . . "as soon as the fourth grave no longer lies empty. As soon as your father's body lies here where it belongs, alongside those who gave him life."

Brook didn't acknowledge the remark but he thought of his father's body. In his mind he saw it again, buried in the rocks below the cliff and yet struggling to rise to the surface of them, begging to be seen. Brook glanced at the trees hovering over the cemetery plot like uneasy mourners. Somewhere in the dis-

144

tance the tumbling water of Left Hand Canyon was a remote ill-formed thunder. "Where do you suppose True Jackson is these days?" he said casually to Etchevarl. "Still working for Ess Cohen, do you think?"

"I assume so."

"Fairplay store? Leadville?"

"I don't know. You must ask Cohen. What is it you want with the black?"

Brook didn't hesitate. "True's the only man I know who's been in those canyons over on the west side, below the cliff where Papa is."

"Ah," Etchevarl breathed, and that sound and the satisfied sag of his shoulders, was all the answer the old man needed to make.

"I can't get down to cliff bottom from up here," Brook went on. "Nobody can. It's impossible."

"So it is," Etchevarl replied, straightening a little where he stood at the fence, removing the goggles from his head and holding them in his hand. "In the days when I herded for your grandfather, I tried every conceivable way to get down into those canyons. I explored each ridge spur, each headwater, each draw and path." He glanced at the immense unbroken bulwark of mountains above them. "Nothing worked. There was no single piece of earth that could be negotiated by a man on a horse or in a wagon. That entire stretch of Divide from Big Red to Guyot is one long escarpment on the west side. It allows no descent. Anywhere."

The day was growing hot despite the wind that had been rising steadily, and Brook removed his cap. "Various people have been in those canyons," he said to Etchevarl. "Miners, surveyors, homesteaders. But True's the only one who's still around. He told me one time that he took a party of government map makers in there while he was stationed at Fort Stanton with the Cavalry. Escorted them in with his whole troop. But he said they went in from the west, from the Blue River side, because that was the only way it could be done."

Etchevarl fussed at his goggles but said nothing. The wind

was picking up everywhere, beginning to stir things that couldn't be seen, becoming a noisy marcher in the upslope timber.

Brook said, "I haven't see True since last winter when Papa sent him packing for stealing that horse money. It used to be he was forever talking about pulling out and heading for New Mexico or Arizona. Rocking chair on a south porch is what he called it." Brook looked at Etchevarl. "I hope the old reprobate hasn't left the Park. People don't come back when they decide to leave."

"Some do," Etchevarl said without the least uncertainty. "Some come back. Your uncle is one. He has left and come back several times."

Brook gave a little contained laugh but said nothing. They left the isolated cemetery plot and started back, the wind momentarily catching Etchevarl's driving coat and billowing it out like something that had been planted there to frighten the stock. The wind followed them in the car, rippling the grass in the meadow as if it were water, as though the road were a sand bar struggling to cross there, making their passage a treacherous thing.

After several minutes Brook brought the talk around to Caleb again. "I was up in the stone shed yesterday," he said to Etch. "I saw the initials that uncle cut in the stone next to Papa's."

"It was more likely the other way around. Caleb would be the first to carve initials, your father second. Caleb was the aggressive brother, the one who initiated things, despite being the younger."

"I studied the initials," Brook said. "I tried to picture them doing it. I thought of them being boys together. They must have been close."

"As young brothers usually are, yes. Even as I was with my own. But brothers grow apart as they grow in age."

Brook turned to him. "Why, Etch? What happens? What makes men with the same blood in their veins become so different? What makes them want different things?"

"Because, quite simply, they *are* different. Birth does not stamp us identical just because of blood. In the same way that a child is not necessarily a duplicate of his parent, so brothers are not twins. Caleb had a separate hunger and he chose a separate way to fill it."

"What hunger? Tell me."

The old man settled back against the peeling leatherette of the car seat, his voice rising to cover the sound of the wind. "Being the second son and not the first seems to have made a difference to Caleb from the very beginning. He was never the shiny red apple to his parents that his older brother was. Caleb was born in the sad time of his sister Elizabeth's murder and perhaps that marked him in some way. He seemed to be forever trying to compensate for something. And he began to argue with his father. Mining companies were extracting millions of dollars worth of minerals from the mountains surrounding the Park but old Julius would not allow so much as a pan on his place, not even in the hands of his own sons. This frustrated Caleb tremendously. He wanted to do more with the land than just feed stock on it. He insisted there was other treasure here besides grass but it was Aaron's right to decide what to do with it all. Aaron was the elder son and would inherit the land when Julius died and Caleb knew it."

"Do you think he hated Papa for that?"

"Not hate, no. There was no hate between them. Jealousy maybe, perhaps even a little contempt, but that was because Caleb never understood your father. He thought Aaron was weak but he wasn't, he was merely passive. He liked reading and music. He loved the land and he genuinely cared for the animals he owned. Then one day Aaron brought home a bride, a schoolteacher from Kansas who was teaching in Fairplay. She was strong-willed, and independent, and beautiful. Very beautiful." Etchevarl studied the wind-whipped breakers of grass they drove through. "Shortly after that," he went on, "Julius discovered Caleb building a sluice on one of the mountain creeks and banished him from the place. Or Caleb left of his own accord, depending on which account one chose to believe at the time. Caleb left immediately of course, and never came back. Oh, he'd write letters occasionally, but there was no pattern

147

to them. And they were never from the same place. He dipped his fingers in many a sack but never found candy in any of them. The world kept beating him wherever he went, thwarting his dreams, whatever they were.

"Then, after Julius died, Caleb began to come home every year or so. I always believed it was to lick his wounds, to get a second wind, as they say. Yet through all this there remained a genuine affection between the two brothers. Aaron worried when Caleb joined the National Guard and was shipped overseas. He thought Caleb too old to be a Doughboy. He nearly was, you know. When Caleb was wounded, Aaron was deeply affected by it. He even considered going over to the French and English hospitals to be with his brother during his convalescence. And he did everything he could to help Caleb when he got home. They seemed to get along well enough, even though there were times when I could hear them arguing about the business, about the hay and the horses, and the timber. Your father believed that whatever you took from the earth you were obligated to give back. Caleb had no such program and Aaron was afraid he would turn this place into Stump Town. But the arguments were not that final and they never quit talking to one another. I think Caleb grew up in the war, actually. That terrible wound. . . ." He shook his head and went on. "When your father disappeared in the canyon that day, Caleb literally tore at the mountains with the one good hand he had left to him. That last night of the search, we stopped at the stone shed on the way down. Caleb was exhausted. He sent the other men out to the truck and then sat against the wall, under the very initials you saw there yesterday, and put his head down . . . and wept uncontrollably. I had to lead him out to the truck." The old Basque fell silent. "But your uncle has recovered well," he went on in an abruptly cold voice. "He has taken charge. That is his way. He has a great strength. He always did have."

Upon their return, Etchevarl parked the Ford in the lot and returned to the employee's building. Brook took up his old station at the periphery of the grounds, avoiding everyone, still wanting to think.

The afternoon waned. The dinner hour came and passed.

148

Just at dark the wind swelled to a concentrated fury and ripped the last jagged flaps of cloud from the sky, exposing the blackness beneath. Brook walked in that blackness. He shook his fist at it and he cried aloud, "Why? Why did you lie about the sound?" At one point, someone turned on a light in a lower room of the house and only that solitary square of window held its place in the darkness. All else—earth, sky, the torn body of the mountains between—all broke apart and flew before the wind.

The house was like a fortress, Margaret thought, withstanding somehow the endless swarming attacks of the wind. She felt abandoned inside it, a sole survivor trapped by an internal stillness even more frightening. As the hours of evening passed and Brook did not return, the darkness of the house turned menacing and she got up from the parlor chair and switched on a light and let her growing dread be assuaged by that false warmth. She didn't know where Brook was, she hadn't seen him since he'd returned in the car with Etchevarl in the early afternoon. Worse, none of the others seemed to care; at dinner, neither Ruth nor Caleb had asked about him.

Margaret decided finally to go outside and wait. She wrapped a shawl around her shoulders and moved to the porch, standing directly in the square of window light, seeing the darkness around her as a sinister place.

And suddenly Brook was there at the top of the porch steps, standing in that same darkness, refusing to leave it as though the frame of window light was for him the real evil. "Brook?" she called, and then she repeated the question, trying to make her voice reveal less of her surprise. "Is that you, Brook? Are you all right?"

"Yes."

"I was worried about you. I haven't seen you since. . . . You didn't come in for dinner."

"I know."

"Has something come up? Something new?"

"No. Nothing."

The wind moaned dismally at the eaves of the house. Beyond the porch railing, in the yawning black pit the lawn had become, the twin firs bent under the blasts. Still, Brook would not move forward into the light and join her. Finally, she gave up waiting. "If things should change," she said, her voice as well as her eyes searching for him in the darkness. "If you need to talk to me about anything. . . ."

But Brook did not reply and she turned and went back into the house.

Brook went upstairs to his room and sat in the chair in the dark and listened to the wind. He thought of Margaret and wondered if the smoke eyes had flared when she spoke to him on the porch. He wondered if the wind screamed as fiercely in the black sedges of Saddle Pass as it did now in the aspen grove behind the house. He lay on the bed and closed his eyes and after a grateful easing time a nurse came into the room and stood beside the bed, holding a wounded soldier in her arms. She was dressed in white and had innocent smoke-colored eyes and was greatly distressed. "Please drink the water," she said to Brook. "If you don't drink this water the doctor will come and report you dead. Please!" she begged. "Please drink!"

Brook groped in the mud for the water but he couldn't find it. When he looked at the wounded soldier he couldn't tell if he were still alive. He could see holes in the soldier's flesh but he couldn't see his face. And he was weeping. Brook could hear the soldier weeping. . . .

He awoke from that and took off his clothes and lay down in the bed again. He fell asleep immediately but sometime in the night he made a journey. Not motive perhaps but a journey nevertheless. His body left the house through the bedroom window and swept up the meadow and over the mill, climbing the long raw defile of Left Hand Canyon, bright now in the light of dreams. When he looked down upon the earth he saw a mountain peak and its topmost line of trees. The trees stood twisted and bent, blasted by wind and cold, writhing in an agony of abandonment. One of the forms that were the trees spotted Brook in the sky and peered up at him. Brook saw that the form had been a body once but was now merely a skulled thing lifting from the earth, rising in air like one who falls in air, the mark of roosting birds visible on the white dais of its forehead and its eyes plucked clean. The lips were teeth, teeth frozen in a grimace of surprise at the death that had come, at the abruptness of it, the dismay.

The form rose swiftly now to meet Brook, its bony jaws bobbing frantically as if it sought to speak. And suddenly it grew a face—lips, nose, cheeks, eyes, all that it had lacked at distance. And still Brook couldn't make it out, couldn't see whose face it was. "Who . . . who are you? . . ."

Brook fought to wake. The need to wake screamed soundlessly in his throat. For long minutes he endured the terror of eyes that would not open and feet that could not flee.

But his eyes opened at last, opened to the blurred realities of his own room where even at that instant, just there and here and there again, the rising form was still visible to the eye, its cry still audible to the ear, the cold of its presence still thick upon the air.

Brook had trouble waking in the morning and went down to the kitchen only when he was certain Caleb and Margaret weren't there. But neither was Ruth. He found her in the dining room instead, doing bookwork of some kind, and when he sat at the table she laid her papers aside and looked up. "Don't tell me my son has condescended to pay me a visit?"

She said it brightly, even smiling a little, and it put Brook instantly off his purpose, made him feel defensive. He hadn't wanted to *answer*, he had wanted to *ask*. He looked at his mother across the table while he waited for the delay to dull her advantage. He could see a tiny nest of lines beginning at the outer corners of her eyes. They did not flaw her face, he saw that as well, they merely gave it a faintly quizzical look, made her appear for a moment like a young girl who has been surprised at an intrusion, and unaccountably pleased. He saw that she had changed her hair. She was wearing it in a way that framed her face, set it in bounds, made it a distinctive thing that has been saved back, not used. Below the bridge of her nose lay a faint runner of freckles. They seemed not to belong to her skin; they were specks of dirt or seed that a careless garden glove had deposited there and she would shortly brush them off, returning her face to the unblemished cameo it was. Etchevarl had been right about the long-ago bride. A strange flutter of anguish moved in Brook's stomach and he turned away. "I need some money," he said.

He did not see her face in the moments that followed but he heard the deflated sound her answer made, as if she had been another person at the table all along, not the altered one with the awkward tentative smile. "You have your own money, Brook," she said to him.

"I may need more."

"More than what? What do you need it for? What are you going to buy?"

"I'm not going to buy. I'm going to find. I'm going to find True Jackson and I'll probably have to go out of the Park to do it." He looked back at her then, part way, enough to watch the surprise seep into her face.

"Jackson? Isn't that the colored man your father ran off last winter for shorting the horse money or something like that?"

"Yes."

"What do you need him for?"

"For a guide. He knows those canyons on the west side of the Divide and nobody else does. He can lead me to Papa's body so I can bring it out." He eyed her. "You *are* interested in that, aren't you, Mother?"

"Brook—"

"You want something to put under the tombstone I ordered, don't you? The marble tombstone, the one that was your favorite?"

"Of course I want those things. Don't question me on them." But she faltered a little when she said it, enough to bring her gaze down. "It's just that I was surprised, that's all."

"You? Surprised? I didn't think you'd allow that."

"Stop it, Brook!" Her voice had been weakening but it firmed quickly now with the old unconscious authority. "Stop talking around things. Stop using words as if they were parts of a riddle. You've been impossible the last couple days. You're surly and rude and you've treated Margaret as if she wasn't wanted here. That's unforgivable. Margaret's been the soul of kindness and understanding since the accident. And so has Caleb. He's been a great comfort to me. I've had to get my head back up and go on too, you know. You aren't the only one here who's suffered a loss." She studied the papers on the table in front of her and her voice softened somewhat when she spoke again, although it may have been from lack of interest. "Your True Jackson may be hard to find."

Brook didn't answer.

"People like that are drifters. They're dead leaves. They stay in one place only when the wind isn't blowing. Even if you do find him, how do you know he'll agree to do what you ask?"

"That's why I need the money. True used to like money, I assume he still does. And I'm sure the Hartman Hay & Cattle Company can afford a few dollars in a worthy cause."

"It could, yes, except for the fact that there is no longer a Hartman Hay & Cattle Company."

He turned fully to her this time. "What?"

"Caleb and I had the name of the business changed yesterday. It's now called Hartman Enterprises."

He stood up. "Why?"

"Caleb thought the name gave a truer picture of us. That it was more representative of what we do, the different lines we're pursuing."

"Does Caleb decide those things now?"

She eyed him narrowly. "I decide them, Brook, if you really need to know. Caleb thought the change was a good idea and I agreed with him. If a new idea is sound I'll accept it. I'm not afraid of the new."

He stood watching her, not speaking. He sensed that something unforeseen had passed between them, something he couldn't absorb yet. And he realized that delay was no longer any help to him. "Will you give me the money?" he said.

"How much?"

"I'm not sure. Maybe fifty dollars."

"Certainly you'll take one of the employees with you. You won't go alone."

"Would that bother you, Mother?" But he didn't wait for an answer. "I'll take Willy Walker. He's good at seeing things no one else sees."

She eyed him. "What's that supposed to mean, Brook? Is it another riddle?"

"And I'll take the Oakland this time. It'll climb the passes—"

"You will take the Model T."

"I see," he answered, taking his time, deliberately letting his emotions show in his voice. "The Oakland's just for Caleb, is that it? I saw him drive it out of here yesterday morning. It's perfectly all right for him to use it whenever he chooses, but just the minute I need—"

"When, Brook?" she broke in. "When do you plan to go looking for Jackson?"

"Tomorrow."

"Fine," she said flatly, not looking at him. "I'll leave the money on your bureau this evening," and she returned to the papers in front of her on the table.

Once again, it was complete dismissal.

That afternoon, Brook told Willy they were leaving first thing in the morning, just the two of them, and Willy's response was to eye Brook suspiciously.

"Pack some supplies in the back seat of the T," Brook instructed him. "Fruit, crackers, blankets. Take extra gasoline, a can of grease, some oil. Fill as many cans with water as you can find and put them in the car. Strap them on the outside if you have to. Bring Mastic. A box of patches. A brace wrench. Pack plenty of tire casings too, all we've got. We're going to track down True Jackson."

Willy whistled soundlessly. "Why would we do that? Old Sarge is long gone by now."

"Is he?"

"He was talking rocking chair on an Arizona porch when he

154

was here last winter. Couldn't get him to talk about anything else."

"While you're at it, check the tool chest to make sure it's got everything we'll need. It's the long black box on the left running board." He studied the dark swollen face under the black hat. "On second thought, you'd better let me do it. You'll pack the damned thing full of horseshoes!" He left Willy and went to the car shed where the Ford was parked, which is where Caleb found him no more than ten minutes later. Caleb didn't waste any time. "I hear you're going looking for Jackson."

"That's right."

"You going to hire him as a guide?"

"Right again."

Caleb pushed his hat back. The hat minimized his face, Brook realized. It was wrong for him and always had been. It made his face look plain and small when what it needed was enlarging; it needed color, distinction, features that would stand out just once in its life. "Tell you the truth," said Caleb timidly, meaning it to be disarming, "I've got some mixed emotions right now. I'm proud of you because you thought of Jackson and ashamed of myself because I didn't." He made a few self-effacing gestures, giving his head a reproachful shake, kicking at a clod of dirt. "I hope you can find him. He was working in one of Cohen's stores the last I heard but you can't be sure, can you? He could just as easily be out of the state. People like that, the wind's always pushing them from behind, never from the front. When they buy their ticket, it's always one way."

Brook looked up from the tool chest. "Some buy round trip. You, for example."

Caleb restored his hat to its original position. "Who are you taking with you?"

"I'd decided on Polite."

"Good choice. He knows car engines in case you have trouble on the road."

"But Polite's hands are still bandaged so I'm not taking him."

155

Caleb coughed into his hand. "I see."

"I've settled on Willy."

"Fine. Have you told him yet?"

"I picked him, I told him."

It was hot in the shed, airless. Caleb laid the index finger of his hand against his forehead and snapped off a streamer of sweat. "Could be I'm a trifle jealous," he said, adding a laugh. "To tell you the truth, I'd like to be going along."

Brook kept busy at the tool chest. "You and I never did take a trip together, did we, Uncle? You were always gone off somewhere, if I remember."

"Well, once," Caleb said. "Once we did. When you were a little boy I took you up to the crooked wood. That's timberline on Big Red. I always called it the crooked wood."

"That was Papa who took me up there."

"No, it was me. You've just forgotten." He pushed at something on the floor with his foot. It was a grease rag. He reached down and picked it up and put it in the tool chest. "How about money? You going to need some money?"

Brook looked up from his work this time. "Have you got money, Uncle? Have you got money of your own to give me?"

Caleb turned and started to leave the shed and then he stopped and came back. "The coon's your man," he said, making it sound like an instruction he'd forgotten to leave with Brook. "He knows those canyons over there. He took a party of map makers into that mess one time—"

"I know. He told me."

"That's mean country. It's all jumbled up. It's like a separate land that's got separate laws. I've known old prospectors who wouldn't touch it. Hell, I wouldn't, nor would I spend the sweat to learn it either." He stuck his hand into his back pocket, pulled it out, fussed with his hat, confessing weaknesses, being vulnerable, striving to establish the common thread. "I know you're hurting about the empty grave," he said. "I've seen it in you the last few days, being short with people, wanting to be by yourself, moving quiet. I understand that. We're all anxious to get our lives back to normal." His voice picked up as

156

though Brook's silence was an encouragement. "But first things first. If you can't locate Jackson, come home. Okay? Use your head. Measure what you want against what it might cost you. Don't go past Leadville, whatever you do. Don't go chasing a tumbleweed like Jackson, he isn't worth it. If something should happen to you it would. . . ." He stopped and began again. "It would destroy your mother. All the progress she has made so far would just flat crumble. She's been through a terrible ordeal. I've done what I could to help and she's starting to come out of it. To tell you the truth, I couldn't stand to see her slip back now."

Brook stood up from the running board of the T. "You're always saying 'To tell the truth'. Is that what you do, Uncle? I mean, what you always do, no matter what it is? No matter what's happened or who's involved? Blood or not blood? Who it hurts? Who it helps? Just the help, just the people, tell the truth?"

Caleb stared, his face tight. "God, Brookers, I wish I could understand what you just said," and when he turned away this time he did not come back.

Margaret stood under the fir trees in the lawn. The sun had long since dropped behind the mountains and shadows were advancing on her everywhere, bringing a light that was grainy and decaying like old wood. She saw Brook emerge from one of the sheds and when he entered the lawn she stepped out from under the trees and advanced toward him. "It's so hot in the house," she said, stopping a few feet away, touching her handkerchief to her neck. "There's no air. What I wouldn't give for some of last night's wind. That's why I came out here to the lawn, it's so much cooler than the house. So lovely here, really, with the grass and the flowers and the pine smell that comes in the evening. Sometimes, when the wind is just right, it brings the smell of the sawmill."

"Yes," Brook said simply. The surprise of her stopping him there in the lawn was clearly visible in his face.

157

And then she said, almost blurting it as if her words were uncontrolled, "You're going to leave, aren't you? You're going on a trip."

"Yes."

"You're going to go searching for a man who used to work for your father. A man who's been gone for six months. Your mother told me."

Brook attempted a laugh. "I can see she did. She didn't leave much out either."

It was difficult for her to see Brook's face as clearly now as she would have liked, the shadows were shrinking the light quickly. "It would be fun to go on a trip like that," she said, trying to force some control into her words.

"You make the trip sound like more than it is. It's not that far really. Fairplay, Alma, a couple of mountain passes. Leadville maybe—"

"Who are you taking?"

"Willy."

"I almost wish it had been me you'd picked. I'd be good company on a trip."

"I'm sure you would."

"What's the name of the man you're looking for?"

"True Jackson."

She repeated the name, more for herself than for him. "That's a strange name. It's unusual, like Virtue or Chastity. I knew a girl once whose name was Christmas. In one of my Bible classes there was an Easter. And a Deliverance too," she added, but when she actually began to hear her own words she stopped immediately. They were flat and empty, inadequate to block the alienation that had threatened from the very first to descend upon them. Brook must have sensed it too for she saw him studying her out of the secrecy that the shadows had imparted to the lawn, and when she spoke again she knew her voice had changed. "It's funny about time, isn't it? What time does to us, the change it brings. A couple of days ago I would have been the first to know about your trip. Now I almost didn't know at all."

Brook watched her, not speaking.

158

"You never would have told me, would you, Brook? If your mother hadn't mentioned it almost in passing, I never would have known. I wouldn't have seen you during the day tomorrow, or at dinner tomorrow night, and I would have had to ask Ruth finally where you were and she'd have said, 'Oh, didn't you know? Didn't anyone tell you? Brook's gone. He went on a trip.'"

Again Brook was silent. The lawn grew hushed. The grass was a black pool that locked their bodies in place as it would dead trees. From out of the aspen grove behind the house a bird called to the lost light. "You sound upset," Brook said. "Are you upset that I'm going?"

"No, I'm not upset. I have no right to be. It's your family, isn't it? What's happened here is your affair, yours and your mother's and your uncle's—"

"I'm sorry."

"It's all right. If I was able to help before, when you confided in me that day you found out, then I'm glad."

"Margaret—"

"It's my fault really. I assumed that if you needed me once you'd always. . . ." She stopped and studied him. "But you don't. How wonderful it is," she added, "to be that strong."

Brook stood quietly. She heard him take a breath and use it for something private and then release it. "How long will you be gone?" she asked.

"I don't know for sure," he said, and his voice sounded distant as though he had moved back from her. "Weather's always a factor. Roads too. And those mountain passes can slow you up."

"It seems such a . . . such a final thing."

"Yes," he said, and she felt immediately that he wanted to say more; there had been a sense of obligation in that single word. "I need to see the body, Margaret. I need more than Willy's story. I told you that."

"Yes."

He seemed far away now, the light had almost completely drained from the yard. The mountain jay called again from its hidden place in the grove and again there was no answer. She could no longer see Brook's face and took a quick unbidden step toward him. "I'll miss you," she said. "It will seem strange without you. You're really all I had here, you know, the one I knew best. The only one, actually." She glanced up at the window of her room and took a deep breath. "Well, I came out for air and now I must go back. I need to write my husband. He's alone in a strange country." She laughed nervously, unavoidably. "Just as I am." She started to move away from him toward the porch.

Brook took a step forward. "Margaret. . . ."

"Good-by, Brook. Good luck on your trip," and she moved up the steps and disappeared into the darker larger loom of the house.

But once in her room she made no attempt to begin a letter to Emerson. She merely sat in a chair and stared at the open window.

CHAPTER 13

The Park lay on both sides of the road like stagnant water, sloshing against nothing, flowing nowhere, making no sound. The only movement of air anywhere was the one the speeding Ford created and it poured back over the hood like water so hot it was close to being steam. The car top was down, as usual this time of year, and Brook had also folded the windshield out in an attempt to get more air. Rain was seldom forecast for July so there was little or no risk of getting wet, but if it did come it was supposed to take one man only four minutes to put the top back up. The "Four Minute Top" was one of the Model T's more popular selling features. One man, four minutes. Grant Pickens had informed them before leaving the house that morning that in light of the adjustments he had recently made to the car with his Convertible Kit, the time required for one man to raise or lower the top would probably improve to around three minutes. "The key thing to remember," Grant insisted, "is that you gotta raise the windshield at the same time you raise the canvas top so that you got something to hook on to."

Grant had covered several other maintenance items with them as well, standing alongside the car with his shoulders bowed and his hands jammed into his pockets like a disbarred racer. He kicked at the tires and rapped the fenders, all in a sour mumbling perversity, and issued several warnings. "If the engine starts to run rough on you," came his first, "then you're gonna have to adjust your spark coils." He eyed Brook and Willy expectantly, waiting for them to ask where the spark coils were located. They didn't ask. "Your coils are in a little metal box under the dashboard," he went on exasperatedly. "There's four of them. Take your lid off your box and tap each one of your coils til your engine smooths out on you."

"Sounds like a xylophone lesson," Willy said.

"If that don't work then go to your commentator," Grant told them.

"You mean commutator," Brook said.

"And don't forget to check your oil," was another instruction. "You forget to check your oil and you'll burn out your number one main bearing sure as rain's got water in it." He would have gone on reciting additional perils that might befall a neglected combustion engine if Brook hadn't rammed the T into gear and shot out the lane, shrouding Grant in a mist of fine dirt and oil-blue exhaust.

Now they were racing south into the glassy mirage of the Park floor, their speed converting the waves of raw heat ahead of them into a long narrow coil of finished dust behind. Far off on the horizon, the peaks of the Mosquito Range held pitted remnants of snow like a face retains the pocks of an old disease.

Around the Puma Hills area the Park turned briefly secluded and full of shadows, hinting of a dark island of outlaws and madmen, but it recaptured its usual openness quickly enough once they drove through. Off to their left they could see the village of Hartsel floating on the endless surface of grass; they overtook it in no time, a desolate wind-banged derelict that leaned in upon itself and pretended not to care that they passed without stopping. Near Badger Springs the road turned stony and the T picked up its first flat. Brook and Willy jacked up the car and removed the casing but they couldn't get the inner tube cement to accept the Kant Kreep patch and it took them almost two hours to make the repair.

It was late afternoon by the time they reached Fairplay. Brook shifted into low gear and they drove slowly down the main street, their eyes full of windsore and glare and their tongues shriveled in their mouths as if they'd been chewing the corners of a dry blanket. The town had a spent air about it, the look of a place where a fair or a gala or an all-day street dance had been held, clamorous and exciting and full of people. But it was over now, they had missed it, it had all been yesterday.

They parked in front of the Fairplay Mercantile and got out, stretching and brushing dust. Ess Cohen wasn't at the store and they talked instead to the clerk, a bandy-legged little man with a scalded look who kept pulling himself up. "Jackson? True Jackson, the colored? Naw, he doesn't work here. He did once but he don't no more."

"Where?"

"Try Leadville. Last I heard he was working in the Leadville store." He tugged at the belt of his trousers and eyed them conspiratorially. "That don't mean Jackson's still there, you understand. You ain't gonna keep coloreds in one place anymore, not since the war. They'll head for the big cities, looking for white women and jobs. Chicago. Los Angeles. Places like that. There's twenty-five hundred of 'em living in Denver right now, did you know that?"

"Either that or I didn't care," said Brook. He took off his cap and blew dust onto the counter. "But obviously you do and I wish I could be more like you." He glanced at Willy. "My friend here wishes he could be too. We both know Ess and the next time we see him we'll tell him what an observant person he's got working here in his Fairplay store. It'll please the shit out of him. Maybe he'll start paying you wages."

The little man hitched himself. "I hate a smart-ass kid!" he hissed, and disappeared into the back of the store.

They left the Merc and ate at a diner down the street and then drove out to the west edge of town and camped, breaking up some dead pinyon to build a fire for coffee. Behind the mountains there was a lurid orange sunset that didn't move for a long time, looking like a design painted on paper. But it crumpled all of a sudden, as if a small fire had gotten to it, and was gone.

163

They spread blankets and took the front seat out of the T and laid it on the ground and used it for a head rest. The night was hot and still and full of crickets. "Tell me something," Willy called from his blanket.

"Shoot."

"What the hell is a number one main bearing?"

Flying down the white dust road to Alma the next morning, the Ford blew a front tire so violently it threw them into the ditch and only Brook's masterful struggle with the steering wheel got them back onto the road without tipping over. The casing was ruined and they replaced it with the first of three spares that were strapped to the left running board.

At Alma they turned left and started the long ascent to Mosquito Pass. The pass crested at slightly over thirteen thousand feet but before they reached it they had boiled over twice, and two additional flats were their reward for dropping too fast down the other side, trying to make up lost time on a road full of chuckholes and boulders.

At the bottom of the Mosquitoes, the road leveled out into a valley where long stately columns of aspen marched arrogantly past scraggly knots of scrub oak. The T forded a creek, ten miles later forded another, and then started the grinding climb of a new mountain range, this time the Sawatch.

The afternoon lengthened. The road became a mere fire lane, the timber an impenetrable wall on each side. Overhead, the clouds were forming into long lumpy ridges the color of old bread dough. The switchbacks of the Sawatch began to squeeze in on each other, shortening up as the gradient increased, going from horseshoe to hairpin. At one point they met a car coming down the mountain and Brook was forced to back up nearly a quarter of a mile before he found a suitable turnout.

Darkness came, thin and cold. A rear tire went flat and they replaced the casing on a slope so steep Brook had to rope the Ford's front bumper to a ponderosa that stood above them on the bank.

But they eventually reached their destination. Sometime

164

after midnight, bone weary and shivering, they chugged into Leadville, the town that sat alone on top the world.

Brook and Willy slept in the car and woke in the morning to the thin washed purity of mountain air. Their teeth chattering, they stumbled into Cohen's store where Ess served them hot coffee and stale pastry and informed them that yes, True Jackson did in fact work there but he wasn't in yet. He sometimes slept late. Ess told them they were welcome to wait on the front steps of the store and watch True ride up the street on his big black horse; a lot of townspeople did. There was plenty of coffee and the morning would warm up as soon as the sun had soaked the mountain top for an hour or so. Or they could drive to Jackson's shack in the alley at the edge of town, it was easy to find, he could show them exactly how to get there.

That's what they decided to do. They drank one more cup of scalding coffee and cranked the T into reluctant life and drove down the main street to the alley Ess had pointed out. They never got the chance to enter it, however, for as they were preparing to make the turn, a horseman on a huge black horse rode out of it.

Brook yanked back on the brake handle and Willy popped up in the seat and blurted, "That's him right there. That's Jackson."

True Jackson hated automobiles—they spit and rattled and occasionally spewed hot water on the unwary; they were unsafe, he was afraid of them—and so he rode to work every day on the back of the big black stallion he had purchased from the United States Cavalry on the day of his mustering out two years earlier. There were people who claimed True didn't actually own the horse, that he didn't have valid papers, that he wasn't 'in legal possession of said animal.' There were others, definitely the majority, who simply didn't care, stating that the horse was all in this world the nigger had, what the hell, let him keep the damned thing. Now the two of them, man and animal, blocked the mouth of the alley like a boulder and Brook cut the Ford's engine and he and Willy sat in the front seat, not moving, not making any motion to get out, staring up at True Jackson.

He was wearing an old bulky army coat and a campaign hat that had probably been camel colored before sun and dirt and sweat had stained it something else. No part of his body moved except his eyes; he was trying to determine if he knew the two men in the car. Watching True watch him, Brook saw that the man's eyes were as much red as white, remembered that they had always been red and that some of the Hartman employees when True worked there had called him Red Eye. The man had a growth of whiskers that was starting to turn white as if he'd been scooping flour from a sack into a store bin and some of it had gotten on his face and he hadn't brushed it off yet. Or perhaps didn't know it was there. Seen on the back of that splendid horse, the whole man seemed shabby and unkempt.

Then he spoke. He had a heavy voice and it boomed at them in the fragile morning quiet, full of sudden recognition. "You two look like a couple remounts that was rode real hard and put away wet."

Willy answered first, still watching the black horse. "How come that animal shines like that?" he asked True.

"All niggers got a shine to 'em, didn't you know that, Chief?"

"You've lost yours," Brook put in drily, taking control of the conversation. But then he realized that Jackson had one hand covering the butt of a rifle that protruded from his saddle. "You won't need the rifle," Brook called to him. "This isn't rifle business."

"What kind is it?"

"Talk mostly. Questions and answers, that sort of thing."

Jackson's eyes continued to search them. "I ain't had nobody come looking for me since my mama needed some wood split one time." His lips barely moved and the words seemed squeezed with belligerence.

"We got plenty of wood," Willy said, trying to joke.

True ignored it. "The last time I was near to a Hartman," he said, fixing on Brook, "it was your daddy. We was working real hard on a misunderstanding. He was supposed to pay me

166

commission for a horse I sold but he didn't. That's how the misunderstanding got started. I don't like it when people don't pay me."

"So you took the money instead, huh True? I forget now how much it was. Twenty-five? Fifty?"

True glared. "Have you come for the difference, boy?"

Sunlight had been creeping down the slope of the street while they talked, coming on inexorably like a watery yellow spill that would have reached them sooner if the cold hadn't slowed it down. When it finally reached True Jackson he slid down from the horse and took off the tattered coat and laid it across the saddle.

Brook watched him. Once out of the coat, the man's body was less than Brook remembered. There was less girth. His neck was thinner; there were cords showing. Some decision passed through the red eyes and True's hand came away from the rifle butt. The rifle was slung in a crude scabbard made of oilcloth, one end held by a front ring of the saddle and the other by tie strings on the rear jockey. "Five dollar saddle on a hundred dollar horse," Brook said to him.

"Times is hard," True mumbled. "Eight dollars a month is what my pension comes to. That'll buy some oats but not a lot of oysters. I ain't thick in the pocket like some people I know."

"That's obvious," said Brook, eyeing the clothes and the saddle. "But I'd expect an old horse soldier like you to at least have a decent scabbard for his rifle."

True made no move. His face remained blank. "You didn't come this far to insult my saddle," he said. "What is it you want with me?"

Brook told him then about his father's death. "Maybe you heard about it."

"I did. I heard it was a runaway horse done it. But I didn't grieve much either way. I left that for his friends."

Brook took off his cap and inspected it and brushed it a little and put it back on his head. "Do you remember Saddle Pass?" he asked True. "That bad place on the Divide between Big Red and Guyot?"

True nodded.

"We figure it happened there. Lightning maybe. Maybe wind. He obviously fell down that west apron and over the edge of the cliff. I saw the body."

True's jaw dropped. " You *saw* it?"

"From the edge of the cliff. Caleb and the others had me on rope. I saw the horse. Seeing the horse is the same thing as seeing Papa. They've got to be together down there."

True waited, studying Brook and the cluttered dust-chalked Ford, and then he said, "When was this?"

"About a week after it happened."

Jackson seemed to relax. He reached in a shirt pocket and brought out a sack of makings and began to build a cigarette. When he had finished he returned the sack to his shirt and looked at Brook with the same lack of expression as before. "And you want me to do what?"

"I want the body. For burial. I need you to take me in there to the bottom of the cliff. I don't know how to get in myself. I wouldn't know if I had the right canyon."

"You and most others," Jackson said, wetting his lips and placing the cigarette carefully between them. "That country's like a virtuous woman. Hard to conquer and harder to leave if you do. It ain't no easy job."

"I haven't asked any easy people to do it," said Brook.

True lit the cigarette and began to scrape dirt with the toe of his boot. He made a ridge first and a small mound out of that, all slowly, and then squashed the whole business with his heel. "What does the big hero say?"

"What?"

"Caleb. What's he say?"

"He doesn't know how to get in there either."

"I mean, what did he say about you coming to look for me?"

Brook swallowed patiently. "I didn't ask him what he thought. The trip isn't his idea. It isn't his money that's financing it. I don't need his permission to leave home and I don't ask him when to come back. I can even take a piss without letting him know."

True set his jaw. "Still got that diarrhea of the mouth, ain't you, boy?"

"What do you say to the job? It'll pay something. Looks to me like you could use the money."

True built in the dirt again, surveying his work through the smoke of his cigarette. "It's a lot of box canyons over there," he said, "and sons of canyons growing out of those. A regular family of canyons is what it is. And there's no water. None running, none standing. There's just the boulders and the sand God put down right at first. Maybe a few rattlers and some horny toads. It's what I call tribulation country."

"I figured you'd have a name for it."

"You'll need supplies," True went on, pushing the greasy campaign hat off his forehead and taking another drag from the fast-burning cigarette. "You'll need plenty of grub. It could take a while to get in there. Some of those canyons can swallow you up." He worked his lips over his teeth and glanced contemptuously at the Ford. "You'll need a truck or a big wagon to make a base camp when the terrain stops you. It's horseback after that. Don't short men nor horses when you draw up your list of things to bring. Best way is the train over Boreas Pass with a couple flat cars."

"I figured that."

"Get off at Breckenridge and follow the Blue to the Swan and work upriver and then pack into that big main canyon where the shaft house sits on the south shoulder. . . ."

"Quit stalling. You coming or not?"

"Then there's the expenses."

"I'll catch those."

"And my fee." He eyed Brook carefully. "It's for the trip in and not the body. You understand? It's just for guiding you to the bottom of the cliff."

Brook patted his jacket pocket and the dust flew. "I've got fifty dollars with me. You get half of that now. It'll give you a little walking around money. The other half you get when you finish."

True said quietly, "My fee is two hundred dollars."

"We'll take Cohen with us," Brook went on. "He's got that Freighter and it should be plenty big enough for the job." He stopped then and his eyes narrowed. "What did you say?"

"Two hundred dollars, that's my fee."

It was quiet in the alley, so quiet they could hear a pack of dogs running in a distant street, nosing at garbage cans. Brook said flatly, "Polite was right. You're a damned nigger."

Jackson studied his boots. "Costs are up, boy. The war did that, I had nothing to do with it. There's rates for everything now. I can get a hundred dollars just for leading a calf through a patch of thistles."

"And I can find ten box canyons for half of that."

True grinned, it was the first animation he'd shown. "Oh, you got the sand for it, boy, I'll give you that. Anybody who'll cross Mosquito and then climb this mountain right afterwards in a little tin flivver with toy wheels has got some sand. But it's funny when you think about it, sand ain't the same thing as experience. They didn't have the same parents." He winked lasciviously. "Hell, one of them didn't have any."

Brook unbuttoned his jacket and flexed his fingers and set the spark lever on the steering wheel. "How about giving us a crank?" he called to Jackson. Then he turned to Willy in the seat beside him. "Say good-by to the general, Willy. We're leaving."

"Good-by, General."

Jackson bent down and gave the crank a single wrench and then walked around to the driver's side. "About that shaft house on the south slope I was telling you about," he called to Brook above the clatter of the engine, "I wouldn't put too much store by that house. As free information it might turn out to be worthless." He gave a wet cavernous laugh, showing the white comb of his teeth, and then his face took on a pained expression. "Lord, boy, nothing's free anymore, don't you know that? Have you priced them Lost Gold Mine maps since you got to Leadville? They're two dollars *each*. Isn't that disgraceful? You can't even buy *directions* cheap anymore."

"Or the truth either," said Brook.

"That too. Harder to find than a two-door outhouse."

Brook shot the T into high gear and had put the town of Leadville a mile behind him before he was finally able to speak. "Can you believe that thieving camp bird?" he shouted at Willy. "Two hundred dollars for one pack trip?"

They were riding the downgrade of the mountain, there was almost no engine noise, just the rush of wind. Willy said, "Seems to me that old burrhead was uncommonly worried about what Caleb had to say about this."

"He was, wasn't he?"

"Still, that don't surprise me much. Caleb always did like to walk the dog with the help. Bossing everybody around, giving orders, laying out the work, pretending to be the big stringer. You never saw it but we did. Sounds like he had True more scared than the others."

"Sounds like it."

"And of course this'll make Caleb look like an A-number-one fortune teller, us coming back empty-handed. I suspect he's been betting good money that we couldn't get the coon."

With all the weight that was in the car, plus the pull of downhill, it took Brook over a hundred yards to get the Ford stopped and turned around. The road had no decent turnout in it anywhere, and no shoulders at all. They lumbered back up the mountain and turned into the alley and True Jackson was sitting on a low stone wall in a little ring of light that filtered down through a copse of scrub oak. Brook pulled the Ford to a stop and set the brake.

True didn't get up from his seat on the wall. "I'd ask you to get out and sit but I figure your rump's too sore for stone."

Brook choked the engine down but he didn't cut it. He dug in his pocket and tossed a fold of bills into Jackson's lap. "Here's fifty dollars. You come to my place for the balance. Two days."

"No, not your place," replied True starchily. "That's bad advice. I'd be like the hen going to the fox's party."

"Como then," Brook said. "Cohen's store. I'll be there with a hundred and fifty dollars and my people."

"I'll be there."

"Promise yourself you will, mister. I've got four motor

vehicles and a hundred horses and if you're not standing on Cohen's steps two days from now I'll use every one of them to ride you down. And you're not a man who can hide easily. You've got an odd color to you."

True Jackson's eyes went raw and he stood up. "Como in two days," he snapped. "On the steps. I'll be the *black* nigger," and he turned his back on the Ford and disappeared into the alley.

CHAPTER 14

They began their trip down the mountain immediately, sailing the easy slopes and dragging the hard, riding the brake and letting it out, coasting one minute and gearing down in a great whine the next, running the tortuous grade of Leadville's massive mountain.

Somewhere past the bottom they stopped in the shade of a willow park and removed their jackets, for they had descended once again into heat, and ate crackers and dried fruit and drank water from a tiny creek that made sleepy sounds. When they finished, Willy stuck the gauge in the gas tank under the front seat and they filled the tank out of the can from the back seat that had the potato stuck on its spout for a cap. The Ford was whitewash now, its shiny Japan Black enamel obliterated by dust. They repacked the gas can and Willy cranked and jumped in and the Ford catapulted out of the roadside shade into the hard blazing track of late morning.

Around noon they turned onto the valley road that led to the Mosquito Range. They ruined a back casing fording a rocky creek several miles later, and pulled a flat in a front tire no more than ten minutes after getting under way again. It was not only their last casing but their spare inner tubes were all used up and the can of Mastic was empty. Brook eyed Willy forlornly. "Are you a praying man?"

Willy's face was waxy with sweat. "Sometimes."

"Then let this be one of the times and pray that this stupid Ford turns into an Oakland before the day is out. At least the Oakland's got tires, not these goddamned rubber bands!"

A thick heat coiled itself around the afternoon. Brook's eyes burned and he grew sleepy but he couldn't let Willy spell him behind the wheel because the swarthy little horseman had never learned to drive. It was only when he asked for a dipper of water and saw that Willy was asleep that Brook pulled off the road under a canopy of cottonwoods and cut the engine. He leaned his head back against the seat and tipped his cap forward and closed his eyes.

He believed he would sleep immediately but he didn't. He had managed to keep Margaret Pendleton pretty well bottled up until then, holding her apart from the places they had gone, but now in the locust-singing silence at the side of the valley road she spilled out into his thoughts. He saw her as clearly as if she had been standing at the front bumper of the car, the wide boning of the face, the pale skin, the slightly large mouth, the eyes vital and gray-black and unconstant. He saw her hands as they had been that day at the corral, the simple unstudied eloquence of them clasped beneath her chin. She kept slipping from woman to girl and then to woman again . . . slipping away . . . coming back . . . and he knew in that moment that he was in love with Margaret Pendleton. More important, he knew that such a love was impossible. He was trapped. He couldn't love her. They couldn't even be friends. A man could not be friends with a woman he had needed in his heart. He had heard of men doing powerful things for a woman, mining a mountain, conquering a country or a business empire, but they were all done out of love, not friendship. A terrible ache passed through him. He would never hold Margaret Pendleton in his arms, could never let his love fill her, this elegant smoke-eyed woman who had come unbeckoned into his days, this minister's wife . . . .

He fell asleep and his thoughts of her passed to dreams. He saw her sitting in the back seat of an automobile wearing a dark blue coat with a lavender hat turned up on one side, trimmed with artificial flowers that glistened in the sun. She was leaving the Park, gliding soundlessly over the meadow to a mountain and beyond the mountain to a prairie where the sky crushed whoever entered it . . . going home, going away, and never saying good-by . . . the vivid smoke eyes lost to him forever. . . .

Sweat running into his eyes woke Brook and he shook Willy awake and they drove on. By the time they had crossed the valley a black bottom-heavy cloud was waiting for them. It clung to the forehead of the Mosquitoes like a soggy bonnet, dropping mist into the canyons like straggles of wet hair. Just as the last of the day's light surrendered and they were well onto the flank of the mountain, the storm broke. Rain poured from the cloud as if nothing but a piece of rotten canvas had held it.

The road quickly turned to grease. Rocks slid into their path from the soaked slopes above. Twice they were forced to stop the Ford and search for deadfall timber with which to corduroy the most threatening washouts so they could advance along the road. The headlights kept flickering out each time they slowed the car for a new hazard and only by clutching the engine and then racing it could Brook keep the lights burning. Without them, they were doomed.

The rain fell unabated. It pounded the hood. It soaked the leatherette cushions in the front seat and the stack of supplies in the back. It drenched the two riders completely; they hadn't been able to find raincoats in the jumble of back-seat gear and the easy Four Minute Top wouldn't budge. Brook sat huddled behind the wheel and Willy beside him, the rain dripping from their hats into their laps and onto the floorboards in a steady stream. "You didn't pray hard enough," Brook muttered to Willy at one point. "This damned Ford's still not an Oakland. An Oakland's got a *top* on it!"

Sometime later, at the very crest of that battered mountain, in the bleakness and the quagmire and the chill, the Ford suddenly skidded helplessly toward the edge of a dropoff whose bottom was blackly invisible. The two men neither moved nor spoke nor scarcely dared to breathe, and after several minutes, when they realized the car wasn't going to topple over the edge, Willy let out his breath in one long quavering squeak and said to Brook, "You've got a thing about trying to fall off cliffs, haven't you?"

Somehow they climbed out and threw a rope on the Ford and pulled it away from the abyss and got back in again, but it took them the rest of the night to cross the mountain. When the rain finally stopped, the wind took over, raging at them, screaming, assaulting them unmercifully from its hiding places in the grim canyons.

They eventually reached the bottom of the mountain and the village of Alma. It was just dawn. The town looked like an old harlot who had gotten drunk the night before and passed out in the street. They drove by her, and didn't stop.

At the far edge of town they pulled the Ford over and got out. They removed their clothes and wrung them out as best they could, and then put them back on. They decided to eat some of the food they had brought but when Willy reached into the back seat and found a box of crackers and held it up, water ran out.

"Shit," Brook exclaimed, "that does it!"

They drove back into Alma and found a restaurant that was just opening for the day. When they crossed the floor to reach the tables in the back, their boots left a trail of water on the linoleum. They ordered breakfast from a waitress who wouldn't look at them and when they had finished eating they drank cup after cup of hot coffee from the pot Brook had demanded the waitress leave at the table. Willy's hat was off, dripping water onto the floor. His hair lay plastered against his forehead and his eyes were swollen nearly shut with fatigue. "You think we ought to check the number one main bearing before we drive any farther?" he mumbled to Brook.

"There is no number one main bearing," Brook replied. "The sonofabitch drowned last night on the mountain!"

But the sun pushed a new day into being, gently at first and then insistently, drying everything it touched, the grass along the side of the road, the men's hats, their clothes, their boots, the gear in the back seat and the sodden cushions in the front. It dried the Ford itself, and as the car raced down the highway toward the heart of the Park it threw off Mosquito mud like a wet dog shaking itself.

Just beyond Fairplay, Willy's bowels began to react to a full stomach and Brook was obliged to pull off to the side of the road to accommodate him. Willy leaped over the car door and disappeared into a stand of ponderosa pine.

The particular stretch of road where Brook parked was situated on a shelf of land that overlooked South Park in its entirety. It was as if the site had been chosen by the Highway Department as the County's official viewing area. It was a perfect choice, the whole Park was visible; all the eye could encompass. At its farthest limits the view blurred and grew fuzzy as if it had gorged itself on distance at the expense of clarity, but below the bench where Brook waited the view was perfect.

As he watched and waited, Brook saw a train creep out of the town of Fairplay behind him and glide onto the floor of the Park. The train was immediate, detailed, he could see the windows and hear the locomotive, but in a matter of minutes the vastness of the land had captured it. As he watched the train shrink gradually into miniature, Brook felt that the Park had never seemed so grand and isolating as it did at that moment, so dwarfing of the puny objects man had put there—a train and its tracks, some roads, a few buildings scattered in the grass like droppings from a meandering beast. His eyes picked up the train again but he knew it would be gone in a moment; the grass would part briefly, and close, and forget the train had ever been there.

Yet Brook knew that eventually, far to the north in Jefferson, the train would reappear. Anyone standing on the depot platform looking south would see something, not motion yet or even size but something, a color perhaps, a spot curiously darker than the grass that bore it. And then, magically, that spot would become the train, become an engine pulling cars. A whistle would rise up from its approach like a sound announcing its own shape, weak and wind-diminished at first but hinting at more to come, going on ahead like a prophet. The train would climb imperceptibly as it neared Jefferson and as proof of its labor the locomotive would send up a slender rope of black smoke. The rope would not rise straight up like a fakir's trick but would trail along the top of the train and become part of it, an extra roofwalk for the cars, a mysterious added weight for the train to carry up the subtle grade to the depot.

But even as he pictured the train's passage, Brook knew that the Park would quickly revert to what it had been before, that a train when it passed only made empty places emptier, that it might cleave loneliness momentarily but could never destroy it. On the silent road where Brook waited, that loneliness rose up and threatened to drown him. He felt adrift, abandoned. Was anyone really waiting for him beyond that ocean of distance? Was Margaret still there? The smoke eyes flashed at him from across the emptiness. *I'll miss you.* Had she said that? Had she meant just for his trip, or forever? *You're really all I had here,* she had said. But had she left? Was her bedroom empty, the door closed and the shades drawn on the fading scent of lilac and the musty warmth of old trapped sunlight? In a rich blue coat under a lavender hat whose flowers glistened in the sun, had she boarded a train and left the Park . . . across the meadow . . . beyond the mountain? . . .

Brook cranked the T and jammed it into gear and just as he was beginning to pick up speed, Willy Walker shot out of the pines and vaulted into the front seat of the car, tugging at his trousers. "You bastard!" he cried. "You were gonna leave me!"

The Ford beat long rolling breakers of dust from the road as they raced into the burning core of the Park. The afternoon became a hot dead summit of time that had ceased to move.

Somewhere near Red Hill Station a smell of burning oil developed and something popped loudly and a thin fissure of steam began to escape the radiator. In addition, a clatter commenced under the floorboards. The Ford's speed gradually diminished after that and no amount of clutching or throttling would restore it.

The sun made a glistening saber of the road and in all that vast arena there was not a single cloud to offer mercy from the attack. A rear casing blew completely off its rim opposite Como and the Ford stood in its own tremble and smoke in the middle of the road while they stuffed the casing with strips of canvas torn from the crippled car top. It failed to hold. When Brook finally turned off at Jefferson and began to climb the east meadow the casing abandoned the rim completely, flopping off into the grass like a run-over snake, and a quarter of a mile short of the lane the T gave a last agonized shudder and stopped dead in the road.

Brook leaped out and ran the remaining distance to the house. When he reached the yard fence he jumped it, racing across the lawn. He glanced up at the window of Margaret's room and his heart sank. The shade was drawn and the panes of glass peered down at him like an invalid who was forbidden to leave the room and could only look out at the world.

Brook tripped along the porch and into the kitchen. His mother was there. Alone. "Brook!" she exclaimed, startled by him, reacting to his presence but revealing no emotion in her face. "Brook, you're home."

He brushed past her, not stopping. He opened the door to the dining room and saw that it was empty. He crossed to the parlor and glanced in and Margaret was not there. He looked in the library. He went to the foot of the stairs and listened. "Margaret?"

No answer.

He ran up the steps and stumbled just short of the top. He pulled himself up and held onto the bannister, still struggling to catch his breath after the long run. The hallway was silent. He opened the door to Margaret's room and it was dusky and air-dead and she was not there, nor could he see any of her things. He moved back down the hall and pushed open the door to his own room and closed it and turned and Margaret was standing directly in front of him, tall and hushed and cool-white with her eyes a tenuous gray-black questioning in her face.

Brook froze with relief and astonishment. He tried again to catch his breath and the effort ripped his chest with pain. "I thought . . . thought you had gone. . . ."

"Oh Brook," cried Margaret suddenly, and all her fragile containment left her. "Brook, I missed you." She seemed instantly pale and uncertain. "I didn't think it was possible . . . I didn't believe I would ever . . . Oh, Brook. . . ." and her voice broke.

He reached out and pulled her to him. "Don't ever leave me, Mag. Please. I couldn't stand it if you left me. . . ."

She lifted her face to him, sobbing a soft wet litany of his name, and he pressed his mouth onto hers. He felt the trembling of her lips and the wetness of her tears. She moved her lips under his and pulled her mouth free and her words leaped at him. "I tried so hard not to miss you, Brook . . . not to love you. . . ." Her voice collapsed into a hot whispering against his face. "Oh, Brook. . . ."

He covered her hushed mumbling with his mouth and her eyes closed. His own eyes closed as well, as if touch were a trigger that brought everything down, his face on hers, his body on hers, all down. There was no conscious sinking to the bed, no lurch of their bodies seeking a place. He reached down and removed his clothing, his flesh gorged with blood and painfully erect. There was a similar disrobing by Margaret as well, a lifting and a drawing aside, but all unseen, their mouths still locked together in the kiss.

Then, miraculously, their bodies joined. His flesh was enveloped instantly in a heat that drew all the purpose of his body to that single place and the rhythmic thrusting that followed was as natural as their sinking to the bed had been. And still he hadn't seen her body. He hadn't glimpsed the breasts and the thighs and the lush buttocks his eyes had once so greedily devoured. He never thought of them. He never opened his eyes, never took his mouth from hers. He could not; they were linked together as though one part of their touching fed the other, their bodies giving in one place and taking in another like a circuit.

There was a finish to it finally, a climax, hers as well as his, a fierce mutual pounding that mounted to pain before it stopped in paralysis. There was an abrupt sinking, a deflation that collapsed the frantic arch their bodies had made and dropped them mute and exhausted upon the bed.

After a moment, Brook opened his eyes and took his mouth from Margaret's and rolled onto his side. He could not feel his lips. He looked and saw that Margaret's lips were compressed and pale and he reached out and touched them with his fingers as if that single act would restore the flow of blood. She kissed his hand and placed it on her breasts. He cupped them gently, accepting their fullness and their warmth for the gift they were.

Softly, she whispered his name.

He laid his face against hers and breathed the lilac of her nearness. "Margaret . . . sweet Jesus . . . Margaret Pendleton."

"Oh, Brook." It was like a cry torn from her body. "I've doomed myself, Brook. I've doomed you. God forgive me."

He lifted her hand to his mouth and held it there a long time. Twilight came and they loved each other again.

Darkness gained the room and covered their eyes with sleep. A night breeze ran down the canyons and crossed the meadows and stirred the curtains at the window. At one point in his sleep, in the warm darkness, he called her name.

CHAPTER 15

Downstairs next morning only Margaret was in the kitchen. Brook kissed her and she hugged him avidly but they didn't speak, purposely, believing that by sheer silence they could prolong this initial wonder they had discovered in one another. They ate bread that Brook cut from a loaf and toasted on top of the stove, and leaving the house and running to the corral they stopped at the springhouse and from a water-beaded crock drank milk so cold it stuck to their lips. At the corral they picked a single horse and rode it without a saddle deep into the aspen grove behind the house. The grove was impregnated with a stillness so intense it was mysterious, perhaps even reverent. Because of it, they still did not speak. They slid from the horse and in the private shadow of the trees they set their mouths upon hard urgent kisses and stripped off their clothing and stroked each other's nakedness to a frenzied excitement. Brook dropped to the ground and pulled Margaret on top of him, sliding her body onto his, guiding her hips up and down and clutching at the frantic undulance of her breasts until in a silent scream of climax she crumpled forward onto him and went limp, her arms about his head and her face in his neck and the rigid nipples of her breasts sucking at the sweat of his chest. And when she finally spoke, only then—"Brook Hartman?"—did her voice expose the drugged quality that her eyes had revealed all the while. "What have you done to me, Brook Hartman?"

He made a nest of his arms and cradled her within them. It was some time before he spoke. "*I met a Lady in the Meads,*" he said then, "*full beautiful, a faery's child; her hair was long and her foot was light, and her eyes were wild.*" When he had finished reciting the lines he held her even tighter.

"Don't break me," she whispered fiercely. "Don't hurt me."

"Not with my arms, I won't. If I decide to hurt you it'll be with the other body parts we just used."

"Then hurt me," she blurted impulsively, "because that's a pain I suddenly can't get enough of."

"On the road from Leadville," he said to her after they had fallen into a period of silence again, "was when I realized what had happened. You were like a pain in me, one I hadn't felt before. And when it went away, a great emptiness took its place. It was frightening."

"Why?"

"Because it was all so sudden. I hadn't expected any of it."

"Why?"

"Well . . . you deny certain things. You don't allow yourself to think about them because you're convinced they can never happen."

"What kind of things?"

"Holding you. Loving you. Seeing your excitement. Feeling it with my body." He pulled back from her a little so as to see her better, still not letting go. "You're not anywhere in my experience."

She laughed impishly and nipped at the lobe of his ear with her teeth. He rolled her over onto her back and laid his face against the low curve of her stomach, his chin resting at the edge of her pubic hair. He rubbed a few of the hairs between his fingers and then pressed the whole mat of them with his hand. "You're silky and soft when I do it like that," he said, "but the individual hairs are like little wires." He pressed again. "And you've got a little mound here, underneath. It's like a padded bone. I felt it earlier."

183

"I'm not surprised. You were deep enough." She extended her arms straight up in the air, lazily, locking her hands together, staring at them but not seeing them. "Coming to climax is a curious thing to happen to the body," she said. "It's like . . . like sitting in the middle of a stream with water pouring over your skin and all of a sudden the water starts to turn warm. Then hot. It floods you with heat everywhere on your body . . . drowns you in heat. And you can't get away because it's made you so weak. You can't move. Your muscles won't work. They've gone stiff with the pleasure. With the feeling."

"Hasn't that ever happened to you before?"

"Not ever. You were the first to give me that, to give me . . . what? . . . my womanness, is that it?" She looked at her wrists, her arms, her hands as if seeing them for the first time. "I think you did it by filling me. I've never been filled like that. Never been touched inside so deeply." She dropped her hands and looked at him. "Fill me again, Brook. Fill me and fill me and fill me." She gave an abrupt cry and pressed her fingertips against her temples. "Good heavens, I sound like a wanton. I feel like one." She drew in a long deliberate breath. "I *am* a wanton."

"Are you?" he said, keeping his voice soft. "I would have expected something different from a wanton. Running sores, stringy hair, a bad smell. And you should know that if I agreed with you I'd jump up and run out of here. Except I'd probably break my big toe on one of the trees."

"I know what you're doing, Brook," she said, turning her face away slightly. "You're trying to smooth over what I've done, take the evil out of it. But you can't. I've still committed adultery. It's still a sin."

This time he waited before he spoke. "Words only define a thing, Mag, they don't change it. What I'm against, I think, is your definition. I don't agree with it. I've got a word that's much better. More honest."

"What is it?"

"Before I tell you, you have to turn your face this way." He extended his arms to her. "And you've got to get back inside here where you belong." When she had done this he wrapped his arms around her and held her tight. "The word is love," he said. "All right?" and he waited to feel her nod of agreement against his shoulder before he went on. "You'll probably laugh," he began, "and I'll accept a giggle or maybe even a slight chuckle, but I'm curious about something. Last night you told me you loved me and no one has ever said that. No one, ever." He felt a flush of embarrassment in his face. "I need to know *why* you do. I hope that makes sense. I need to know what it is in me that's . . . that's worthy."

She disengaged herself and reached up and traced his mouth with her finger as if she were acknowledging the question but asking him at the same time to be patient. The earlier tightness was gone from her face, her voice was soft. "That'll be hard to explain," she said. "I'm not sure I . . . people don't go around making lists of the things they love about someone." She gave a kind of faint incredulous laugh. "In my case there wasn't time for a list. It all happened so quickly, an explosion really. We were friends, and then strangers, and then this." She dropped her hand from his mouth and uncertainty thinned her voice. "I have to change my way of looking at you, Brook. What I thought of before, when you were away on your trip and I began to realize . . . to feel the emptiness, were the reasons *not* to allow this to happen."

"Was the age difference one of the reasons? The four years?"

She turned her face, taking her time, looking back at him, looking away, not being afraid so much as private. "I was aware of the age difference right at first, when I first arrived here. I could see the four years but they didn't mean anything. They were just a number that registered on my mind for a moment and then disappeared. You're four years older than a cousin, you've had a particular hat for four years. The number four *that way*." She looked closely at him. "That's all changed. I think it depends now on what the two of us did with those four years. If I had spent mine filling myself with wisdom and you hadn't, then I'd be ahead, wouldn't I? It would create a gap. But I don't feel a gap. I don't feel the numbers. It isn't that they went away, but that they don't matter."

He watched her face. "That's a nice bright answer but it isn't the one I asked for."

"I told you it would be hard," but it was in her face that she hadn't given up. After a moment she went inward. He could almost feel it, feel the separate tensing motion her body made to go within herself and find the answer. "Because there's no guile in you," she said finally, looking at him intently. "You don't pose. You don't study what you're going to say or what you should look like when you say it. You don't look ahead at effects. There's something in life that hasn't touched you yet. I'm not sure I even know what it is."

He worked up a smirk of sorts and started a comeback but she saw it and stopped him. "Oh, but there's arrogance in you," she said, putting a protest in her voice, making the exaggerated face they both expected. "And pride. And selfishness."

He smiled widely, showing the crooked teeth. "All that?"

She smiled back at him and then went sober again. "The truth is, you're still strange to me. I don't know you. I don't know what you are, what you like. The personal deep-down things about you. . . ." She trailed off.

"I can get a catalog made up if you'd like. My name in block letters on the cover. Table of contents. A good picture on the flyleaf."

"For example," she went on, "have you actually read all those books of poetry in the library? And why do you like poetry? Most men don't, or won't admit to it."

"If you'll give me time to organize a—"

"Do you ride that buckskin horse because you love him or is he simply better than the other horses?"

"I'll be damned," he said, and tried to make another diversion of her words but she wouldn't let go her newfound seriousness. "When you went to Denver," she said, "did you like riding the train? Do you like big cities? Did you like Denver?"

She managed eventually to lure him into her sobriety. "I'm not sure," he answered. "I thought for the first couple days that Denver was the greatest place in the world. But it changed by the end of the week. It was like going to a puppet show and

186

seeing the wires. All the illusions vanished. The city became full of people who drank wood alcohol and laughed a lot and went around saying things like 'Yes, we have no bananas.' There wasn't a one of them you would really want to know, or call a friend."

"At least the people you met."

He waited and then went on. "There were some sad things too. The crippled veterans, the soldiers who came back from the war all shot up. A few of them had no legs. They would scoot up to you on those little padded dollies and salute and call out their serial numbers and then hold up their hats for money." He shook his head in an abrupt anger. "Jesus, that's a hell of a way for us to treat our heroes!"

"Are they heroes, Brook?" She looked closely at him. "Maybe they're just the unfortunates, the victims of accidents. Wrong place at the wrong time, that sort of thing. The farmer in Kansas who loses his hand in a corn shredder, is he more noble than the farmer who didn't? Is he noble at all? Why should an accident change what he really is? Is Caleb a hero simply because he got his arm shot off? Is Caleb—?"

"Hey," he said, grabbing her playfully. "No farmers. No Caleb. No anybody, okay? I don't need them now. I just need you."

Quickly, with an almost desperate intensity, Margaret burrowed against his chest. "Oh Brook, need me *always*. Please! There's nothing left for me now except that. I gave up a marriage for you. I gave up my chance at . . . heaven."

He held her within the circle of his arms but it was more casual than protective, and his voice when he spoke was mocking. "My God, Mag, do you suppose there really is such a place as heaven? A place where we can hide if the going gets rough? If the Fates decide to come looking for us?"

They ran naked to a new place in the trees, hiding from each other behind the chalky columns of aspen. So still and solemn was the grove that it seemed an altar place; the trees were giant candles and the sun a candlelight somewhere above them, secretive, isolating. "Do you know what I'm remembering right now?" she said to Brook from the hidden side of an aspen.

"What?" he asked from the other.

"I'm remembering the day they brought you back from the mountain after you'd fallen off the cliff. Ruth set you down in a chair and took your shirt off and you were naked from the waist up. We bandaged you, remember? Later, I touched your skin and it was hot. It gave me goose pimples. Shocked me. I didn't understand what was happening. I didn't know what to do."

His hand reached around the tree for her. "I remember that day too," he said. "Only with me it was your breath on my face, you were standing so close that one time. And the smell of you. Like lilac. I didn't know what to do either. All I could do was blush. I blushed so hard I was sure you could feel the heat. That's what I remember about that day, being scared of you."

"Are you still scared?"

Again he reached for her around the tree. "You want to come out here and find out?"

"If I did, would you still not know what to do? Would you still blush if I stood close?"

"How close?"

It grew suddenly very still in the grove. "*Like this!*" and she leaped out from behind the aspen and faced him. "Blush for me, Brook," she breathed. "Please. I want to see it. I want to see all of it." His nakedness flew at her as if it were a reflection of her own. She stepped toward him and stood close. His breathing was the only sound anywhere. She reached out and touched his skin, stroked it. It was smooth, hot. With a soft cry she pulled him down to the cushiony leaf-matted earth and fed her new hunger back to him with her body.

"What would your mother think if she knew about us?" They had dressed finally and she was leading the horse out of the aspen grove, Brook at her side.

He snorted. "She already does. She couldn't help but know.

188

I didn't exactly tiptoe into the house when I came home yesterday."

"Do you think she'll say anything to us?"

"Probably. But she'll wait until there are people around. Then she'll start a lecture about young men and morals and behavior and—"

"No, I don't think so."

Brook glanced at her. "Why?"

"Because I think you've repeatedly misjudged your mother and you're doing it again. Ruth isn't that concerned about morality. About traditional reactions. Not innately." She delayed purposely, forming her thoughts. "I've been able to understand Ruth a little better lately. She's strong, Brook, stronger than any of us realize. Nothing turns her aside. She won't allow it. It's as if she's made a pact with herself never to be broken, no matter what happens."

"Well, if Mother thinks I—"

"Wait, let me finish." She reached out and held his arm. "Your mother lets people see only what she wants them to see, what suits her purpose at the time. It's the surface things she shows, not what's inside her."

"Inside?" His voice rose. "My God, what *is* inside her?"

"Brook—"

"I'll tell you what's inside her, Margaret. *Secrecy.* She thrives on it. It's the key to her, to everything she does. She never talks about the timber or the mill. She never once opened her mouth on the Bulldog, whether she wanted it or not. She's kept that to herself from day one. And she changed the name of the business and didn't say a word. God only knows what else she's keeping secret."

Margaret studied Brook's face and then burst into laughter. "Well, she wouldn't be the only one with something to hide, would she? I know of at least two others. They're right here actually, in plain sight, walking a horse out of a grove of trees." She could see her laughter catch at Brook, gather him in. He lifted his hands in a defensive gesture, but playfully. "I'm not hiding anything." He turned and faced the trailing horse. "You, horse, am I trying to hide anything? I just chased Margaret

Pendleton naked through the trees but there wasn't anything I tried to hide."

"Good thing too, huh, horse? Because I don't think he could have hid it." She laughed excitedly and threw herself at Brook, the reins dropping from her hand. "Oh, you terrible man," she cried. She encircled his neck with her arms, smothered his rising laughter with her mouth. "You terrible blushing man!"

When they returned to the lot, Margaret went riding in the east meadow and Brook went with Etchevarl to one of the sheds, for during their absence Ess Cohen had unexpectedly delivered the tombstone and Etchevarl wanted Brook to see it. The crate lay propped against the door and Brook pried loose the boards and together the two of them inspected it. Etchevarl seemed genuinely pleased with it, remarking to Brook that it was a superb stone, worthy of its purpose. "Once again you have done your duty."

Brook was staring at the tombstone. "What?"

"Your duty. You have done your Christian duty."

Brook continued to stare. "I think the duty I want done now," he said, "is for my mother to see this stone. After all, it's her husband's, isn't it? That's his name engraved there. And it's marble. She said she preferred marble. She should see it."

"I would not expect much attention from her," Etchevarl offered listlessly. "Not now."

"What do you mean?"

"While you were gone looking for Jackson, Caleb gave up the summer kitchen. He moved into the house, into the bedroom off the parlor. Your mother has been busy getting the room ready for him."

Brook turned without a word and walked back into the depths of the shed and stood for several minutes. Then he came out. Still he didn't speak.

"In one sense," Etchevarl went on, watching Brook's face closely, "the house is Caleb's more than it is your mother's. It was his old room he moved into, the room where he was born.

His wanting it again would be a difficult petition for your mother to deny."

"Not if she wanted to," Brook said clearly. His eyes were still on the tombstone. It looked elegant and ceremonial in the sunlight, the name and the dates finely hewn, the surface richly polished. Yet a coldness emanated from it and Brook looked away. "You won't be going on this trip to the other side," he said to Etchevarl. "I need you to stay here and look after things. Right now I want you to get some people together and start loading the Double T truck with the gear that Ess brought out the day I came back from Denver. The truck's got to be packed up and ready to go by tomorrow morning."

"Why use the Double T? Why not the Bulldog?"

"The what?"

Etchevarl pointed across the lot. "There, beside the shed. The new Mack Bulldog. Caleb brought it back from Denver while you were gone."

It was true. The truck was there, wrapped in its red-white newness like a gift opened too soon, looking pugnacious and resolute beside the sleepy shed. Abruptly, Brook left the old Basque standing in the doorway of the shed. But he did not go to the house, even though he knew Ruth was sure to be in the kitchen. Instead, he jumped into the Double T and drove up to the sawmill and motioned for Polite to cut the power and climb down from the headrig. When Polite came out to the car Brook told him about the trip and informed him that he would be in the party.

At first, Polite seemed startled by the announcement but he recovered quickly. He told Brook he'd be glad to go along, however he'd have to check with Caleb after work and get permission.

"You just got permission. The only permission you need. Mine."

Polite worked his cheeks into a bulb and let go with a powerful splat of tobacco juice, then looked at Brook and grinned, showing his stained teeth. Actually it was more smirk than grin. "Explain something to me, Itty Bitty. Who's supposed to tell me when to get up and dance and when to sit down? Is it you or is it Caleb? I'm confused."

"You confuse easy, Polite. That's been your biggest problem. Don't come up here to the mill in the morning, just be ready to go with me. Is that simple enough?" He left the mill and drove back down the meadow road and found Willy Walker in the employee's kitchen drinking coffee, his eyes swollen with unfinished sleep. "On this trip to the other side," Brook said to him, "you're going with me."

"No," Willy drawled. "I ain't going nowhere with you. The last time I did that you tried to leave me behind. And you burned out the damned car."

"You're going, so get yourself ready. And I want you to stay close."

"What are you talking about? How close? When?"

"I've got a plan I'm working on. We'll need to talk before we reach the cliff bottom where the body is."

"What's wrong with talking right now?"

"On the trip. I'll tell you when." He left the room and located Grant Pickens in the forge. The building was fiery hot. Grant's leather helmet was pushed back and his forehead was gummy with melted pomade. "I'll need you tomorrow," Brook told him. "Little trip over the top of the mountain."

Grant straightened up slowly and skinned his lips back from his teeth. "Caleb's put me on this job fixing chain," he answered, puckering his mouth as if it tasted bad. "Job could last a couple days."

"Then you're in more trouble than I thought. You can't count and there won't be anybody here to tell you when the two days are up."

Grant's face flamed and he swore wetly. "The day I go anywhere with you is the day pigs fly!"

"Help Willy with the horses in the morning. Volunteer yourself. Make up a string of six and be sure the buckskin is one of them." He studied Grant's smeared forehead. "And leave your helmet here. The pigs will want to shit in it and improve the smell."

Still, Brook did not go to the house. He walked to the edge

of the lawn and stood for several minutes, looking in at the summer kitchen, studying the faded red flagstone walk that separated it from the main house.

Then he went to the kitchen, only then, with the anger churning in his stomach like acid. Ruth was alone in the room with its disarming spaciousness, its comforting smells. He took a chair at the table and watched her but she did not open the conversation; he guessed that her avoidance of him was intended to be a reproach. She was dressed in an unusually bright skirt and blouse and wore her hair loose at the shoulders, giving her face an unpent temporary look. His stomach cramped with a curious disgust and he said sharply to her, "Now that the tombstone is here I thought I might find you in widow's black. It would be more fitting than that dancey business you're wearing."

She looked at him but it was oblique, almost indifferent. "Widow's black is not a cloth, Brook. It's a condition."

"I didn't know that."

"Now you do. And when I choose to wear black I will wear it. Or white. Or burgundy. And I won't ask you beforehand whether you like it."

"But there might be another you'd ask, right?"

"Don't riddle me, Brook." She was no longer looking at him. "Ask or say, but don't be a riddler. It's not a role you play well."

Instantly his mind flashed a picture of her the night he returned from Denver, grim and clenched in a darkened corner of the parlor. "Roles can be easy to play," he said. "Harder to understand." But she did not answer and he knew he had not reached her with the remark. He was caught with his thinking unfocused and the anger of the afternoon wasting in him. "I need a two hundred dollar draft," he said.

Her head came up. "For what? I just gave you fifty dollars a few days ago."

"It's True Jackson's fee for the search."

She stood even straighter. "Two hundred seems high."

"What should it be, Mother?"

"Things have a relative value."

"What value should we place on Papa?"

She let out a bit then, relaxing her shoulders. "You know I didn't mean it that way."

He saw it as an opening. "How *do* you mean things lately? I never know anymore."

"Brook—"

He coughed loudly. "You forgot I ordered the tombstone, didn't you? You forgot it until just this minute when I mentioned it. Should we forget what it's for too? Should we have Etchevarl just plant it in the ground over an empty grave and save True Jackson's two hundred dollars? Is that what you want?"

She set herself and her jaw tightened. "I'll sign the draft tonight. You need to sign in front of Mr. Cohen in the store tomorrow. It needs both our signatures." She didn't go on with anything but he could tell she wasn't through with him, he knew from the way her eyes held him with the old familiar mix of plea and demand. "I'm glad you found Jackson, Brook. I'm proud that you initiated the search and made a success of it. That's a kind of courage. Courage is mostly persistence anyway. If I haven't talked to you about what you've done it's because I haven't seen you." She didn't look away but her face seemed to soften a little, taking on an air of acceptance, perhaps even resignation, as if these last words, the quiet ones, were all that she had spoken, as if there had been no harsh or hurting talk before and there would be none to follow. Watching her, Brook marveled at it. He sensed that he had just witnessed the essential strength of her, the remarkable talent she had for turning away another's indignation with merely a look, weak and strong at the same moment, never without dignity. It made him furious. "Yes," he snapped, "I understand you've been busy too. Busy getting Caleb's bed ready."

He thought the remark would shatter the quiet of the room like a dropped cup but it did not show in her face. Her head came up a little. "Now you've said what you came to say, Brook. Finally. Did you want to discuss it or did you just want to say it?"

"One of the employees told me that Caleb moved into the house. I wish you'd told me first."

"I wish so too. Last night when you got back from your trip I wanted to talk to you but you didn't have time. You had to get upstairs. You didn't even say hello."

"If we had talked, would it have changed anything? Papa isn't even in his grave yet and the man moves into his house."

"It is my house, Brook, as much as anyone's. I will decide who lives in it. And while we're talking about your father and his grave, why the sudden conscience? Isn't it just a little tardy? Up until a week ago you couldn't be bothered. You made absolutely no attempt to arrange for the body to be brought back. Now nothing will divert you. Money, terrain, risk, nothing. You're suddenly the dutiful son who feels he must show moral outrage at everything that happens. Except for what he does himself, of course."

Brook pushed his chair back and got to his feet. "Of all the people to talk about morality, you're not the one."

Her shoulders stiffened. "What do you mean?"

"To itch this soon after your husband's death is one thing. But to scratch the way you're doing is another. It stinks!"

She came toward him across the room with her eyes blazing. "Don't you talk to me that way!"

"Hell, I don't know what suit to lay out first, the black pin stripe for Papa's funeral or the white flannel for your wedding."

She slapped his face so hard that for a moment he feared he would lose his balance and fall backward. But he did not, and he reached out and grabbed the hand that had slapped him and squeezed it until her whole face drained to white from the pain. "There might be blood in that bed you've been making up, Mother. How can I tell who spilled it and who's just rolling in it? Or is there a difference?"

It was the shock that sprang into her face, more than any relaxing of his fury, that broke his grip on her. "What blood? What are you talking about? Is this another of your riddles?"

He released her and stepped back. "You're right, there is a riddle. But I'll have it solved by the time I get back and then we'll talk. We'll talk about the blood and a lot of things. That's a promise."

He left the house immediately but he knew the confrontation had been a failure; it had not purged him of his anger. He tossed a spade into the bed of the Double T and drove up to the cemetery plot. To one side of the three graves he began to turn ground for a fourth but he stopped after a few minutes. He leaned against the fence and lit a cigarette and studied the graves at his feet, trying to penetrate the sod and visualize the coffins there. Did the coffins still exist or had the years dissolved them back into the dirt that covered them? How long could bone survive? Flesh was brief, he knew, but how long for bone? The baby Elizabeth was certainly chalk now but was there still shape under the grass to the longer heavier skeleton of Julius Hartman? Brook could remember his grandfather quite well, an old man with a lonely voice who seldom came out of the room off the parlor. He sat in his rocking chair with his trouser legs tucked into his socks, the sleeves of his sweater pushed up to the elbow and the buttons not closed evenly, hoarding gaudy trinkets to show Elizabeth and talking to people whose names Brook had never heard, his face like a candle that has melted. In the end the old man became like the room his years had trapped him in—stale and rumpled and worn, rocking endlessly in a creaking chair under a wall plaque that read, in an old-fashioned flowery script, *I will work hard, and watch, and my chance will come.*

When he himself was old, Brook thought, would he talk to Margaret if she had preceded him in death? What would it be like to live on after she had gone? Would he finally forget the flowered scent of her and the throaty way she laughed? Forget her mouth and the smoke eyes? The lush body? Could he sit dry and old in a quiet room with the sun fading the hooked rugs and speak her name until the sound of it became as lost as the dying mill whistle? Better to be cut off young with the touch and the sound of her still upon him, the warmth of her inside him like a second life. Better that.

He left the cemetery and returned to the lot and when he had parked the truck and was coming around a corner of one of the sheds he saw Margaret standing in the shade with her back to him, looking at the mountains. He crept up behind her and slipped his arm around her waist, gently, to catch her surprise, and said, "But you're here now, Mag, and there's no reason to think about it anymore."

She didn't understand his words, but asked for no explanation. She leaned back against him and her laugh was that of a child who is pleased about being startled. She freed herself from Brook's grasp and turned to him. In her eyes he saw the aspen grove, thick, hot, pulsing. His hands reached out and touched her body.

They ran to the corral and caught out two horses and sped across the grassy toe of the mountain into the cool rising of Right Hand where the hoof sounds of their passage thundered on ahead and then came echoing back down the canyon as though to urge them on. In a manger on the horse side of the shed they fell into the hay and fed the desire that had driven them there. They lay naked and resting a long time, listening to the jays berate the stillness, watching the twilight cast shadows on the windows of the shed like a giant bird, hovering. They rolled into each other, pinching and giggling, but their noise brought a horse suddenly, a sad-eyed querulous bay who hung his head over the edge of the manger and looked down on them. Margaret squealed and Brook cried jauntily, "*Look, look, a horse at the door, and little King Charlie snarling! Go back, my Lord, across the moor, you are not her darling!*"

When the horse had withdrawn, Margaret squeezed Brook happily. "You *have* read all those poetry books, haven't you? Was that Byron?"

"Tennyson," he answered. "I know a lot of Tennyson. I know a lot of everybody. Memorizing poems was the easiest thing I ever did." He burrowed deeper into the hay of the manger and hugged Margaret to him. "When I was little we'd have music and reading sessions in the parlor nearly every Sunday. I always did poetry for my part of the program. I'd stand up and recite a poem and everyone would be impressed. Every time. Never failed. Etch would laugh and my dad would clap, and Caleb would sort of hug me, if not there in the parlor, at least later in the kitchen or some place, and he'd invariably say 'Hey, good job on the poem, kid!' " He stopped. "At least when he was home he did that."

"How about your mother?"

"Mother was different. As always. She'd wait until the applause had ended and then say something like 'Straighten your collar, Brook.' Or 'Brook, your nose is running. Wipe it, please.' "

Margaret didn't respond right away, picking chaff from his naked shoulder. "When I came back from riding," she said, "I went up to my room and I could hear you and your mother arguing in the kitchen. I couldn't make out the words but it was quite loud at times."

"Yes."

"You argue with her a lot. All the time, in fact. Why?"

He shrugged.

"There's no warmth between the two of you. You treat her as if you were . . . cold . . . unloving. And you're not. You're not at all."

"If I treat her that way it's because that's the way she always treated me. It's what she wanted, I guess. Like with the poetry. I did a jood job but she wasn't interested. It was that way with everything. How warm and loving should that make a boy growing up?" He started to tell her more and then stopped. "But to hell with that," he said. "I don't memorize poems anymore. I've got more important things to memorize." He turned in the hay and faced her. "Your body, for instance. Your face, your hands." He grabbed her hand and raised it playfully to his mouth. *"I kissed her slender hand, she took the kiss sedately; Maud is not yet seventeen, but she is tall and stately."*

"Bravo, Lord Tennyson!" Margaret cried. "Bravo!"

"I don't think that verse is quite right. I believe that one line should read *Mag is not yet twenty-six, but she is aging greatly*.

Margaret gave a moan of mock indignation and then fell quiet in the way of people who are contemplating mischief. Suddenly she bent over Brook and kissed him and pushed her tongue between his teeth. He bit it gently and in return she bit him on the lower lip, sharply, and a tiny trickle of blood appeared. But she kissed it away with a soft cry in his neck, and then reached down and stroked him to erection. He rolled over and entered her and again there was the flood that broke, full of pain and a smothered crying, and their bodies made the old burning lock of one another. She moved rhythmically beneath him, up and down, up and down, now in languor and now in frenzy, watching his face until she saw reflected there the paralyzing ecstasy of her own orgasm, and when they kissed and rolled apart their mouths were sticky with the blood from his bitten lip. "You've wounded me, Mag," he whispered to her.

"We've wounded each other, Brook. Forever."

They dressed and left the shed and the last reluctant wisps of sunset light followed them down the canyon. In the yard it deserted them completely and in Margaret's room there was only blackness and the numbing silence of a mountain night when there is no wind. They lay uncovered, not speaking, not moving. He slept briefly and then woke. The moon rose sometime later, more a softening of the darkness than any light of its own, and a coolness came into the room and Margaret reached down and covered their nakedness with a sheet. Brook turned and lay on his side, watching her. He could barely make out her face, but the way she breathed, the ease and the privacy of it, made him suspect that he was in her thoughts, gathered in, safe. It was true, for after several minutes she spoke, calmly, without passion or alarm. "You know what's wonderful, Brook?"

"What?"

"It's wonderful not being afraid of you." She pressed her fingers against his lips. "No, don't laugh. Every man who's been in my life I've been afraid of. My father. My husband. Uncles. Both grandfathers. I don't know why, I just have. But not you. And it's wonderful. I feel free. I feel that I've accomplished something very important in my life. In my growth as a woman, as a person."

Brook squeezed her hand and kept silent. A great night hush crept into the room, and they slept.

The dawn came at last and the gauzy light touched their eyes with its infinitely tiny shock and woke them. Margaret lay for several minutes watching Brook and her hand came out

199

and felt the back of his neck. "Your hair has grown long," she said. "You're much prettier with it long. When you first came home from Denver your hair was too short. Your cap didn't fit right. You looked like a little chicken that a sombrero had fallen on."

"Little rooster," he corrected her sleepily.

"But it's shaggy now and needs to be trimmed."

"Yes," he said, still not opening his eyes. "When I get back, then you can do it."

Daylight filtered gradually into the room, delicate, weak, not strong enough yet to support the heavy forms and outlines that the day would eventually demand. Margaret reached out and touched Brook's face cautiously. "Tell me why you're going away again, Brook. I keep forgetting what it is that takes you away from me," but when he started to answer she covered his mouth with her hand and held it there.

With the fullness of light came sound, and with sound the reality of life beyond the window, and Brook rose and dressed and left the room.

But later, when the search party was made up and waiting in the lot, Brook walked over to Margaret where she stood at the yard fence. "Good-by, Mag."

"Brook," she said, "we have a whole life ahead of us. We need to be together to live it. Promise me you'll come back."

"Yes."

"That's not enough. You must promise me."

"I promise." Her hair was not combed and her eyes were soft and sleepy. "Come here, Mag," he said, removing his cap, and when she had stepped close he ran the tip of one finger along her cheek. "*I met a lady in the Meads, full beautiful, a Faery's child; her hair was long and her foot was light, and her eyes were wild.*"

She reached out and held his hands in hers. "Go bring back the dead, Brook, so the living can begin to live."

Brook crossed the lot and started the Double T truck and led the party down the lane and through the gate and out into the road that arrowed whitely away into the rising heat of the Park floor.

200

CHAPTER 16

Grant Pickens was the first to speak when Brook's group found True Jackson standing on the steps of the Como Mercantile. "Well, you ain't got no uglier since I seen you last," is what Grant said to him.

"You Mississippi people always were quick to flatter," True answered, and he fixed on Grant, not acknowledging anyone else in the bunch. At one point, Caleb nodded at True but didn't say anything. Polite sprayed a storm of tobacco juice onto the sidewalk but didn't speak either, and when Brook left the Double T and walked up the steps and into the store, True followed promptly.

The first thing Ess Cohen did after Brook made his request for the Freighter was to take the two men aside and explain that he would be more than pleased to accompany the party as a contracted supplier but did they understand that the store could hardly be expected to pick up Jackson's salary for the actual days the search would take. "I mean, the man won't be in *my* employ on those days, will he?" Cohen asked, looking from one to the other.

Both men agreed and then Brook asked True to supply Ess with a list of the additional supplies that should be loaded into his Freighter, and in what quantity.

True did exactly that, exultantly, as if he had turned some mysterious tables on the storekeeper. "I want fifty feet of half-inch rope," he began, "and again as much three-quarter. I want slings, a pair. I want axes, three of them, double bitted. Blankets I want, one for each man. Nobody ever brings enough blankets when they go into mountains. They must think it's the seashore." He glanced reproachfully at Brook. "And we'll need more food. I know without looking that what the boy brought in his Lizzie won't be enough. I count seven men in the party and I'm well acquainted with the way most of them eat. I want to see more fruit, more biscuits, more beef, some dried meat and some tins. And a big bale of straw."

Cohen's head came up from his order pad. "Did you say a bale of straw?"

"I did. And add a sack of oats and two quarts of whiskey to that list."

"Whiskey?"

"Now don't tell me whiskey's against the law, Mr. Cohen. I've sold six bottles already this week from your Leadville store. I work there, remember? I don't care grits about law, I just want to find the two bottles when I go to look for them." He called out several more items and when he had finished, Brook cashed the draft, paid Ess Cohen, and surrendered most of the remaining money to Jackson.

While the men loaded the Freighter, Brook drove to the offices of the Denver, South Park & Pacific Railroad on the north edge of Como where he was informed by the yard master that the next train to Breckenridge was the High Line over Boreas at two P.M. Brook signed an invoice for the rental of two railcars and then left the office and waited outside. A few minutes later a door in the roundhouse slid open and a locomotive appeared, looking from a distance like a hibernating beast emerging from its cave, shaking off sleep and coughing up the spit of long idleness. It lumbered sulkily to a wye of adjoining tracks and began to shunt railcars back and forth until it had miraculously isolated from the others a stockcar and a flatcar, which were then nudged forward onto a siding. About the time Ess arrived in the yards with the fully loaded Freighter, the switch engine had given a last grumble and retreated to its cave.

With the help of a special ramp Ess drove the Freighter onto the flatcar, where it was chocked into place and chained down front and back. The seven horses were loaded into the stockcar, the seven men trooping in behind them, but just before the two o'clock train climbed up from the floor of the Park into the Como yards, Ess Cohen and Polite decided it was too crowded in the stockcar with all those horses and they crawled back to the flatcar and sat in the front seat of the Freighter.

After a few minutes the High Line train backed down the branch track and coupled the two extra cars onto its rear with a resounding jolt that sent the horses stumbling into each other, wild eyed and fearful. Caleb laughed nervously. "*40 Hommes et 8 Chevaux*. Makes me wonder if I'm not back in France."

The train eventually got underway and the men sat quietly except for Grant Pickens who scurried back and forth between the open doors of the car, swinging his arms and gawking. When the train reached a stretch of severe switchbacks he stuck his head out one side and announced in his chirpy voice that he could see the goddamned front and the goddamned back of this train all at the same goddamned time. "She's puffing and grunting like a mouse passing a stalk of rhubarb," he cried, his dull toothy face red with excitement.

"You'd better sit down," Caleb called out. "You're going to spook those horses. Haven't you ever ridden a train before?"

"Well, you know, I thought I had when I was a kid," Grant answered, addressing all of them where they sat against the walls, "but I must have gotten it mixed up with just watching them go by." His sudden candor was painful. "That can happen, you know. You can watch a thing so many times you actually commence to think—"

"Sit down!" Caleb barked, and everyone stared at him as though they expected to see the command suspended in the air like a separate object. The only one who didn't stare was True Jackson. He sat propped against a stack of saddles at the far end of the car with his soiled campaign hat pulled down over his eyes.

The train passed through a mosaic of meadows and timber, the meadows increasingly showing a lighter green than the timber as though they had melted out from the trees. At a spraddle of shacks that once had been a mining camp the tracks made a tortuous horseshoe up to Windy Point, where the train slowed but did not stop. It climbed to Peabody and then climbed an equivalent distance to the husked shell of Selkirk, and just when it seeemd the train had climbed as far as it could, it climbed again. The meadows gradually vanished. Like exhausted hikers who couldn't keep up, the trees straggled and finally disappeared altogether.

Abruptly, the earth turned darkly colorless. At an elevation of twelve thousand feet the High Line grade mercifully leveled off and the train entered Boreas Pass proper. A house and a shed stood alongside the tracks, as well as some coal bins and a pole for a telegraph that had lost its wires, and a dilapidated water tank. Shortly after that, where the roadbed crossed the base of a steep treeless slope, the railroad tracks disappeared into the protective tunnel of a snowshed.

As they rumbled through the shed, it occurred to Brook that man was at his most audacious when he erected buildings on a mountain pass. They were puny and insignificant and more than buildings they looked like pieces of a rocky peak that had broken off and slid down the slope. Or perhaps an avalanche had swept them along for a time and then dumped them there when the slope gave out. Why did man build that high on a mountain? Who did he think he was that he felt compelled to proclaim his presence in that overwhelming place?

The train emerged from the snowshed and as if it had been waiting to attack, an angry black cloud blew down at them from the peak above. The wind shook the car and the rain whipped through the slatted walls and drenched men and horses alike. Willy Walker peered disgustedly through the sodden mat of hair in his eyes and muttered wearily to Brook, "Why is it that every time I go anywhere with you I get soaking wet?"

After several minutes the rain stopped, but not the wind. It was furious and raw and it rippled the standing water on the floor of the car to show its wrath. "Boreas," muttered Brook, wringing water from his cap, "God of the North Wind. They sure named it right!"

The train rattled through the notch of the mountain for another quarter of a mile with the sky crowding it all the way, and then True Jackson got off his haunches and stood up. "Get the horses to the west end of the car," he ordered. "We're gonna start down the other side of this mountain directly, and I do mean *down!*"

No sooner had they shifted the horses than the train tilted forward and began quickly to pick up speed. The stack of saddles slid the length of the car and slammed into the tangle of horses and knocked two of them completely off their feet. In the middle of the open door Grant Pickens stood riveted with fear. "Get out of that door!" the black ex-sergeant boomed at Grant over the scream of the horses. "We hit a curve and you'll go flying out of here like a wad of shot!"

But Grant remained frozen and only an opposite lurch of the car saved him. His feet went out from under him and he shot across the wet floor and slammed headfirst into the wall. "It's a pure blessing," Jackson announced, kneeling beside the stunned figure. "Now he won't piss his pants!"

Quickly the train settled into a frightening rhythm. It would speed up on a straight stretch of track and then career sickeningly when it reached a curve, teetering for a moment on a breathless lip of space and then righting itself and racing on. On the speeding flatcar, Ess Cohen and Polite sat transfixed in the front seat of the Freighter, their faces bloodless and bulge-eyed, their mouths locked on a scream of terror that no one in the stockcar could possibly have heard. Behind them, in the body of the Freighter, drawers would shoot out of the merchandise cabinets with each new curve in the track, whipping and banging in a kind of mechanical dance as the train tipped first left and then right, the drawers of one side slamming shut just as those on the other side flew open, the contents streaming joyously behind like bunting on a Holiday Special.

But the nightmarish descent ended at last and the curves straightened out into a long diminishing grade. Grant Pickens recovered his senses. The two fallen horses regained their feet and Willy Walker moved reassuringly among them, scratching their manes and rubbing their noses, crooning sweetheart names at them, gentling them down. Tɩue Jackson stood back from the door of the car and contemplated the approaching town. "Breckenridge on the Blue," he announced matter-of-factly.

It took an hour to disembark the horses and the enormous Freighter. When the job was finished, the men stood in the empty railyards and watched the train disappear into the narrow mountain-cramped valley of the Blue River. "We'll angle off to the east from here," True announced, mounting the big stallion, "and try to pick up French Gulch before it gets dark."

Brook stopped him. "Why east? Shouldn't we follow the Blue north until the Swan joins it? Isn't that the route you mentioned to me in Leadville?"

Jackson shook his head with an exaggerated disbelief. "Lord, boy," he said, easing the words with a mawkish grin, "I told you not to put no stock in that story. Don't you know when somebody's waxing your rope?"

They found their way to French Gulch easily enough but when they reached it they stopped immediately. It was involuntary, for what lay before them was a scene of utter desolation. Hydraulic placer mining had churned the stream bed into such a wasteland of gates and channels and sluices that nowhere could be seen even a hint of the original river. Huge piles of gravel tailings rose up from the maze of ponds like trolls demanding tribute from anyone foolhardy enough to seek passage there.

But in a kind of empathy with the stream, perhaps out of mercy, twilight began to veil the butchery of the miners' hoses and the party circled around to a far edge of the gulch and made camp. As they sat around the fire and ate their meal, a few pink fingers of sunset still clung to the crest of the Ten Mile Mountains to the west. It wasn't for long. The fingers lost their grip and slipped down behind the range and a full blackness descended upon the devastated river. Nightlong, no mur-

mur of moving water sounded there. In the morning no beaver scurried about, and no birds came down to meet the sun.

They cleared camp early. The Freighter led the procession with Brook sitting next to Ess in the front seat and True Jackson riding alongside on the big black stallion. Polite and Willy Walker made a pair of horsemen directly behind the truck while Caleb and Grant Pickens brought up the rear.

The day was destined to be hot. The sky looked like a pewter bowl that someone had hammered on and then discarded. To the east, the mountains appeared timid and inconsequential, giving off no sense of mass, reflecting no light. The road skirted the south edge of the ravaged creek but it had trouble holding its track in the numerous washouts and the Freighter's progress was slow. Sometime during the morning Caleb rode up alongside, dour and tight-faced, wanting to know why they hadn't crossed to the other side of the gulch. "It looks like better going over there to me," and he glanced at Brook for confirmation.

Brook refused to intercede. True Jackson obviously heard the remark but ignored it, and after a few minutes Caleb let his horse drift back to the rear of the line.

Gradually the hills began to steepen on both sides of the gulch. Old mining camps rose here and there out of the encroaching scrub with their rotted roof beams thrusting up into the sky like the hands of the dead trying to signal the living as they passed below. The timber thickened and piles of tailings began to spill out onto the slopes in gray lobate shapings; they resembled chunks of cow liver that had been tossed aside at a gigantic butchering and then forgotten. On the point of one of the hills stood a deserted cabin, its windows empty and querulous like the eyes of an abandoned child. The frail structure seemed to be waiting for someone.

They never came, whoever they were.

Midday passed and a baked airless heat rushed down the gulch to meet them. True Jackson kept swiveling around in his saddle, glancing repeatedly behind him and to both sides, and Brook finally called him over to the Freighter. "Seems to me you spend a lot of time looking around."

Jackson's voice was subdued. "Not looking, boy. *Watching*. You been looking. There's a difference."

"Are you going to give me some tracker's savvy now? Will this be a lesson from the grizzled old scout in reading wilderness sign?"

"Pieces," True answered, sliding over the remark, not bothering to look at Brook, "I'm watching for pieces. And not just one piece by itself. There's got to be two or three together to mean anything. That old gallows frame this morning, for example," and he acknowledged Brook now. "I seen you studying that frame like you was going to put it to memory."

"So?"

"This country's got a hundred gallows frames in it. Question is, which one's the right one? Which is the one that tells you you're in French Gulch and not Lincoln Draw?"

Brook didn't answer.

"As it turns out, you had the right frame but you didn't know it. You didn't pick up your companion piece. Your positive proof."

Brook merely looked at him.

"It was that rock outcrop on the hill directly across the gulch from the frame. The one that looked like a cat's head. You didn't see it. I did, that's the difference. They go together, those two pieces. Cat's head and gallows frame. If they're not together then you're not in French Gulch and your ass is lost." His voice had picked up some intensity. "Do you see what I'm saying, boy? Pieces. Pieces together. You use them right and they'll draw you a map in your mind that's a hundred times clearer than any drawn on paper."

Later in the afternoon they came to a place where a minuscule rivulet of water had trickled down into a rock terrace and formed a pool big enough to water the horses, which they did. The road gave out a short time after leaving the terrace and an island of brush rose up and split the gulch like a boulder splits creek water, but it sank back into the earth after half a mile and the gulch veered noticeably to the southeast. Brook transferred from the Freighter to his buckskin and rode ahead with True into the gulch to inspect it, and when they came back out True called for a stop. On their left stood a hill that was shingled from top to bottom with tailings, and at the base of this hill they made a cooking fire and prepared a meal.

When they had finished eating, Willy cleaned up the area and Ess filled the Freighter with gas and checked the oil, wanting to make sure, he said, "that the vehicle was in good morning order." Apart from the occasional pop of the fire, the stillness in the gulch was total. Shadows crept in and formed a circle around them like nightriders who had drifted down from the hills, hoping to share their camp. What talk there was was flat and brief and sprawled with fatigue, like the men themselves. Ess Cohen quickly fell asleep in the Freighter seat. Grant produced a pint bottle of whiskey which he emptied quickly and broke on a distant rock. True Jackson fussed with his black horse. He fed the animal a half-bucket of oats and then broke open the bale of straw and rubbed him down with it. In another bucket he prepared a mixture of whiskey and water and washed the horse all over, then rubbed him dry with more of the straw. Next he shook out two blankets and covered the stallion with one and himself with the other, stretching out on the ground beneath the animal's belly.

Caleb sat across the fire from Brook, its light dancing in his eyes, giving the bland face a vital quality it ordinarily lacked. Without True Jackson to watch, without anything to watch but the fire, Caleb was obviously moved to start a conversation. "Wouldn't you like to be home right about now, Brookers?"

"Who wouldn't?"

"Sitting on the porch swing or on the bench in the lawn, talking to Margaret?"

The question struck Brook as more of an impertinence than a pleasantry and he wouldn't answer, but Caleb was intent on continuing. "Have I detected on your part more than just a passing interest in the lovely young lady from Kansas City?"

Again the words scraped at Brook and this time he made no effort to keep silent. "You'd have to be blind not to see that." He looked across the flames at Caleb. "You're not blind, are you?"

"We can all be blind," Caleb answered, "especially where the fair sex is concerned." His tone had changed. He didn't seem offended by Brook's bluntness but his words were stiff now, almost embarrassed. "You just need to be a little careful, Brookers, that's all I'm saying. After all, Margaret's . . . married. Married and working at it, I'm sure. Minister and all. A situation like that could be awkward if it got away from you."

"I don't think that's any of your business."

Caleb went on talking as if he hadn't heard. "You might do better checking out some of those Denver girls. Did you ever think of that? There's some real lookers down there, as I'm sure you noticed." He attempted a laugh. "Good material to build a nest with. Start a family, that sort of thing."

Brook had been leaning back on his elbow and now sat up. "Good advice, Uncle. Why didn't you follow it yourself? I should think you'd have wanted a wife and kids at one time. Settle down, feet on the floor, bed of your own, that sort of thing. How come you didn't practice what you preach when you had the chance?"

The fire spat pine resin nervously, heightening the silence around them. Caleb sat stonily, giving himself to the fire again, gripping his coffee cup. Watching him, Brook was reminded of a snapshot Caleb had brought home from the war. He and several Doughboys from the Rainbow Division were mugging for the camera in front of a canteen they had captured from the Germans, holding up battered metal drinking cups under a sign which read *Kantine 2 Kamp Batl 61*. The Americans were clowning and cheery and Caleb was clutching the Kraut cup in his right hand like a desperately won trophy. Now he was half a world away, sitting grim and circumspect at a dying fire in a darkened gulch, and the cup was in his left hand, the only hand he had.

* * *

Breakfast was a hurried talkless affair. Once they were underway, the road disintegrated into no more than a crude trail. Ahead of them the heat rose up from the earth in bulbs of cloud that tumbled feverishly across the sky, darkening as they rose.

Sometime later the gulch narrowed and the brush clotted up as though in some peevish conspiracy to block their way. Ess Cohen swore at the terrain and the truck and the whole endeavor in general. Beside him in the seat, Brook's eyes stung with sweat and the gasoline-sweet smell of the laboring engine threatened to make him sick. The American flags on the Freighter's twin struts hung straight down in the heat. Somewhere far ahead a roll of thunder sounded.

After another hour's going, True Jackson rode up alongside the truck and removed his hat and wiped at his head with a rag. He sat his horse heavily and without grace, his eyes puffed and rheumy. The old cavalry jacket he wore had never been washed; sun and rain and too many summers of sweat had faded it to a mottled gray. Watching him, Brook realized that True Jackson had grown old, old and harried in a life that had lost all its fixed points. This frayed dumpy horse soldier was a relic of an obsolete time, a man clinging to a history that was losing its relevance. Pointing at the horizon, he spoke to Brook in a voice thick with fatigue. "You'd best get ready for a new way of seeing things, boy. What I'm showing you is the back side of the Divide. What you been looking at all your life is the front."

"Right."

"That peak off to your left, there in the north, you know which one that is?"

Brook didn't answer.

"That's Guyot." The extended arm moved south. "What you figure the next one is, that bald one?"

"Big Red."

"Right. And that finger ridge connecting the two, would you say that was your Saddle Pass?"

Brook peered intently, then nodded in agreement.

True restored the hat to his head with an air of resigned

accomplishment. "That's where you wanted to go, boy," he mumbled grittily, "to that cliff bottom below Saddle. And that's where I'm taking you."

Thunder sounded intermittently, petulant and indecisive like an old dog growling from beneath a porch, unwilling to come out into the sun and take a stand, not yet, not at this distance.

At some point in late morning a grave appeared abruptly at the base of the east bank, an ancient grave with its bed sunken badly but with the rusted metal bars of its cross still intact. It slipped quickly behind the caravan but in the heat and the drowsy hypnotic grinding of the Freighter's transmission, Brook's thoughts stayed with the grave. In a big land where location and event were almost accidental, someone had insisted on erecting a cross, a cross not of wood but of metal, knowing metal would endure, wanting it to last. Why? Why in a life often wayward and haphazard did man insist that its end be so precisely remembered? What was there about death that man had to honor and commemorate it? Or was it death at all?

The thunder growled again, and again after that, stalking their caravan now like a beast they could not see. Sometime in the afternoon, long after all hope of ever leaving that blistering tunnel of heat had faded, the banks of the gulch abruptly disappeared and the floor lifted and they drove up and out of that plodding mole run of earth into the free space and vision of a mountain meadow. It was a magic escape. An unbelievable puff of breeze struck them. The horses shook their head harness at it and the men looked up in unison, seeking its source. They saw immediately that it came from where the thunder had come, from the mountains. The sky above the Divide had gathered into a purple mass—knotty, pendulous, looking like the swollen udders of a dreadful she-beast who had slouched across the mountains searching for a birthing den.

They climbed the meadow for a quarter of a mile and then disappeared into a timbered cathedral world that enveloped them completely. The floor of the forest was a carpet of needles, its dome the towering top growth of lodgepole pine, and their caravan of horses and motor truck wound soundlessly through the rays of almost spiritual light that occasionally broke through. It was a welcome sanctuary, however unreal. They had hidden for a brief moment from the hovering storm; the prowling dogs of thunder could not find them there.

The refuge was short-lived. The forest thinned and they were out of it quickly, breaking onto a ridge full of dead bristlecone pine and a scatter of bone-white snags. Brook watched True Jackson ride out onto the ridge alone to scout the terrain and then turn to come back. The great black stallion reared and screamed and pawed the air and just for a moment, silhouetted against the storm, he seemed some fierce portentous steed from a dark mythology. "We'll camp here," True announced when he had rejoined the main party at the Freighter. "That way, we'll be close to the timber in case those clouds yonder decide to do something ugly." Even as he spoke, a dense roiling lobe of the storm broke off from the principal mass and began to move slowly toward them, a double rainbow out in front.

They built a fire and made a rope corral in the edge of the trees for the horses. After he had eaten, Brook caught Willy Walker's eye and motioned for him to follow and they moved downslope from the camp and sat on the ground next to a pad of dwarf willow. Darkness had begun to well up from the canyons below them like a flood of black water. "Sometime tomorrow," Brook began, "we'll reach that cliff bottom where the body is. It's time to go over the plan I've worked out."

Willy shrugged tiredly, his face as stained and blotched as sweated leather. "Why?"

"I need some evidence. I've got to have more to go on than what you've told me about it being Caleb who heard the sound."

"Christ, you still on that?"

"What the hell do you think we came over here for?"

"To get your old man's body out of those rocks so we can bury it. What else?"

Brook lit a cigarette and took a couple of quick drags. "The way the plan works, it's like a play, only I'm not the leading actor. You are. I want you to listen good because there won't be time tomorrow to go over it again."

Willy moaned grumpily.

"The minute we spot the body I want you to go right up to it. You've got to be out in front of the group and get to the body before anyone else does."

The blackness from the canyons below had finally reached the top of the ridge. The stillness around them was unnatural. There was no air. Nothing moved. Brook could no longer see Willy clearly, he was a shadow beside him in the grass, nothing more. "Why the hell do I have to be the first one to the body?" Willy demanded. It was pure whining resentment.

"If there was a murder that day instead of an accident then it had to happen on that first split when Caleb and Grant rode off by themselves after the storm—"

"What murder? What are you talking about?"

"Listen to me! If those two were in this together I figure they had to separate for a minute or so, one to stand guard and the other to kill Papa and push him and the gray off the cliff. They didn't dare shoot him because the rest of you would have heard the shot."

"What are you saying?" Willy's voice had become shrill. "Why in hell would they want to push Aaron Hartman off the cliff, for Christ's sake? Caleb and Aaron were *brothers!*"

"Keep your voice down, damn it!"

"Well, make sense then! You talk like you been chewing peyote buds."

"Damn it, Willy, will you trust me just once to know what I'm talking about? You don't have to agree, you just have to listen. Can you do that for me?"

Willy grunted but said nothing. Out of the darkness, thunder rumbled like a heavy wagon moving on an unseen road.

"The plan is this," Brook said, beginning again. "The minute you reach the body you bend over and act like you're studying it. Understand? Then you stand up and shout real loud so everyone can hear—*Aaron was shot! He's got a bullet hole in his head!* You really sing it out."

214

"How could he be shot, for Christ's sake? You just got done saying—"

"He wasn't shot, damn it! It's make believe we're doing here. A skit. A play. Papa wasn't killed with a bullet but we're going to pretend he was. When you holler out that he was shot, the man who stood guard that day is going to be so confused that for a second he'll forget himself and look right at the killer." He paused for breath. "Do you understand, Willy? He'll look at the killer and I'll be able to see his face. I'll know who it was."

In the fragmented vision that the lightning allowed them, Brook could see Willy shake his head. "That's all the plan you got?" He took in a ragged breath and let it out. "Jesus, man, that ain't much."

"I never had much to begin with. Just what you told me about the sound. It all comes down to that. It was either a lie or it wasn't. There was a murder done that day or it was an accident. But I've got to know."

Willy didn't answer. Without the lightning flashes he was merely part of the night.

After a few minutes of silence, Brook ordered Willy to turn in and get some sleep, and when he had gone Brook spread his own blankets just inside the timber. The wind moved restlessly in the tops of the trees as though it had seen the campfire from a long way off and had come to investigate, but clumsily, not knowing what fire was or how to approach it. Brook watched the lightning make a slide show of the trees surrounding him and then closed his eyes and let his thoughts fill with Margaret. It was a relief to think of her, this woman who was so delightful naked, bigger everywhere than she looked with her clothes on, but not big, this woman whose eyes could darken instantly when she was angry or excited . . . flat black hair so prim at the neck . . . smooth upper arms . . . the surprising breasts. . . .

Suddenly she came to him, vividly, cleanly, like a white dove flying out of thunder. *Go bring back the dead, Brook, so the living can begin to live* He reached for her but she became a black horse whose eyes were made of lightning, a bolt of lightning that split his sleep before the sleep closed over it. Another bolt came, tearing apart the wind. Fiery rods of light ripped the sky and suddenly six white riders filled a mountain canyon. One of the six, a specter, raised his hand and a black fork of storm dropped down and speared one of the riders and plucked him from the earth. Death for him. Irrevocable. *Go bring back the dead, Brook, so the living.* . . .

A blade of lightning slashed a nearby pine and split it with a great roar and burst of fire, tumbling Brook out of the timber into the darkness. As if the doomed tree had contained water, rain exploded onto the ridge in a torrent of fury. The men raced to the truck and struggled to don their slickers. The lightning struck again, cracking open a second tree, and the horses screamed in terror.

"Get . . . horses . . . out of . . . the trees!" Brook shouted, but his words were drowned in the tempest.

Full of the earth's heat and tortured by surging columns of air, the rain turned to hail and flayed them viciously. Stumbling and cursing, the men managed to lead the horses into open ground where they reared and pawed the air at each new stab of lightning. The air smelled burned and coppery. Electricity danced on the metal edges of the truck, on the barrel racks, the windshield posts, the louvers in the hood. Huddled among the horses, the men could feel it stir their hair and see it hop in thin blue arcs along the line of rivets in the bridle harness. Like a crazy man shuttering a lantern, the lightning caught the men and the animals and the great spires of timber in a weird montage of silver images.

The wind was the first to stop. Sometime after midnight the mix of rain and hail subsided and the lightning strikes grew weak and the storm slunk away into a distant part of its own darkness, as if it feared the dawn.

When the first light came the men counted the horses and inspected the Freighter and in a tiny space between where the campfire had been and the edge of the timber they found the round-faced prairie horseman, Willy Walker, dead on the ground in his yellow slicker.

They buried him at full light just inside the trees, in a shallow grave they spaded out of the sodden pine-smelly earth.

They removed their hats and Caleb spoke a few words, mumbling them badly: "Man cometh forth like a flower and is cut down. Seeing his days are determined, Thou hast appointed him bounds that he cannot pass. . . ."

"Jesus," Brook whispered. "Jesus Christ, Willy."

CHAPTER 17

After the burial they ate tinned meat and biscuits and fruit and drank hot coffee and no man there looked directly at another, nor did he speak. Before they finished breaking camp a wind came up briefly and blew the last remnants of cloud from the sky as though it meant to allow no witnesses to the night's events.

The caravan followed a crude road down off the ridge and immediately entered a wasteland of sand and rocks and barren canyons. There was no evidence that rain had ever fallen on this part of the earth. It seemed an alien place, a land protective of its seclusion and enraged at the encroachment of strange horsemen and a clamorous motor truck, and it expressed that rage by greeting them with a savage heat.

True Jackson had a choice of main canyons but settled on one that angled southeast. No trees grew within it. There was no grass, no brush. The canyon floor was hot sand and the walls were columned and combed like burned out coal. "Jesus Christ in the creek bed!" Grant Pickens exclaimed. "This ain't no canyon. It's a furnace!"

"I figured there might be one or two natural wonders you hadn't come across yet," True replied, but the sarcasm in his voice was muted. It was the first conversation of the morning and he seemed pleased with the chance to talk. His black face shone like wet pitch and his tunic was already spotted with sweat. He glanced into the depths of the canyon and up at the Divide and then to Ess Cohen in the Freighter. "How much water we got left in them barrels, Mr. Cohen?"

"Less than half what we started with," came Cohen's reply, his voice tight with concern. "I don't know if it'll last in this blasted inferno or not."

"It might last," True answered, savoring his position, his authority, "and then again it might not. This country ain't like no other. The Mexican, he named it *malpais*. My old troop in the thirteenth called it Bad Duty. But whatever name you give it, it just flat don't belong here. Arizona maybe, maybe New Mexico, but not here." He eyed the line of riders waiting for him. "What it is, actually, is one of them tricks God plays on His children from time to time. I figure He doesn't want us getting too comfortable. He tells us we need water to live and then makes us travel through land that don't have any. Maybe it's a tribulation He's putting us through instead of a trick. That's what He did to the children of Israel, you know. Aggravated the hell out of them. No way they could figure out how to please Him."

From the front seat of the truck, Brook laughed derisively. "This is no search party, it's a Free School. Geography lessons, map reading, Bible texts, you name it, we got it." He zeroed in on True then. "But I suggest that for right now you teach a class in not wasting any of the water we've got left."

"Waste not, want not," True came back, obviously trying to keep the conversation going. "Isn't that how the old saying goes, boy? Isn't that from the Bible? Are you acquainted with the Bible?" He grinned impudently, seeming to invite a reaction not only from Brook but from the others as well, something that might work a delay. It didn't succeed. Brook reached over and released the truck's huge hand brake and instructed Cohen to move ahead.

The Freighter's tires dragged heavily at the sand, slowing the procession considerably. A thread of breeze would occasionally unravel from the spool of heat in the canyon and flutter tantalizingly around them, but it wouldn't last.

After another hour's going they stopped completely, their

throats choked on the cotton of heat. The horses shook their heads angrily and tongued the harsh bits that gagged their mouths. A sliver of shade protruded from one side of the Freighter and the riders congregated there. Cohen took down the buckets and watered the horses while the men sucked at pieces of dried fruit and gulped down a rationed half-dipper of the tepid water. "Damn," Polite groaned, refilling his mouth with shreds of pouch tobacco, "I wish I'd saved some of that Columbia River water, even the stuff I soaked my feet in. I'd dump it all over my head. Right now!" He worked the tobacco up in his mouth and managed a preliminary spit that looked like a tenuous brown vine had sprouted from his lips and was seeking the ground. "How much further we got, Itty Bitty?" he asked, wiping his chin, snipping the vine completely.

Brook nodded toward Jackson. "I suggest you ask our Bible quoting guide that question."

But Polite wouldn't look at Jackson, let alone ask for information, and the caravan gathered itself reluctantly and crept forward again.

In a matter of minutes they came to their first tributary canyon. It stretched straight east to the base of the mountains, scorched and brittle. Above it, a raven coasted on an unseen column of air. He belonged to the canyon, he was part of the heat, part of the silence.

"Drier than granny's tits in there," Grant exclaimed, peering in, shielding his eyes from the sun. "Let's keep going."

The caravan passed in quick succession a pair of identical canyons and then intersected a third. It was narrow and rock-jammed and at its far end stood a sheer cliff face, its bottom lost in rocks and the watery ripples of heat, its top a towering cliff edge a thousand feet high.

"That's it," True Jackson announced, looking directly at Brook. "That's your canyon."

The entire party shifted apprehensively in their seats and studied it. A line of boulders sat in the canyon's mouth like a set of broken teeth. "We ain't getting no truck in there," declared Polite bluntly. "No horse either. And no man, unless he's skinny enough to scootch sideways between those boulders."

It was an accurate assessment. The canyon was completely blocked by boulders, although those at the north end appeared to be smaller. Grant Pickens tugged importantly at the straps of his leather helmet and pointed at the smaller boulders. "We can jump the horses over."

True grunted contemptuously. "You never was wrapped real tight, Pickens, otherwise you'd see that can't be done. Those rocks ain't only higher than they look, they're deeper. We'd high center the first horse we sent over. He'd just teeter back and forth and wiggle his legs at us, even the ones that was busted." True surveyed the line of boulders embedded in the canyon sand. "Horses can't jump over, truck can't drive in, and we got to have one or the other. So what does that leave us?" He removed a rag from inside his tunic and wiped fretfully at his neck. "We brought those slings and pullies." It was as if he were alone now, talking to himself. "If we rigged the ropes properly we could maybe raise the horses over those rocks at the south end and drop them inside. That's one possibility."

"And a foolish one," Brook broke in. "Even if we could rig the slings it would take too long." He turned to Ess Cohen in the seat beside him. "You've got half a dozen planks chained to the sides of this truck. What kind of condition are they in?"

Cohen answered that the planks were in excellent condition, that he had used them on several occasions to ford creeks and shore up bridges, as well as to build a temporary ramp over railroad tracks so he could cross the Freighter.

"Then that's how we cross those boulders," Brook declared. "We build a ramp. We build it out of those planks and some of this sand and we walk the horses over one at a time. Anybody want to argue?"

It took an hour of steady labor by the whole party and half that time again to reassure the horses and lead them across the narrow planking to the other side. True Jackson was the last to cross and when he was safely on the other side Brook walked back to the Freighter with Cohen. "Whatever happens," Brook said to him, "don't leave this spot until I get back."

Cohen started to speak and then didn't finish. When they reached the Freighter he stood at the steps to the cab and studied Brook from beneath the brim of the floppy hat he wore. "You'd better prepare yourself," he said to Brook. "Your father's body won't be what you expect. It won't be very pleasant for you in there."

"I know that."

"I don't think you do. I think there's a lot of things you don't know. I doubt if you ever saw what time and this kind of heat can do to a body that's been all busted up. You'll smell it long before you see it. It won't be anything you recognize from the family picture album."

Brook stared at Ess. The man's face was streaked with dust and sweat and the narrow deepset eyes glistened with tiny points of light. It struck Brook that there was a private Ess Cohen that stood apart from the public merchant everyone knew, and that he was seeing him now. Some strange sort of discipline marked him, a history Brook could only guess at, and for a moment he was strengthened by it. Then he walked back to the boulders and crossed over and joined the four mounted men waiting for him on the other side.

Heat clotted the canyon. There was an overpowering smell of scorched sand, of the peculiar sweetness of plants that grow without water. A dust rose up from the ground as they rode over it, clinging to their sweat like metal fines to a magnet.

Caleb and the two others rode ahead with the spare horse and Brook and True Jackson followed fifty yards behind. They had penetrated the canyon perhaps a quarter of a mile when True's black horse abruptly lurched to the side. True went flying off and struck the ground hard, his breath exploding from him, his saddle breaking free and landing on top of his body. Brook slid from the buckskin and ran to him, pulling the saddle off. "What the hell?"

"Cinch," True grunted, struggling up, his eyes big with surprise. "Cinch gave way." He stood on one leg but nearly fell when he attempted to put weight on the other one. "Hip," he muttered, clutching Brook's shoulder. "Feels like she's pushed in." He tried stepping down again but the pain stopped him. "The leg won't take no stepping on, boy," he said with a grimace. "Better leave me."

"Bullshit. I need you."

"Not anymore. You're where you wanted to go. There's less than a mile left." He peered up the heat-smothered canyon to where the three riders had stopped and were looking back at them.

"Why would the damned cinch bust loose?" Brook wanted to know.

True shrugged heavily and in the stillness it was practically a sound. "I'll wait for you here," he said. "Nothing's broken but the hip's popped for sure. I can pop her back but it needs time. You go on."

Brook got back up on the buckskin and rejoined the others, pushing immediately to the front. After several hundred yards the canyon floor climbed a slight talus slope and then leveled off again and ahead of them Brook could see the cliff face clearly. No jut or crevice or stunted tree broke its surface at any point. It exploded straight up out of the earth, catching the sun and flashing it back like a giant mirror. Brook closed his eyes and an old dreamlike terror projected the vision of two bodies slipping silently over the edge of the cliff, infinitely tiny bodies tumbling end over end in a grotesque slow motion, sinking into air that would not hold them, growing in size to become at last the brown twig of a man and the gray ball of a horse, both doomed to perish on a merciless ground before they ever struck it.

But they weren't there.

In all those acres of rock at cliff bottom the two bodies were nowhere to be found. There was no trace of them, horse nor man. Brook searched frantically among the boulders but not a shred of flesh or cloth or bone revealed itself. There was only the heat and the blinding glare of the sun against the cliff, and the ancient violated stillness.

The three remaining riders drew up in a line across the edge of the empty rock field in front of Brook and glared at him. Polite worked his jaws and then spoke. "There ain't no Aaron Hartman in this canyon," he said, sending a surly splat of tobacco juice onto the surface of a nearby rock. "There ain't now and there never was."

The four riders turned away from the cliff and headed back out of the canyon, picking their way over the little talus step and across the desolate empty dust toward where they had started. As they rode, Grant Pickens gradually eased his horse alongside Brook's. "You lied," he hissed acidly. "You lied about seeing your old man's body at the bottom of that cliff."

Brook yanked his feet from the stirrups and pushed off from his saddle and threw himself at Grant, knocking him from his horse and onto the ground, Brook on top. He grabbed Grant by the straps of his helmet and pushed his face into the scalding dirt of the canyon floor and held it there. But immediately an arm encircled Brook's neck from behind and pulled him off, twisting his arm behind him so that he was powerless to move.

It was Polite.

Grant flopped over onto his back, tearing at his throat with both hands and blowing sand from his mouth. Caleb got down from the little roan gelding he rode and approached them. "Anyone can make a mistake," he said, addressing the struggling Grant. "He can believe he saw something that wasn't there. That's what happened to Brook. Now get back on your horse and let this be." He watched Grant obey the order and then turned to Brook. "Are you all right?"

Brook grunted.

"Do you think you can quit jumping people? If the answer is yes than I'll ask Polite to let you go." Brook grunted again and Polite released him. "Now let's get back to the truck," Caleb said, "and get us a dipperful of that water. It may be warm as piss but it's bound to be wet."

The four of them remounted and rode back without speaking further. Ess Cohen was waiting for them at the Freighter but True Jackson was not. "Where is he?" Brook asked.

"Strangest damned thing," Cohen replied. "Jackson came riding out of the canyon and up over the planks on that big black stud looking like one of the Furies. Scared the hell out of me."

"*On* the horse?" Brook demanded. "*Saddled?*"

"Hell, yes, saddled. What else would he be?"

"He couldn't be saddled. He had a busted cinch. And a hip to go with it."

Ess Cohen pushed his hat back from his face. "Not the Jackson I saw. He didn't have a busted anything. He filled a couple canteens with water and grabbed a bag of grain and got back up on the horse."

"What did he say to you?"

"Nothing. Not a word. He just jammed his heels into that stallion and raced the hell out of here. And he didn't look back, I can guarantee you that."

None of them spoke. Caleb had a curious look on his face. From somewhere far off there sounded a plaintive whistle of wind.

They watered the horses and recovered the planks and Ess got the Freighter turned around somehow in the soft sand and they started back, retracing their path of the morning. Brook rode by himself in the rear of the procession, watching the tracks in the sand. Just before they reached the end of the canyon a rock dislodged from the rim somewhere behind him, but he did not look back. He heard the rock hit the wall of the canyon and stop and fall again, and then strike once more lower down, going from silence to sound and back to silence sporadically, like the breathing of someone who is dying.

CHAPTER 18

"The simple truth," Brook said to Margaret, "is that Caleb's not involved. He never was."

It was late morning of Brook's first day back and they were in Margaret's room. Brook had come in from Como around midnight, driving the Double T Ford he had left at the Merc that first day, and once in her room he had collapsed on the bed with his clothes still on. Now he was awake and sipping the cup of hot coffee she had brought up from the kitchen for him. "This trip proves it, Mag, once and for all. We were just flat wrong about Caleb."

She sat quietly on the edge of the bed next to Brook, smoothing her skirt over her knees, watching the level of coffee in his cup and resolving to keep even a hint of suspicion out of whatever she said to him. She failed. Brook's renewed defense of Caleb returned her unavoidably to her original stand. "But so many strange things happened," she said, trying to mute it, not looking directly at Brook. "Willy Walker's death. True Jackson's running away."

Brook tipped the cup to his mouth again. "Caleb had nothing to do with them. It was just coincidence. Things can be coincidence."

Again she chose her words with care, trying to keep her voice free of argument or protest. "Caleb told your mother and me in the kitchen this morning that we had to be patient with you now." She waited for an outburst from Brook but none came, and she went on. "Caleb said that things would eventually get back to normal but that for the time being you were going through a period of doubt and confusion and that we had to be patient. He said he knew you hadn't lied about seeing the body of your father at the bottom of the cliff, although it might seem that way to some. You had only a fraction of a second to see anything before you fell over the edge and he believes that the light color you saw at the bottom was probably a boulder rather than a horse. He said the rock field over there had a few such boulders in it, that he'd seen them himself." She watched Brook drink. "Caleb asked us to be understanding. He said you were ashamed and disappointed both, that's why you attacked Grant. He called it pure old-fashioned frustration."

Brook kept his mouth pressed against the rim of the cup as though he were resting it there.

Margaret was equally quiet for a moment, equally reflective. "Still," she went on, the suspicion finally breaking free, "Caleb had to be surprised that the bodies weren't at the bottom of the cliff. Regardless of anything else, guilty or innocent, whether he was party to pushing the bodies off the cliff or honestly believes the storm did it, he had to be surprised when the bodies weren't in the rocks." She looked at Brook and waited. "Was he, Brook? Was Caleb surprised?"

Brook drank from the cup. "I don't know. I didn't watch his face. I'd hoped to see both his and Grant's because I had this plan worked out with Willy, a kind of trick for when we came onto the body. But I never got the chance. Willy was dead by then."

"Do you think he was deliberately killed? To protect himself, could Caleb have—?"

"Protect himself from what?" Brook turned and looked at her, the old incredulity thick in his voice and his face. "Caleb didn't do anything. He wasn't involved. Why would he be afraid of Willy?"

"Because it was Willy who stumbled onto the lie in the canyon that day."

Brook took in a breath and let it out. "Caleb didn't know

about Willy's story before and he didn't learn about it on the trip, so how could he act on it?" He shook his head at her. "No, Mag, the lightning got Willy. It could have gotten any one of us but it picked him. The Fates reached in. Willy was in the wrong place at the wrong time and it burned him out pure and simple." Brook started to take another sip of coffee as a sort of summation but then he stopped and began to stare into the cup instead. "Think about this, Mag," he said, turning to her, a new intensity in his voice. "Just for the sake of the argument, let's say that Caleb actually did kill Papa. Okay? Let's say he did it so he could have this place for himself, so he could take over the business." He eyed her sharply. "Concentrate on that a minute. Look at it real hard. Is Caleb home free? Has he got the place? No, he hasn't, because he's still got *me*. He's still got the murdered man's son. I'm alive and kicking and smack dab in his way. If Caleb murdered Papa why hasn't he murdered me too?" His voice rose. "He's had half a dozen good chances, my God! He could have gone down to Denver and slipped a knife in me while I was asleep in my room. He had the address from my letter and could have been back before morning. Not only that, he could have ambushed me on Mosquito Pass when I went to find Jackson. And how about the biggest opportunity of all? How about that day on Saddle when I fell over the edge? He could have finished me off in front of witnesses, for God's sake! All he'd had to do is not grab the rope, just let it run down the apron and I'm dead and gone just like that!" and he gave his fingers an emphatic snap. But he quieted immediately, as if he were capable of nothing more than that short burst of energy. "No, Mag," he said, and the resignation was back in his voice, "what we've got here, what we've had all along, is coincidence."

Margaret repeated the earlier deliberate smoothing motion on her skirt. "I wish I could convince myself to put as much faith in coincidence as you do."

"It's just another word for pieces," Brook said, looking out the window now. "Pieces can mean something or they can mean nothing, it all depends on what you put with them. True explained that to me and it made sense."

She shot Brook a quick glance. "And that's another problem. How about True? Why did he run off on you? Is that a piece like the others? Another coincidence?"

Brook didn't delay. "I think True got scared. Scared about what happened to Willy and about us burying his body on that godforsaken ridge. Scared of the other body he expected to find at the foot of the cliff. All of a sudden there's too many bodies and he can't handle it and he runs away." He gave a weak laugh. "Reminds me of that blackface skit I saw at the Pantages in Denver. The main comic was always scared and whenever something especially spooky happened to him he'd stand there on the stage and begin to roll his eyes. Then he'd flap his arms and pump his legs and just before he started to run he'd holler *Feet, don't fail me now!* That's what happened to True Jackson, Mag. The only difference is, True had a horse." Brook pushed himself up from the bed and placed the empty coffee cup on the dresser and slumped down beside her.

She took that moment to ask Brook what his plans were, what he was going to do next.

"I've got to find Papa. He's still up there on the mountain somewhere. This trip proves that. I want to bring him back and bury him next to Grandpa and then I want to forget it. Forget everything. I want to get back to normal again, like Caleb's always saying. I want to take you to Denver for a weekend. Maybe a whole week. We'll get a nice room at the Oxford Hotel. I'll take you to Boulder on the Electric. Show you the prairie from the top of the D & F tower. You can see practically all the way to Kansas. And I want to go out to School of Mines and enroll for the fall term." He tried a smile. "I still can't tell pyrites from gold. I never will if I don't get working on it."

"Brook—"

"I didn't make it out to Mines when I was in Denver before, when I was there alone. I guess I don't do well alone." The smile died and a perplexed look took its place. "God, that seems so long ago. Like something I did when I was young." He lifted his hands and rubbed his eyes and then let his hands collapse into his lap.

She immediately took hold of his arm. "Oh, Brook, you look so tired! Won't you try to sleep some more? Please?" She pulled his head down into her lap and stroked the hair at the back of his neck. "I forgot," she whispered. "I forgot your hair. It seems as if it's grown twice as long. I need to trim it."

"Yes," he said, and closed his eyes.

She could feel his whole body start to relax against hers, feel the submission of it. "Those things you mentioned, Brook, Denver . . . Golden . . . we'll do them. But we won't stop there. We'll do more." Her words began to tumble. "We'll drive into Fairplay so I can register to vote. I need to do that now that I've got the right. We'll go to one of the pastures and look up the colt, the one we weaned, the one that tripped you. Remember? We'll ride up to the crooked wood again and I'll show you I'm not afraid of things as I was. And we'll stop in Left Hand and look for our mountain lion, our cougar. Maybe she'll be lying out on that ledge with her babies this time. In the sun." She gave a tiny contained sob and buried her face in the mat of his hair. "I love you so, Brook. You're what I waited for all my life. I knew you were out there in the world but I couldn't find you. I didn't know how to look. How to wait. Now I don't have to. You're here and I'm here and we can start our life together. From this moment on, Brook."

But he didn't hear her words. He couldn't. He was asleep.

Brook slept until late afternoon, still in his clothes, and then got up and changed and left the house. There was no one about that he could see. He saddled the buckskin and caught out an extra horse and tied them both to the rear of the Double T stake bed truck. Then he drove to Right Hand Canyon.

It was strange, the way the thing developed. It was a miraculous unfolding, some logic was involved certainly but mostly it was pure chance, and Brook marveled at it when he thought about it later. It had started with his remembering almost idly a conversation he'd had with Etch on the train coming back from Denver that Sunday.

Ponds.

The old Basque herder had mentioned getting into a gulch during the search that had a string of ponds in it. Brook remembered because Etch's description had been so unusual, colorful almost, which was rare for him. He'd said that the ponds—two or three, he couldn't remember the exact number —were so incredibly blue that it was as if tiny pieces of the sky had fallen to the earth, that the sky was actually ice and the pieces had melted there to make the ponds.

That was a lot of poetry for Arranz Etchevarl.

Now, driving in the lower stretches of Right Hand Canyon, the memory of that poetry and that conversation gradually edged back into Brook's thoughts, and remained there. Maybe it was the Double T's engine noise bouncing off the canyon's narrow walls that coaxed up the recall, that made him think of that noisy Sunday train and the old man's imagery. Whatever, the picture was in his mind now and would not go away.

Blue ponds.

It was a piece, he supposed. Was there another that went with it? True had said there had to be. And where? Brook knew the area left of the canyon quite well but vaguely now he remembered a slope somewhere on the less familiar right, heavily timbered, deeply gulched, forming the more primitive Jefferson Creek headwaters under the eastern lip of the Divide. Maybe the blue ponds. . . .

Brook decided that to go all the way up Right Hand was the best approach. Go to the top and then turn and come down. Better vision that way. Easier going.

He left the truck at the stone shed and mounted the buckskin, leading the spare. He crossed Saddle Pass and then stopped to get his bearings beneath the single rock pinnacle that stood at the opposite end. The rock was perhaps sixty feet high and surrounded at the base by a cluster of boulders that looked as if they'd been put there deliberately to support it against the wind. The rock was granite and the tiny flakes of mica would sometimes catch sunlight and reflect it back, Brook remembered, as if the pinnacle were a jeweled tower marking the entrance to a fairyland. But when in shadow the pinnacle stood stark and forbidding, more the grim outer fortress of a

mysterious kingdom than anything. What actually did lie beyond the rock pinnacle were the stands of Englemann spruce
that Polite and Caleb favored, and additional meadows.

Brook left the shaft of rock—magic tower or brooding fort,
it didn't make the difference now that it had when he was a
boy—and turned to the right and followed the edge of the
lowest meadow. Several gullies led off from it, born and nursed
by the steeper grades on that side. They were sinuous and
narrow and gorged now with summer's brittle growth. Brook
dismounted. In the second gully, he saw the ponds.

There were two of them and he almost missed them, for they
were blue no longer. Summer had gutted them, leached them
out, made of them dank scummy pots that only midges would
attend.

Brook got down from the buckskin and approached the first
pond. It was much diminished, its edges shrunken and its banks
exposing concentric rings of dried mud like a healing ulcer.
Breaking the pattern on one side of the pond was what appeared to be a large shapeless bag but what was in actuality,
when Brook walked up and stood over it, the carcass of the
Alma gray.

Death had shrunk the horse's body into a pouch of hide that
was the same color as the mud it lay in. The head seemed
sealed, the eyes and mouth sewn shut against the water that
once had held it. The chest and belly and the back of the horse
were visible, with the saddle still attached, but the hind quarters remained immersed in the dead black water of the pond.

Perhaps forty yards downslope lay the second pond and
Brook walked to it. It was almost identical in size and appearance with the first, but there was nothing to be seen. He
turned to go back to the upper pond and it was then that he
spotted the sluice. He had walked right by it earlier and hadn't
seen it. It stood exactly midway between the two ponds, not a
sluice anymore but merely the remains of one. The loamy
sand of the gully floor had reclaimed most of it. There was a
toppled gate that was recognizable, tilting like a tombstone in
a devastated graveyard, and a few shards of rotten timber. That

was all. But it was old, Brook knew, perhaps the very sluice that the young Caleb had secretly built when—

It was then Brook saw the grave.

He knew immediately that's what it was. In some bizarre fluke of vision his eyes caught on a piece of material sticking out of the earth on the other side of the sluice, caught on it and moved past and then came back. Even as he stared at the material and saw it for the corner of weathered canvas it was, he marveled at the incredible mischance that luck really was, for without the special spread of events that had allowed an employee to witness the single flaw in a desperate plan and get the chance to tell of it, without the intrusion of an old man's unexpected imagery, without that precise combination of light and time that had revealed a canvas where no canvas should be, without these. . . .

Brook walked back to where the horses waited and removed a spade from the pack horse and returned to the grave. Carefully, he shoveled and scraped the soil away and then bent down and lifted up the corner of the canvas.

His breath caught in his throat and his eyes locked onto the inextricable colloidal mass that lay in the hole at his feet. He saw the remains of a hat and the shape of a head, and perhaps a torso, and arms and legs folded brokenly over the body as if in some pathetic attempt to cover its shame.

Brook looked away. His stomach lurched and his throat opened, but he did not retch. After a moment he looked back.

Sometime after that he reached down and pulled his father's hat forward so that it would completely cover what was left of his face. When he did, a large piece of the brim tore off in his hand, and he didn't drop it into the grave as he first thought of doing, but kept it. Immediately afterward, he spotted something caught in what he believed was one of his father's hands and he bent down and pulled the object free. As he did, a flutter of air escaped the body.

Brook thought it sounded like a name.

Eventually, Brook maneuvered the canvas back into place and covered the hole with dirt, not packing or tamping but

233

mounding it only, for it was not a permanent grave he intended. He covered the mound with several large rocks from the adjoining bank and when he had finished he removed his vest and laid the fragment of hat brim and the other object inside it and placed the vest inside his shirt. He turned his back on the grave then and walked to the sluice and stood over it, staring down.

"You sonofabitch," he said then, directing a kick at the weathered remains of the sluice gate. "You precious sonofabitch, you did it! You killed him!"

Brook picked up the spade and slammed it against the toppled remnant of gate, shattering it. He stomped the rotten lumber into pieces and scattered the pieces across the gully floor. He lifted the spade above his head and held it there, squeezing the spade in both hands as if to crush it. Then he began in his chest and his throat and in his mouth a cry that started raggedly and then rose in an uninterrupted roar to rupture the air everywhere around him. It soared out of the banks of the gully and swept through the surrounding trees, echoing on the far wooded slopes that lay beyond the mountain. . . .

Brook rode up out of the gully and into the meadow, and then he crossed Saddle Pass and turned down into the shadowy cut of Right Hand.

At the stone shed he switched to the stake bed and at the bottom of the canyon he drove into a dusk that was sooty and unlifting, like a great fire that has burned well all day and then gone faulty at the end. He coasted down into the lot and went directly to the smith shop and lit a lantern and removed the vest from inside his shirt. When he unfolded it the odor of the pieces assaulted him instantly. He regained his breath and transferred the piece of hat to a small square of oilcloth he found on a bench, and the second object he carried across the shed and washed in a bucket of water that stood by the forge.

The object was coated with a gummy mix of humus and dirt but when it finally washed clean Brook saw that it was a leather tie string from a saddle, approximately ten inches in length. Inspecting the tie in the light of the lantern, the picture of a full saddle flashed through his mind, but it disappeared immediately and he returned to the oilcloth and laid the tie next to the fragment of hat. Creasing the oilcloth once from each side he tucked in the ends and made a final fold, then hid the package under a roll of canvas. As he did so, the image of a saddle presented itself to him once more.

He walked through the darkness to the harness shed, where he closed the door and lit a new lantern. Turning the wick up, he moved along one side of the saddle rail and inspected each saddle that hung there, seeking out each pair of tie strings, both front jockey and rear, running the thongs carefully through his fingers. When he returned along the opposite side of the rail he performed the identical inspection, checking to see if the pairs were complete. They were.

Finishing this, he blew out the lantern and went to the house, groping his way up the blackness of the stairs and along the hall to Margaret's room.

She met him with a burst of surprise, and a kind of wonder that had become part of their greetings, and then closed the door and held him briefly before he took a seat on the bed. She did not switch on the light but sat next to him in the darkness with her hand touching his.

"Margaret," he said to her, "I found Papa."

"Oh, Brook!"

"In a grave, Margaret. Under canvas and dirt in a gully near the top of the mountain."

Margaret shuddered without a sound and the emotion coursed through her hand into his. She mutttered something prayerlike under her breath and laid her head against his shoulder and did not speak for several minutes. "Did you bring the body back with you?" she asked finally, lifting her head and looking at him.

"No."

She wanted to ask why but she didn't, he was too quiet, too controlled. She asked instead, "Have you told Ruth?"

"No."

"Will you tell her?"

"Yes, but not now."

No sound came in through the open window, no sound rose up from the inner house. The bedroom was so black it seemed the two of them were suspended in a void, linked to reality only by the act of their hands touching.

Yet, gradually, a light from outside began to form and gather at the window. It was a suggestion at first, a glow so faint it could not be detected by looking directly at the window but only peripherally, to one side or the other. But it grew steadily and became at last a force strong enough to give outline to the curtains and the window sill, to the night stand with its pitcher and bowl looking like a still life, to the floor and the walls and finally to the bed where the two of them sat watching it. "The moon," Brook said simply, as if only simple explanations would suffice in this complex darkness.

Later, he went to the window but returned quickly to the bed and sat again. After a few minutes he again approached the window but when he left this time he sat in the chair next to the bed.

"Are you thinking of your father, Brook?"

"I'm thinking of something I found."

She could see the form of him in the chair plainly enough, but not his face; the moonlight, striking one side of his body, had put his face into shadow. "In the grave?" she asked.

"Yes. In Papa's hand. A piece of tie string."

"Like on a saddle? That kind of tie string?"

"Yes."

"Do you still have it?"

"I wrapped it in a piece of oilcloth."

"Oilcloth," she said, and it was almost musing, "that's a funny thing to use." She hadn't taken her eyes off him, she had been watching him as he talked, fascinated by the disconnected way his words issued from the shadow of his face. But then he made a sound in his throat and stood straight up from his chair. "Seven," he said, and it was fiercely constrained, almost a hiss. "Seven men in Right Hand that day, not six. The seventh man was True Jackson. He was already there. Waiting." Brook's

236

head swiveled toward her and for the first time she could see his face. "Sweet Jesus," he whispered, "that's how they did it."

Margaret rose from the bed. "Brook?"

Brook rubbed his hands together slowly. It was an unconscious gesture. "Caleb had True planted in the canyon. That's why he stopped the party, why he made up the sound. Willy Walker was right all the time. Only True didn't do the job the way Caleb told him. He didn't push Papa off the cliff. He buried him."

Margaret reached for Brook through the slatted shadows that the moonlight made in the room. "Brook, that's why Jackson ran away. He knew all the time that your dad's body wasn't in the rocks at cliff bottom. Caleb thought it was, which is probably why he went along with True guiding you in. It would look perfectly natural. But True knew better. He was afraid to face Caleb when he found out. So he ran away."

Brook sagged back into the chair as though his legs had failed him. "That morning in Leadville," he said weakly. "When True came riding out of the alley he had his rifle trussed up with a sling made of oilcloth. I told him it looked shabby, that an old horse soldier like him ought to have a decent scabbard for his rifle. But there was something else, something missing from the saddle. I looked right at it but we were both talking smart and I didn't see it. It didn't register." He swore softly. "The tie I took from Papa's hand will match the busted tie on True's saddle. He must have torn it loose when he was falling, while True was smashing his head in." He rubbed his hands together again. "Sweet Jesus, it's as if Papa gave me the name of his killer right from the grave."

Margaret was standing over Brook now, reaching down for his hands, trying to quiet them. "But there's nothing we can do now," she said. It was strong, direct. "Jackson's gone. He's a fugitive. He's far away by this time. After all, he had money. He got paid well for what he did."

She had located Brook's hands but he would suddenly not be held. "Maybe," he said, and it was icily quiet. Before she could fully discern his meaning he had scooped up his cap and jacket from the top of the dresser and started out the door.

She followed him, her whisper a slashing violation of the black stillness in the hall. "Brook, you're not going to Leadville now? Not at night? Oh, Brook, no!"

Brook pounded down the stairs and onto the porch, vaulting the railing onto the lawn. Margaret raced after him and at the gate she caught him. "Brook, listen to me! Please! Don't do this! Wait until morning and then go to Leadville. Talk to the sheriff there and tell him you have proof that Jackson killed your father. Take the leather tie with you and show it to him. The sheriff can prepare the necessary warrants or bulletins or whatever's needed. The law will find Jackson, Brook, and put him in jail. He'll stand trial for murder. And maybe the County Attorney can persuade him to confess and implicate the others."

It was as if Brook hadn't heard, as if he were alone in that incongruously romantic moonlight at the edge of the lawn. He took his watch from his pocket and studied it. "If I take the Oakland I can be in Leadville by dawn." But it was to the watch he spoke and when he turned away to cross the lot, Margaret was forced to follow after him like a spurned suppliant. "Please, Brook," she pleaded, "don't do this. Stay here with me, at least until morning." But the futility of it won out finally and she gave up, letting him go on without her, watching helplessly from the dumb cowering shadows of the lot.

Brook retrieved the oilcloth package and from a cabinet in the tack house he took the Enfield rifle with the attached bayonet that Caleb had given him, and put them both in the front seat of the Oakland. The keys were in the ignition. He backed the car out of the shed and when he reached the lane he stopped and got out and looked for Margaret.

"Oh, Brook!" she cried, running to him from the shadows, exploding into one last plea, "don't take this on yourself. Please! Telephone ahead and notify the authorities that you're coming. Get some help. It's too dangerous for you alone!"

He pulled her to him and held her wordlessly and then slid in behind the wheel of the Oakland and drove away, the car turning instantly to a black fleck on the moonlit road, blurred and imperfect like a shadow on water.

CHAPTER 19

The way to Leadville was by moonlight. South Park was a sea of moonlight, cream-white, soft as cotton. It was as if a decree had gone out to the kingdom that only the Oakland could navigate that sea. And so it did, elegantly.

Then too, there was the sheer scale of the thing, the magic of a minute vessel sailing across that immense ocean in the moonlight, isolated and distinct like a black seed on a white cloth. The sky helped. It appeared to be less intrusive than usual, more tolerant of tiny earthbound things. Even the mountains seemed awed. They watched from their circle in total silence, reluctant to assert themselves, creating no shadow anywhere that might impede the Oakland's crossing.

In the front seat of the car, the sense of being alone in the middle of a mysterious sea gradually deserted Brook and he began to feel the steering wheel in his hands, see the wheels track the road. The Oakland was an automobile after all and it made him think of other automobiles, of other places and other days. He thought of the Race About he had liked in Denver, of the Stutz Speedster he had wanted to buy. He remembered the Marmon 34 Twelve Cylinder with its crimson body and white wheels that had carried him down another moon-wet road. He thought of the splendid Pierce-Arrow Opera coupes on Curtis Street, of the fluid horns and the sweet exhausts of that endlessly moving Great White Way, the headlamps like a million silver moths converging on their own allure. He remembered the girls passing in the touring car on Seventeenth, heard their voices and their laughter, saw the lifting arms and the rich streaming hair and the faces brighter by far than any moonlight.

He turned at Fairplay. He turned again at Alma. He climbed the massif of Mosquito and the moon guided him the entire way, over the light-burned mountain top and down the far side into the dark expectant woods that waited like a lover in the valley beyond. Then a final climb, a final mountain, the earth slipping past the windows of the car as effortlessly as misplaced time.

When at last he reached the alley in Leadville, Brook switched off the Oakland's engine and cut the headlights. He sat unmoving in the front seat with the windows rolled up against the cold mountain air. It was extremely quiet. The world was asleep. The night was a smooth blue-steel box he alone could sit in while he waited for the day. He waited a long time until the moon, unfaithful at last and without the least remorse, ran off across the mountains. The birds began to sing. On both sides of the street Brook could see outlines forming—chimneys, roof peaks, the blind eye of upstairs windows. Then the packed dirt of the street emerged. Sidewalks. Hedges.

Brook stirred then. He opened the oilcloth on the seat beside him and put one of the items inside his shirt. He made certain the bayonet was securely attached to the rifle barrel and then got out of the car and closed the door carefully and started walking up the alley, the dawn air thick with pine smell.

Yet it was not totally dawn, there was light sufficient for shapes only, and dim at that. As he groped his way into the alley, Brook bumped into the open door of what he guessed was a small barn sitting behind what he believed was a small house. There was a window visible in the house; he knew because there was a light showing in it, flickering weakly the way a coal oil lamp does at dawn.

Brook stepped around the door and into the barn and stood absolutely still just inside, waiting for full light to come and

240

show him where he was. He heard a horse flutter somewhere in front of him and he experienced the prickly feeling of being watched from the darkness.

The day came swiftly when it came. It rushed the alley and the barn and washed out all interior densities but one—a huge black horse.

True Jackson's horse.

Brook's heart leaped. Behind the wide-eyed stallion stood two docile mules loaded with box packs. Slowly, taking care not to startle the animals, Brook eased himself into an adjacent stall and stood motionless.

In a matter of minutes the figure of True Jackson loomed in the doorway, made shapeless by the bulky coat he wore. He was carrying a blanket roll which he proceeded to secure to the front of the stallion's saddle, all the while making a whistled crooning sound in his teeth.

From out of the decaying shadows of the stall, Brook spoke: "I see you fixed that busted scabbard, Trooper."

True Jackson's mouth music froze in his throat and his body locked into a rod. Brook could sense him struggling to place the voice, and when he turned finally and saw Brook standing in the stall his whole face blew open with relief. His shoulders dropped and his mouth split so wide it pushed everything else out of his face. "Lawdy Lawd, Mistuh Brook," he breathed, "you liked to scared this ole nigger right down to his *knees!*" His head cocked itself like a feeding bird's and he laughed a thin exaggerated cackle of a laugh.

Brook waited until the performance was over and then he said, "Have you ever seen any vaudeville, True? The real stuff, I mean. I have. I went to several shows when I was down in Denver. The best were at the Pantages over on Curtis Street, especially this one Midnight Ramble skit that had the two blackface comics in it. One's name was Lester, he was the bright one, a guy who'd made a profession out of avoiding trouble. The other man was called Toby. Toby was the dummy, the one who was always screwing up, you know the kind. Real doofus. I remember Toby grinned a lot and showed his teeth, and he did this sort of funny little shuffle with those big fakey shoes he had. He did some Lawdy Lawds too, pretty much like you did just now. He was really comical, especially when he was trying to figure out a way to make money. Not a lot of money, you understand, just enough to get out of town. And Toby scared real easy, did I tell you that part? It was probably the funniest part of the show. When something would spook him real bad he'd stand there on stage with his eyes rolling and his knees shaking like crazy—getting ready to run away, you know—and he'd say in this high trembly voice, 'Feet, don't fail me *now!*' Oh, he got a lot of laughs with that. Golly!" Brook's eyes swept over the waiting stallion and the pair of packed mules and then setled on True's face. "You aren't like Toby, are you, True? You wouldn't be thinking of running away, would you?"

The fear started then in Jackson's face, in the eyes mostly. They quit focusing on any one thing in particular.

"Good," said Brook pleasantly, "I was hoping you'd stick around this time. We've got a little business to take care of. We didn't get it all done before. You fell off your horse in that canyon and popped a hip, remember?" He waited and then went on. "What we've got here now, True, is some pieces. Pieces that go together, like you told me about." He reached inside his shirt and brought out the broken tie and with his other hand he raised the rifle so True could see the bayonet. Its tip had been honed to a point sharper even than the needles Etchevarl sewed canvas with, its blade glistening with a pure brilliance in the early light. "On the rear lay of your saddle," Brook began, "you've got two long string ties and forward of that you've got two short ones. That is to say, you should have." His eyes moved to the saddle on the big stallion's back. "I can see that both long strings are in place, but one of your short ties is missing. This one," he said quietly, and held it up.

Jackson's face sagged, starting to take on a look of doom the way twilight takes on darkness. Irrevocably.

"I imagine you've got it figured out by now," Brook explained, "where I found the busted tie. It was in my father's hand. At least I think it was his hand, it was hard to tell for sure. It had begun to rot and looked like black leather, a lot

like your hand looks. I damned near didn't see the tie string."
He scanned True's face. "You never did see it, did you? When
you were beating Papa's head in and he started to go down I
figure he grabbed hold of whatever he could. You know how
a hurt man will grab, don't you, True? What Papa got was
your scabbard and that old rotten tie. Of course, all you saw
him get was the scabbard. You buried the tie with the body and
didn't know it. Now I've got it." Again his eyes swept the
black stallion and the two mules. "And my having it is what's
going to cut short this trip you're getting ready to take."

True's face looked like it had started to drain down into his
body. In some bleak hopeless way his eyes sought the rifle in
Brook's hand.

Brook saw it and stepped forward quickly and placed the
tip of the bayonet under Jackson's chin. "Mister, I can have
your tongue on this point before you ever get a hand moved.
Do you believe that? Nod your head if you believe that."

The man couldn't have nodded, didn't dare move his jaw
the least bit. Only his eyes moved, rolling obediently as if
Brook had asked to see the whites.

"You told me once, Trooper, that you didn't like it when
people didn't pay you. I know now what you were talking
about. Caleb hired you for a job and you held up most of your
end but he hasn't paid you for it. I came over here to the mountain top this morning to tell you that he can't. He hasn't got
the money yet. He has to marry the widow to get it." Brook
dropped the broken saddle piece into his jacket pocket with his
free hand. "The chances are real good now that the wedding
will never take place. I think you can see that, so if I were you I
wouldn't bother getting your tux cleaned and pressed. About
the only thing you've got left, True, is to tell me who was in
this business with you and Caleb. It might work a world of
benefit if you could give me the name."

Brook stopped talking and waited. The big cavalry mount
whisked his tail impatiently, slapping both mules across the
face. They batted their eyes but never once moved their heads.
Brook put a slight pressure on the bayonet and True's head
jerked and a trickle of blood appeared on the blade. "It was

Pickens and Caleb together on that first split, wasn't it, True? What did they do, get there in time to watch you do it?"

Still no answer. Brook bumped the rifle again and Jackson's eyes flared like the eyes of a large animal caught in a trap that had been set for a smaller one; there was humiliation in them. A drop of blood ran down the blade of the bayonet, destroying the glisten, and then another. Still Jackson didn't speak and watching him, waiting, Brook realized that he never would. In some unfathomable way the refusal had to do with codes, with fixed points, and with what was left, some last stand in a whole lifetime of humiliation. In his greasy hat and decrepit coat, True Jackson looked like nothing more than another failed rag man from the streets of Denver.

Brook let out a breath and then, answering a sudden unexplainable rush of pity, lowered the bayonet. "Turn around and put your back against this blade," he said to True. "And remember, I can easily spear a kidney if you make a bad move. And you'd better say good-by to that rocking chair. It won't fit in a jail cell." With that he marched True Jackson into the alley and up the street to the jail, past Cohen's store, past the empty dawn porches where the townspeople ordinarily liked to watch the aging black cavalryman ride to work on the big shiny black stallion that no one was quite sure he owned.

After he left the sheriff, Brook went back to the little barn in the alley. With the bayonet still fixed to the Enfield he sliced through the stallion's belly strap and let the saddle and blanket fall free onto the floor. He removed the bridle as well and then slapped the great black rump enough times to send the horse clumping through the open door of the barn. He turned next to the mules and while they stood with their eyes scornfully averted, he removed their rope halters and cut their box packs loose. "You guys don't need a rocking chair either," he shouted at them. "Now get the hell out of here!"

CHAPTER 20

Brook was watching for Margaret through the windshield of the Oakland, scanning the lane for movement, color, form. Suddenly he saw her. She did not emerge from the approaches so much as she simply materialized in the center of the car tracks, already in motion, running toward him with the wind of her race pressing her clothing against her body.

He stopped the car and got out. "Brook!" she cried when she saw him, her voice thin with distance and exertion, the single braid of her hair bouncing jubilantly across her shoulders. *"Brook!"*

He waited for her in front of the car and then swept her into his arms when she reached him. *"Oh Brook, you're back! You're home!"* and her face was a hot wet flush of laughter and tears. He whirled her completely around, pressed his face into her hair and her neck, whirled her again and would not let her go. "Ahhhh, Mag!"

Set on her feet at last, Margaret held him at arm's length while her eyes searched his face eagerly. "Was he there, Brook? Was Jackson there? Did you find him?"

"Yes."

"Did he cooperate? Did he tell you—?"

"The sheriff's got him, Mag. He's got him locked up tight in a cell in Leadville. True Jackson's been charged with murder and conspiracy to commit murder."

Margaret's breath exploded in a wild exhalation of relief. "Oh Brook," she cried, and her voice broke with emotion for just that moment. But she recovered quickly and asked if there had been any trouble, if he was all right. "Are you all right?" she asked, repeating it, inspecting his face, his mouth, his eyes. "Your eyes look so strange."

"It's because I haven't slept. That's a long trip. A lot of road to watch."

Her eyes remained fixed on his face, devouring his reassurances. "Oh, Brook, it's over," she cried. "It's over and we're intact. We're whole."

"Not quite over," he said. "There's one more thing I've got to do."

"I know. You've got to bring your father's body down." She leaned into him and buried her face in his chest. Fiercely. Tenderly. "Then, sweetheart. Then it's over."

He lifted her off her feet once more and held her against him for a long time. "Margaret Pendleton . . . Mag . . . faery beauty of the Meads . . . sweet Jesus!" Finally, he set her down. Happiness shone in her face like sun on water. "There's something I want you to do for me," he said.

"Tell me."

"I want you to go to your room and rest. Get out of this heat. Sleep if you can. You're the one who looks tired."

"It's a happy tired."

He reached out and gripped her wrists and looked into her face. "Wait for me, Mag. Will you do that? I'll go up and get the body and then I'll come to you when I'm finished. All right?"

She rode with him in the Oakland and when they reached the end of the lane she kissed him with a gleeful cry and ran into the house.

Brook backed the Double T out of the shed and parked at the gate and then crossed the lawn to the kitchen. Ruth was there, sitting alone at the table. He crossed the room and stood opposite her, holding his silence so long that she was forced finally to glance up. There was no interest in the act, no warmth, no surprise, nothing but the old insulated imperious beauty.

He asked her where Caleb was.

"Why did you go back to Leadville?" she said, and the indifference of it deadened her voice.

The question startled him. "How did you know that?"

"Margaret mentioned it. Caleb had asked where you were."

"Where is Caleb?"

"I don't know. He's been gone several hours."

Brook left his side of the table and came around and stood beside her. "Do you know what this is, Mother?" he said, removing the fragment of hat brim from his pocket and presenting it to her. "Do you recognize it?"

Her eyes touched it but her hands did not. Her nose turned up slightly with the old mannered revulsion she had always shown whenever he brought her something unusual, a deformed puppy, a baby bird fallen from the nest, something she didn't want. She didn't want this. "It's a piece of a hat," he said to her. "I found it in a grave. Yesterday. Up on the mountain."

She had looked away when he first started to speak but now she looked back at him, directly at him. There was a terrible anticipation in her eyes.

"Your husband's grave, Madam. I thought you would want to know."

A substance false-white and tubercular flooded into Ruth's face. Behind her eyes, something previously unbreakable seemed to be breaking apart. She started to speak and then stopped and gave a little gasp. "Oh, it's Papa's hat all right," Brook said. "Papa's grave. Hat in the grave. It's like a riddle, isn't it, Mama?" He waited, watching her. She had always hated him calling her *Mama*. "Aren't you going to scold me about the riddle? You always have before. I've come to expect a scolding on nearly everything." Still she didn't speak, she merely stared. "Isn't it a shame that Caleb isn't here now to comfort you, Mother? He's good at that, isn't he? And I know he'd want to see this hat again, poor fragment that it is. He hasn't seen it for some time, not since he threw it into the grave. Now it's rotting. The worms have been at it. At Papa too. You wouldn't recognize him in that tiny little hole they put him in."

A terror came to his mother then, spoiling the eyes utterly, pinching her face, twisting the mouth into a pain that needed a voice and still could find none. She was like a mute trying to tell a tale of horror with only her eyes. Her hand came out and gripped Brook's arm and he looked down at it as if it were something *she* had brought *him*. And he didn't want it. Not now. He said quietly to her, "You want to share this with me, don't you? Now, after all these years. But it's not your grief you want to share, not your love. It's just your horror. And another disappointment." Her face resembled an expensive silk the heat had wilted. He bent forward to her. "You left me out, Mother. Always. All my life. You brought me here but you didn't want me to know you. I tried but I didn't know how. You were the adult and you had the advantage. It was like you were afraid I would . . . diminish you. Now we're all diminished. You. Me. Papa. Uncle. All of us. My God," he said, and reached down and removed her hand from his arm. "My God, the waste in that."

He stood looking down at her and for the first time in his life he heard his mother cry, saw her cry, saw the tears.

The canyon lay impaled by heat, scalded, helpless. No birds sang from the timbered rims. Caught between the blazing rock walls, the creek struggled weakly to escape. Brook had hoped for a breeze as soon as he gained the heights but it did not come. Overhead, the sky was the blue heat of forge fire but far to the west there were clouds. They resembled a wad of dirty wool that wouldn't fluff up, like the stuff he had shaken out of an old mattress he found one time in the attic of one of the sheds.

When he had crossed Saddle he turned right and followed the edge of the meadow around to the head of the gully where the grave was located. He dismounted and walked the pack horse down through the choke of brush to the grave. He took the body bag from the horse's saddle and spread it on the ground. He removed the rocks from the top of the grave, spaded the dirt aside, lifted the canvas-held body, placed it inside the bag and closed the bag up and hoisted it to the horse's back. He led the pack horse out of the gully to where the buckskin waited, mounted, and rode back across the meadow. When he was some fifty yards from the rock pinnacle he glanced up for some reason, probably remembering the unexpected hoofprints in the sand next to the grave, and as he did he caught a flash of sun on metal.

Instantly, he threw himself backward out of the saddle, pulling the buckskin to the ground with him, and in that same instant he heard the rifle shot and the *whennng* of the bullet singing over his head. He pushed free of the tumbling horse and grabbed the Winchester out of the scabbard, all in one motion, and pumped the lever once and peered back up the slope to the rock tower.

A man's head popped up from a notch in the boulders at the base of the rock, a head wearing a bowler hat and followed by a bright mackinaw shirt. Brook took a sight on the leaning figure and pulled the trigger.

It was odd how dreamy the events became then, how they merged and broke apart, how when the bullet struck Polite his rifle flew up, errant and weightless like a stick falling in the wrong direction. How Polite's hat bounced once on his head from the impact but didn't fall off. How his body started to lean farther and farther out from its hiding place in the rocks as if he were seeking a new position to watch from. But he leaned too far, much too far, so that he fell out upon the ground and the bowler hat came off his head for good this time, and rolled away.

Brook rose and got the buckskin to his feet and walked up to the rock, holding the reins in his left hand and the cocked Winchester in his right.

Polite lay motionless on the ground just out from the rocks. Blood was flowing from the base of his neck, soaking the front of his shirt. Brook stopped and said, "You know what'll happen if you make another wrong move, don't you, Polite?"

Polite's voice sounded bewildered, but strong. He'd always

had that booming voice. "Can't move," he said. "Nothing's working right all of a sudden. Arms, legs . . . nothing."

Brook knelt to a squatting position but remained an arm's length away.

"Ah, Itty Bitty," Polite said, and already the voice was straining. "I broke bad on this. I shot too late and got curious too soon."

"Bad day for you, good for me. It goes like that sometimes. But you surprised the hell out of me, Polite, I'll give you that. I didn't think you were in on it." He glanced around. "Where's Caleb?"

Some of the bruised plum color of Polite's face had started to leach out. His mouth twisted as if he were making the effort to lift his arms and inspect the wound. But he hadn't moved. Nothing moved below the hole in his neck. "Damn," he grunted, and tried to spit but it hung on his lip. His head lolled to one side and then came back. He took a breath that sounded watery. "You mind that day you slipped off the edge of the cliff here and I caught your rope and tore my hands up? You mind that day, Itty Bitty?"

"Where's Caleb?"

"I didn't have to catch that rope. I could have let it run on by me, natural like, and none the wiser." His eyes moved but his lips hardly at all. "I saved you, Itty Bitty. Will that stand for me now?"

"Make sense, Polite. Nothing'll stand for you now. You've got a hole in you and everything you are is running out of it. What you did or didn't do one day with a rope doesn't matter." He studied Polite's slowly yellowing face. "It's like with Papa. It didn't matter that he took True Jackson in and fed him and trusted him and paid him decent wages for the first time in his life. True still killed him."

Polite's eyes rolled up and he stared into the sky as though he were looking for something at the far end of it. "That nigger . . . screwed up."

"So did some other people."

Polite's eyes rolled into a search for Brook's face. His voice was much weaker now. "Nigger was supposed to push man and horse off the cliff. That was the plan. Caleb wanted it . . . done that way. I go left, Caleb right, draw everybody off . . . leave Jackson plenty of time to do . . . his job and get away. Black bastard . . . changed the plan."

"Why would Caleb want to draw Grant off? Wasn't he in this with you?"

"No. Little pissant . . . too dumb. Spooks too easy."

"Who killed Willy?"

Polite's eyes flutttered. "Storm killed Willy. The lightning."

Brook watched the stricken face drain all its color into the shirt, the ground. "That day up here on the apron, why *did* you grab the rope? You could have finished me too."

"Not you. Caleb wanted you . . . safe." Polite blinked rapidly and rolled his head back and forth as though he were fighting sleep. "Always safe."

Brook bent closer. "Why, Polite? Why a man like Caleb? For the business, for Christ's sake? For a bigger stack of lumber and a new truck?"

Polite's head stopped rolling and the rapid blinking stopped. The flow of blood from his throat slowed thickly. "Not business. Not truck. Caleb wanted your . . . loved your . . . mother."

A single bead of sweat dropped from Brook's chin onto Polite's face but it never moved once it struck. It didn't swell, didn't glisten, didn't run off. Brook stood up from the gaudily dressed figure on the ground and removed his cap and wiped his forehead and when he knelt down again, Polite was dead.

Brook rounded up the buckskin and the pack horse and when he had ridden halfway across Saddle he detected movement ahead of him and glanced up.

It was Caleb.

He was horseback, picking his way across the pass on the little blunt-nosed gelding he favored. When they were only a few feet from each other, both riders stopped. There was no wind and it was very quiet. Brook said, "It's all a matter of odds, isn't it, Caleb?"

Caleb tried a smile but it was brittle, like something that has hung too long in the wind and dried out. "Brook, listen to me—"

"Sweet Jesus, a man like you."

Caleb started with something new but Brook stopped him with an upraised hand and edged the buckskin forward until he was directly abreast of Caleb's horse. Caleb's eyes were restless and unfixed, his face flushed for once. Brook could see the tiny patch of untouched whiskers beneath his nose. "When True jammed Papa in that grave he had to break his body up so he would fit." He kept his eyes on Caleb's face as if to hold him in place, and pulled the Winchester from the scabbard. "Broke Papa's legs. Back. Arms. Everything. You thought you'd been saved from knowing about that, didn't you, Uncle?"

A visible pain ripped through Caleb's face. "Baskets, Brookers . . . Almighty God, I couldn't do baskets!"

Brook swung the rifle and struck Caleb on the stump of his arm. Caleb went flying off the gelding into the sedge of the west apron, tumbling almost playfully at first and then more quickly, more certainly, as the grade captured him. He grabbed at the thin brown grass but it failed him, failed the single frantic hand consistently, time after time.

Suddenly there was no more time, no more room. Caleb was far down the apron, already growing formless and then faceless as well. He gave a cry that might have been a name, or perhaps a last rush of terror, and then shot over the edge of the cliff and was gone, disappearing from the sedge like a flawed seed it could no longer tolerate.

When he turned down into Right Hand, Brook saw that a few clouds had begun to form overhead and it seemed that the heat had broken somewhat. He removed his cap and wiped the sweat from his face with a bandana and put the cap back on. Shadows were beginning to lean into his path when he turned at the rock face. When he came in sight of the stone shed he saw Grant Pickens step out from the shadows and peer up the canyon at him.

"Hey you, Grant Pickens!" Brook called. "You frog-eyed sonofabitch, come up here and help me!"

He saw Grant lift a rifle from behind his body and shoulder

it and he heard the sound of the shot. But that's all Brook saw, and all he ever heard. The bullet tore through the wrist of the hand he had raised in greeting and slammed into the exact center of his forehead. He toppled off the buckskin and landed on his side on the ground. He was dead long before he stopped rolling but for one so tall and thin, the way he rolled right up to the edge of the creek was a languorous sort of movement, a kind of grace.

CHAPTER 21

Etchevarl heard the single rifle shot the way one would hear such a sound. It was more intense, more singular for not having to compete with any other, but it was a long way off; if anything diminished the sound, it was distance. Had he been inside a building, Etchevarl never would have heard the shot at all. But he was at the yard gate, heading for the house, when it sounded.

He listened instinctively for a second shot, satisfying the unconscious expectation for things to happen in pairs, but none came. He turned from the gate and walked back to the stake bed truck and cranked it over, for he knew this was a sound he would have to check out.

He drove toward Right Hand and had penetrated perhaps fifty yards into the canyon when the mounted figure of Grant Pickens swept into view, clattering madly down the canyon road, his body locked in the reckless speed of flight.

Etchevarl braked the truck and stepped out into the narrow roadway and Grant's horse slid to a desperate skewing stop in front of him. Grant's leather helmet was missing and his shirt was plastered with sweat. "I saw it all," he screamed at Etchevarl, sawing at the reins. "He killed them both! Polite first and then Caleb. Pushed him *over*, for God's sake!" His eyes burned wildly and he blew spit with every word. "I had to do it! He was coming for me. Calling me out! Jesus Christ, I'd have been *next!*"

The horse was as crazed now as Grant, and Etchevarl tried in vain to grab its headstall. "Stop screaming!" he commanded Grant. "You are making no sense at all. What has happened? I must know!"

Grant gathered himself, his face ragged with fright. "Get out of my way, old man!" and he threw up one foot and struck Etchevarl in the chest. Etchevarl fell backward into the dirt and Grant jumped his horse over the prostrate form and raced away.

The old man regained his feet and ran down the road until he reached the canyon mouth where the rock walls spread open and his vision of the meadow and the house and the whole expanse of South Park unfolded before him.

Hair flying, arms and legs flopping like a faulty carnival toy, Grant Pickens fled the place and never looked back. He cleared the meadow and raced past the house, picking up a first veil of dust in the lane and a second in the road until, at last, time and distance absorbed them both.

Avoiding the kitchen, defeated in the airless hallway upstairs where Ruth had inexplicably locked herself in her room, Margaret sat on the piano bench in the parlor and waited for Brook, listening to the stillness of the house. There was nothing else to listen to. The floor clock in the dining room struck its hypnotic unvaried seconds but such monotony is a part of stillness. At one point in her waiting, Margaret heard the pounding tattoo of a running horse and hoping it was Brook she ran to the window and parted the curtains. It was not Brook. She didn't know who it was. There was a clot of impenetrable dust far out in the road and nothing more.

Then later she caught something. Not a sound exactly, nor even that eerie sense of movement that often precedes sound, but an indefinable awareness of something beyond, outside, impending, and she left the parlor and went out and stood on the porch.

She saw easily then what she hadn't quite heard before. On the road that trickled out of Right Hand Canyon and crossed the north meadow she saw a convoy of sorts—a skeletal stake bed truck with a pair of horses following behind. Just that, one truck and two tied horses.

She moved down the porch steps and crossed the withered grass of the lawn, keeping her eyes fixed on the approaching caravan. In the truck seat only one figure was visible to her, the driver, and on the horses trailing the truck there were no riders.

She started to walk faster and once she penetrated the meadow she began to run, holding her skirt off her knees and concentrating not on her feet nor the possible entanglement of deep grass but on Etchevarl's slowly emerging face in the front seat of the truck, for she suddenly felt that to look away from that mournful countenance would be to lose the whole oncoming procession to distance, to something unspeakably absent.

When she reached the truck she stopped. Her eyes ran past Etchevarl initially and then came back to where he sat in the seat gripping the wheel and staring out at her, not in recognition but in desperation, as though he too dared not look away. "Where's Brook?" she called to him, and the dread in her voice startled her. "Why isn't Brook with you?"

It startled Etchevarl as well, for he spoke much too shrilly, much too loudly, his single utterance thrusting at her in a voice she had never heard before. "Madness." In a voice she would hear forever. "Madness."

"Etchevarl?"

The old man shook his head at her and she shook her own head back at him, numbly, forming over and over at her mouth the word that could find no sound. No. No.

The queer shattered voice flew at her again from the front seat. "In the back . . . back of the truck."

"No!" It was like flesh torn from her body.

"The yellow slicker."

Somehow, she managed to circle around to the back of the truck. Bodies were laid out there with a terrible neatness. A line of them, boots to the rear. How many? Who? Not Brook surely. Brook had placed the bodies there, gotten tired, stayed in the mountains. One last incredible coincidence. She saw that one of the bodies was encased in a rubber bag. One was uncovered and drenched in red. One lay beneath a yellow slicker with a cap protruding from it, stuck on the toe of a boot. Brook's cap. Brook's boot.

Something exploded inside her body at that moment, tore loose the reality of what she was witnessing. With an awful wrenching agony, her voice replaced it. "Oh, Brook, I was so frightened there for a minute. You forgot to promise me you'd come back. You always promised before, remember?" She reached out and touched the cap. "But it's all right, babe. You're here now. I'm not angry, really I'm not. You must think I'm always angry." The truck started to move forward and she ran after it, keeping up easily, one hand at her skirt and the other on the truck frame. "It's over now, Brook. The dead are all here. You've brought them home." Suddenly she heard sobbing. "You musn't cry, love. Please. We can start our own lives now. It's our turn. We waited." The grass caught at her feet but she would not look down at it, she would not look away from the loading of the truck bed in front of her. "There are still things I don't know about you, Brook. There's so much we never talked about. You never told me if you really did like to ride the train. If you have a favorite poet. And what about the buckskin horse? Did you pick him to be yours because you loved him or just because he was the best? You love animals so, I know that. I've seen it." The sobbing increased. "Oh, please, Brook, answer me. I need to know about you. We need to know about each other—"

But the sobbing swelled unbearably and her throat could not contain it. She released the truck and dropped back, letting the frail vehicle with its yellow burden go on through the meadow without her. Then, in a moment made of tiny cries of comprehension, she dropped to her knees. "Aahhh," she sobbed. "Aahhh. . . ." and fell forward into the grass.

Etchevarl found her in that precise spot perhaps an hour later, doubled up in the grass, clutching her knees to her body. She was mumbling a little, moaning, but mainly she was quiet.

He lifted her in his arms and carried her back to the house, walking carefully through the sad hazed unreal light that is a summer evening in the high mountains.

Polite was buried by the County in the public cemetery at Jefferson but Etchevarl dug the remaining three graves himself in the family plot at the top of the west meadow. Two he filled immediately of course, and one, Caleb's, remained empty. No one stood with him at the interment except Ess Cohen. Cohen had come out at Etchevarl's request to take an order for two headstones and to contract for a search party to recover Caleb's body from the base of the French Pass Cliffs, which was how Etchevarl referred to the precipice on Saddle.

The old Basque herder visited the two new graves daily, tamping the dirt down, removing the small pine branches the night winds sometimes blew onto them, checking against animal damage. It was the small inquisitive night creatures one had to protect against primarily; the larger animals such as cougar and bear did not bother man's grave sites. Etchevarl had always thought that peculiar.

He had picked no flowers for the graves, nor placed any. The grass would cover them soon enough. The grass grew lush in that corner of the Park and Etchevarl was sure the grass would have reclaimed the graves by first snow, which was ordinarily mid-October at that elevation.

He mentioned none of this to Ruth, for he scarcely saw her those first few days. She came out one evening to the porch and stood for a few minutes and then retreated into the house. He never saw Margaret Pendleton at all. He began to worry about her and one evening when Ruth came onto the porch a second time, Etchevarl hurried into the yard and stood at the bottom of the porch steps, holding his beret in his hands like a homemade gift he had finally gotten nerve enough to bring her. "I do not see the young lady, Señora," he said. "The Reverend Pendleton's wife. Is it certain she has not gone home and left you alone?"

"She won't speak to me, Arranz," Ruth answered abruptly, and to Etchevarl her voice was unrecognizable. The face too was much changed, not swollen exactly, not what one might expect tears to do to it, but empty more, suspended. "She won't come out of her room. I can go in but she won't respond to me. She sits in a chair or stands at the window and stares at the mountains."

"You must help her."

"I can't," Ruth answered simply in her dead voice. "I don't know how."

Etchevarl was back at the porch the following night, the conversation continuing almost without interuption. "Will Mrs. Pendleton not speak even of the deaths, Señora?" he asked.

"The first day. The day after it happened. She spoke then, just that once. 'The horse,' she said. 'I heard a horse running. Why? Whose horse was it?' "

Watching from the bottom of the steps, Etchevarl realized that Margaret's questions would also be Ruth's. He knew too what his answer must be. "Grant Pickens," he said to her. "It was Grant Pickens's horse Mrs. Pendleton heard that day. He is responsible for the tragedy. I was in the lower end of the canyon and he flew by me like the wind. I continued on up toward the ridge. I found Brook lying by the creek near the rock face where the canyon turns," and he drew it for her with his elegantly gloved hands. "Caleb's horse was standing alone in the middle of the pass but Caleb was missing. Polite's body was at the rock tower. It is certain that Grant Pickens ambushed all three of them, pushing Caleb's body off the pass for some reason." He waited for Ruth to learn of his deceit by questioning him, but she did not. "You must take Mrs. Pendleton home, Señora," he said gently. "Home to her husband. There is nothing for her here. It is finished."

Unexpectedly, Ruth agreed. "Yes," she said, looking down the steps at him. "Will you make the arrangements, Arranz? Please." She turned and went into the house, more determinedly than she had come out, Etchevarl thought, and the following night she came again to the porch. This time she watched Etchevarl cross the lawn and then invited him to sit with her in the swing. "I have packed," she told him. "Margaret's trunks and several cases for myself."

"I understand. Tomorrow morning I will drive the two of you to Jefferson for the train."

Ruth asked then about the mill. Was the mill completely shut down? Were the boilers cold? Had the fires in the wigwam burner been allowed to go out and damage the brick?

Etchevarl answered quickly. "There has been no damage to any of the equipment. I saw to that by organizing a maintenance crew the very first day. They are still stationed at the mill."

"Arranz," Ruth said after a long preoccupied silence, "I want you to begin the necessary inquiries and see to it that a new headrig man is hired as soon as possible." She continued resolutely in that vein, touching briefly on renewed production schedules, price clauses that might possibly be in effect and lumber deliveries to be made accordingly. "All the contracts Caleb had out, verbal and written, must be honored. That's most important. Our integrity must not be jeopardized." And then she said, in total surprise to Etchevarl but in a perfectly normal voice, looking directly at him, "It wouldn't do if Brook had somehow . . . killed Caleb himself. I couldn't bear it."

Etchevarl caught himself revealing more of his surprise than he intended. His head came up sharply and he felt his mouth open enough so that he had to consciously close it before he spoke. He felt a quick indignation as well, but he managed to keep it out of his voice. "Why would Brook do such a thing, Señora? He would have no reason."

Ruth didn't answer. Her eyes drifted momentarily toward the upper end of the west meadow, just below the timber. The fence-ringed plot could not be seen from the porch; there was a gauzy sunset light blurring it, blurring the edge of the trees, causing even the mountains to look temporarily unmoored. "That empty grave. . . ." she said, but there was no musing in it, no reluctance. "You'll recover Caleb's body first, Arranz, before you get involved in the mill. Is that agreed?"

"I have opened preliminary discussions relating to the search party. I expect to recover the body while you are returning the young woman to her home in Kansas."

"Good," Ruth said, and her hand came out and touched Etchevarl's arm. "Brook should rest beside his father."

"He does."

"No," she said, and put a deliberate pressure of fingers on his arm. "Not yet. Not until you bring him back from the other side."

In the morning, with Margaret waiting wordless and unparticipating in the parlor, Etchevarl loaded the trunks and the suitcases onto the bed of the Double T. Ruth was dressed in a black outfit much too heavy for late July, and Margaret wore a rich blue coat and a lavender hat that was turned up on one side and trimmed with artificial flowers.

Etchevarl was slow driving out of the lane and into the road, intentionally so, for he was always acutely aware of his responsibilities for any passengers riding in a motor vehicle he was driving. He wanted very much for the trip to Jefferson to be completely uneventful. No flat tires. No overchoking that would kill the engine. No locking of the brakes. No severe lurching in case he had to cross the ruts. He even wished the sawmill whistle not to blow. It could be such a melancholy sound. The maintenance crew had been in place every day and they hadn't once bothered to blow the whistle. So why would they now?

But they did. And he had been right, it was wrenchingly melancholy. He thought it sounded almost human, a poignant wail for things that were gone and would never come again. A cry for something that was lost forever.

But it ended finally. One of the women gave a tiny anguished sob just before it died away, Etchevarl couldn't tell which one, and he pretended not to hear and concentrated even more earnestly on his driving. The truck bounced badly in the baked ruts, even with its extra weight of trunks, and Etchevarl accepted his responsibility and steered off the road and drove in the meadow where the going was much smoother. It was a good decision, enabling him to look around a bit. He saw that the day was going to be hot but it was early yet and the cool morning freshness still surrounded them. The dew was deep in the grass, abundant and blue-white and sparkling in the sun like a Park drifter's dream of riches.

Raised and educated in the West, William Dieter lives presently in Denver where he is at work on a novel of Arizona.